**Also available from Kaylea Cross and Carina Press**

*Tactical Strike*
*Lethal Pursuit*
*Darkest Caress*

# Kaylea Cross

# DEADLY DESCENT

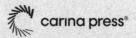
carina press®

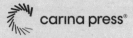

carina press®

ISBN-13: 978-0-373-00236-8

DEADLY DESCENT

Recycling programs for this product may not exist in your area.

www.CarinaPress.com

**Printed in U.S.A.**

Dear Reader,

If you're at all familiar with my books then you already know I'm a huge fan of our military. The idea for the Bagram Special Ops series came about because I wanted to write books featuring both men *and* women currently serving in uniform in Afghanistan.

*Deadly Descent* is the first book of the series, and it was a whole lot of fun to research. I also had to overcome a big personal obstacle to get the job done. Due to a classmate being the sole survivor of a horrific plane crash back in high school, I've been terrified of flying ever since. Yeah, I realize it's not a rational, logical fear, but it's a pretty severe phobia for me. However, to make sure I got my facts right for the book, I made myself go up in a helicopter several times (feel the fear and do it anyway!) to get the feel of it and learn about the controls in the cockpit. I'm so happy that I lived to tell you about it! I also interviewed flight instructors and a navy pilot who'd been in a severe helicopter crash (uh, that may have set me back a little in my efforts to overcome my fear of flying).

The best part, though? I got to interview both an army reservist Black Hawk medevac pilot, *and* a recently retired air force pararescueman (PJ). Holy awesome! Since there are just over three hundred active duty PJs out there, it was incredible for me to be hooked up with one of these rare and amazing airmen. My contact has patiently answered each and every annoying research question I've ever sent him since, so I hope you learn something interesting in *Deadly Descent* and the rest of the series because of him.

I'm so excited for you to read Cam and Devon's book! I hope you enjoy it and the rest of the Bagram series.

Happy reading,

Kaylea Cross

www.KayleaCross.com

This book is dedicated to the amazing men and women of AFSOC, but especially to my very favorite heroes, the selfless men of United States Air Force Pararescue, who stand ready to go into harm's way so *That Others May Live.* Hooyah!

# DEADLY DESCENT

It is my duty as a Pararescueman to save life and to aid the injured. I will be prepared at all times to perform my assigned duties quickly and efficiently, placing these duties before personal desires and comforts. These things I do, that others may live.

—Pararescue Jumper Code

# PROLOGUE

*Bagram Airfield, Afghanistan*
*Mid-October*

CAPTAIN DEVON "SPIKE" Crawford's hands sweated inside her flight gloves as she awaited the tower's response to her request for clearance. Through her night vision goggles she watched the relentless wall of fog outside the cockpit thicken. It crept over the ground like a shroud, swallowing everything in its path.

Her pulse drummed in her ears. Visibility was bad here, but even worse where they were going.

The answer she'd been waiting for finally came over the radio. "Angel one-niner cleared for takeoff."

She let out a slow breath. "Roger that."

Her co-pilot, Will, glanced at her but she ignored the questioning look. Heavy fog made the flight dangerous, but American soldiers were dying in that remote mountain village. They were counting on her to evacuate them to a hospital.

Willing her pounding heart to slow down, she raised the collective until the wheels were clear, checked her center of gravity and pushed forward on the cyclic. The Black Hawk lifted off the tarmac and cruised forward, gaining altitude. The pitch of the engines changed, rising with the power increase. The bird climbed steadily into the night air, strong and smooth. Above the occasional traffic on the radio, her three crew members remained deathly silent.

Their unspoken tension weighed on her with each passing kilometer. As pilot commander, she was responsible for the safety of her aircraft and crew. Their lives were literally in her hands.

But so were the lives of the wounded out at the distant LZ, waiting and praying for medevac extraction. She owed them her best shot, no matter how bad the visibility was.

The steady hum of the engines filled the cabin as they left the relative safety of Bagram behind and banked southeast toward the darkened mountains. Their snow-capped peaks were obscured by the ever encroaching fog. It made navigation next to impossible and increased the chance of clipping a rotor blade when they cruised through the narrow mountain passes. By the time she hit the first waypoint, near zero visibility made any further attempt practically suicidal.

Her damp hands tightened around the controls as she put the bird into a hover. "I can't see shit out there." She clenched her jaw, battling the gnawing fear and guilt. "Will?"

He glanced over at her for a moment, and then shook his head. "This is crazy. Call it, Dev."

*Dammit.* Her gaze strayed to the south. Out there somewhere beyond the crippling low cloud cover, men were dying. It tore her up that she wasn't going to get them out, but she had no choice.

She spoke over the intercom to the crew chief and medic. "That's it guys, I'm calling it off. We're outta here." Was it her imagination, or did a collective sigh of relief follow her words? She dialed in the frequency for the ops center. "This is Angel one-niner. Visibility is compromised. We're returning to base." *Sorry*, she added silently to the men she was about to abandon. But she couldn't risk her crew and the bird by going any further.

"Copy that, Angel one-niner."

With a heavy heart, Devon turned the Black Hawk back. The fog continued to roll in on the return trip, and when she finally touched down at Bagram her hands and armpits were soaked with cold sweat. She reached overhead to shut off the power and removed her helmet. Damn, she was glad just to be on the ground without incident after flying through that.

A hand settled on her shoulder, and she looked over to meet Will's knowing stare.

"Hey. We gave it our best."

*Yeah, but tell that to the wounded men in the village.* She rubbed her gritty eyes.

"We'll still be on standby, and we'll get out as soon as the viz improves."

"That's not going to happen, and you know it." By then another crew would have taken their place. And it would be far too late for those men back in the mountains.

"Then the Night Stalkers can give it a shot." He squeezed her shoulder in a firm grip. "At least you tried, Spike. Most pilots wouldn't have even attempted a flight in these conditions."

The respect in his tone did little to soothe her conscience. She nodded stiffly and climbed out of the bird, heading straight for the ops center to find out if anything else could be done for the wounded on the ground. No one told her much but she hung around anyhow, until a Night Stalker crew was finally dispatched. She stayed in the empty briefing room for hours, waiting for word about the operation. Had they managed to get to the extraction point? Had they evacuated those men she'd been forced to leave stranded?

Heavy footsteps coming down the hallway made her jump. She headed for the door, but it swung open when she was halfway to it. Her heart did a crazy roll in her chest when she saw Cam standing there, tall and gorgeous in his desert camo utilities. She hadn't seen him in months, and to run into him here at this hour was unbelievable.

"Cam!" Ignoring the nervous butterflies fluttering in her belly, she gave him a delighted smile. "What are you doing—"

His grave expression and the tense set of his shoulders cut off her words like an axe. Her hand flew to her throat. This was no accidental meeting. He'd come looking for her.

"What?" she asked, swamped by a sense of impending dread. Her heart pounded dully in her ears.

Unmoving in the doorway, Cam stared back at her with haunted blue eyes. "It's Ty."

# ONE

*Arlington National Cemetery, Washington, DC*
*Ten days later*

SHIVERING IN HER Army National Guard dress uniform, Devon flinched when the Air Force honor guard fired their twenty-one gun salute beside Ty's grave. His flag-draped silver coffin sat suspended over it, waiting to be lowered into the dark hole.

The haunting strains of Taps rang out, and her skin erupted in goose bumps. When the last note died away in the crisp fall air, the honor guard folded the flag into a perfect triangle that showed part of the blue field and white stars. Across the grave, seated with her husband's comforting arm around her shoulders, Ty's mother accepted the flag from his commanding officer. She clutched it to her chest and stared with swimming eyes at the box that held the remains of her only child. Her shattered expression alone made Devon want to weep.

She jerked when her friend Ryan put an arm around her, but after a second instinctively moved closer to him. Away from the other man flanking her. Both wore their dress blues, and both had borne Ty to his grave. She was grateful for their presence, but standing this close to Cam hurt almost as much as knowing Ty was going into that hole.

Because they both knew the truth about why he'd died.

The wind gusted through her dress jacket and over her legs below the hem of her skirt. She barely heard what the chaplain was saying—she didn't care what he had to say. Nothing could ease her pain. Or the suffocating guilt that came with it.

When he stopped, the family stood to say their final goodbyes. One by one they placed yellow roses atop the silver casket until the lid was smothered in flowers. Ty's mother trembled beneath her husband's arm for a moment, then let out a keening wail of grief so sharp it made the hair on Devon's neck stand up. Struggling to hold her composure, she bit the inside of her cheek until she tasted blood.

As his family left the graveside Devon stood there, rigid in the cold, staring at her ex-boyfriend's coffin. *I'm so sorry, Ty. So very sorry...*

Ryan stepped up to the edge of the grave. He saluted, bringing his right hand to the brim of his scarlet beret. His square jaw was clenched tight. After a few silent moments he dropped his hand and walked away without a word, leaving her with Cam. The lump in Devon's throat threatened to choke her.

Cam came forward next and raised his salute against the maroon beret that marked him as a Pararescueman. Like Ty had been. She risked a glance at him, and the grief etched in his face stabbed at her. He took something out of his pocket and turned it over in his fingers. Her throat tightened when she realized what he held. She automatically put a hand to her neck, touching the chain that held the lucky quarter's twin over her heart.

Cam stared at the keepsake a moment longer before hunkering down beside the casket. The quarter flashed briefly in the weak afternoon light as he placed it gently on the lid. "See you on the other side, buddy." He rose and took up a position behind Devon, staying at a respectful distance to let her say her final goodbye. Killing her with his presence and not even realizing it.

The tears were there, just as they'd always been since she'd been notified of Ty's death. But tears didn't relieve her suffering, and didn't change the fact that Ty was gone.

Devon squeezed her hands into fists, her short nails cutting into her damp palms. She wished Cam would leave so she could say goodbye properly. So she wouldn't betray Ty more than she already had.

Cam didn't move, but she'd known he wouldn't leave her to face this alone.

Fighting to ignore him and the unsettling effect he had on her, she tried to think of something to say to Ty. She'd already said the most important things while sitting next to his zipped body bag in the morgue at Bagram.

She snapped a smart salute and held it while she stared down at his coffin. "Bye, Ty," she whispered, easing her trembling hand down to her side.

Cam's hand settled on her shoulder. She flinched, and he dropped it. She couldn't bear his touch right now. It hurt too much.

"Come on," he said quietly. "It's time to go."

She swallowed and managed a nod, but couldn't look at him as she turned from Ty's casket. Walking away from his grave was the second hardest thing she'd ever done.

The hardest had put him in it.

She walked through the rows of pristine white headstones. So many of them, and many more still to come before the war on terror ended. If it ever did.

With each step the heels of her pumps bit into the damp, meticulously-kept grass. She kept her eyes focused on Ryan standing at the line of their cars, but she was acutely aware of Cam's undeniably magnetic presence a few feet behind her.

Ryan forced a tired smile when she neared him. "Okay?"

"Yes."

"We'll follow you back."

"Are you sure you're okay to drive?" Cam's voice was full of concern.

She didn't look at him. "I'm sure." The last thing she needed was to be trapped in a car with him.

Devon climbed into her rental car and drove to her hotel, wondering what the hell she was doing hosting the reception for some of Ty's military buddies.

*You're tough. You can handle this.*

BACK IN HER bland hotel room, she ordered Mexican takeout because Ty had loved it. Cam and Ryan went out to pick it up and find some beer while she took a shower and changed into her civvies. The guests arrived, and the PJs told stories about Ty as they ate, but Devon couldn't relax. They should blame her, hate her, but they didn't. She wished they would. It would be easier for her to bear.

They finished eating, and Cam raised his Corona, Ty's favorite beer. "To a hell of a PJ, and the best damn friend anyone could have."

"Hooyah," Ryan and the others chorused, holding up their bottles.

Devon's throat was too tight to speak. She tapped bottles with guys around her and avoided Cam's gaze while she took a sip. She was doing fine. All she had to do was hold it together for a little longer.

She was still okay when the other guests filed out and left her with Ryan and Cam. But when Ryan stood to leave, she jumped up with him, assaulted by a wave of dread. Given the way she was feeling, being alone with Cam was *not* a good idea.

She knew it, but couldn't summon the will to ask him to leave with Ryan. Truth was, she didn't want to be alone right now. Not when she'd just been reminded that death stalked all of them. Their professions ensured that.

Beneath the vulnerability that came with knowing how fleeting life was, she was all too aware of Cam's Pacific blue eyes resting on her face as she walked Ryan to the door. Cam's presence had always unsettled her, right from the first time she'd met him.

While she'd been dating his best friend.

Pulling on his shoes, Ryan smiled up at her with his endearing bad-boy grin. "Wish I could stay longer."

She wished that too. "Can't you stay for one more beer?"

"Wish I could take you up on that, darlin', but I can't. Flight leaves in two hours." His mahogany gaze moved to Cam over on the couch. "See you over there."

"You know it."

Just the sound of his deep voice sent traitorous shivers of pleasure up her spine. "You might see me there too," she blurted to Ryan, wishing she could leave with him.

Ryan's brows shot up, but it was Cam's gaze zeroing in on her that she noticed. The touch was almost physical, so strong it made the skin at her nape tingle.

"For real?' Ryan asked. "You just got back."

"I heard a rumor that they might extend my tour." She shoved her hands into her jeans pockets and shrugged. "Not sure, though."

He paused, studying her face. She held her spine straight and kept her expression blank, refusing to show even a hint of the paralyzing doubt she carried with her now.

"Well let me know if you're coming, so I know to look for you." He hugged her. His arms were warm and strong, offering the comfort she badly needed, but it wasn't what she really wanted.

Damn her to hell, she wished with everything in her that Cam was holding her. The knowledge made her feel sick.

"You sure you're okay?" Ryan asked quietly against her hair.

She nodded, fighting the sting of tears caused by equal parts grief and guilt. "I'll be fine."

He released her and stepped back. "No wonder Ty was hung up on you."

More guilt settled in her belly, but she forced a smile. "Don't do anything I wouldn't do over there."

His eyes twinkled with mischief. "Now what fun would that be?"

Devon shut the door behind him, and it seemed like he took all the oxygen with him. Being alone in the same room with Cam made it hard to breathe. Especially now with the silence building between them like a wall.

"Why didn't you tell me?"

She tensed. The low timbre of his voice brushed over her nerve endings like a caress.

Bracing herself, she turned around and met the vivid stare that threatened to suck the remaining air out of her lungs. He had one muscular arm draped over the back of the couch, and his dark blond brows were pulled into a tight frown. She couldn't ignore him now, yet she couldn't summon the courage to go sit beside him. She stayed where she was. "It never seemed to be the right time. A lot's happened over the past few weeks."

For an instant she thought the muscles in his jaw clenched, but it was gone so fast she told herself she'd imagined it. Cam never got annoyed. He was easy-going personified. And the sexiest, most mouth-watering man she'd ever met, much as she hated herself for thinking it.

"Did Ty know you might be extending your tour?"

She nodded, fighting the urge to rub her suddenly damp palms on her jeans.

Cam tilted his head. "There a reason why you're still standing next to the door like that?"

"No." She forced herself to walk over, grab her Corona off the low table strewn with takeout Mexican containers, and sit stiffly on the opposite end of the couch. She searched for something to say to fill the awkward void stretching out between them, but nothing came to mind.

Cam watched her in silence for a long moment before making another attempt at conversation. "Ty once told me you became a pilot because you were afraid to fly. That true?"

The change to a more neutral subject helped. "More like I was afraid of crashing." For good reason. She shrugged, pushing the memory away. "I went to therapy for a while, and thought learning to fly might help me overcome it. Seemed like a good idea at the time."

Cam grinned, flashing a dimple in his lean right cheek. "Helluva way to conquer your fear."

"Yeah. I know it sounds stupid, but being in a helicopter always feels safer than being in a fixed wing. I'm closer to the ground, can land pretty much anywhere if I need to." She shrugged. "I like being in a helo better."

"Especially if you're at the controls."

"Yeah," she said with a reluctant grin. "Especially then."

"You'll have to take me up sometime."

She shot him a bland look. "Right, because you don't get enough chopper rides already."

"Never been up with a female pilot, though."

Because she was tempted to keep staring, she looked away from his beautiful face. "Well, we fly pretty much the same as the boys do." *Only better.*

"I bet you're great at it."

"I'm not bad," she admitted, brushing at an imaginary piece of lint on her jeans. "I love flying medevac. I like knowing I might give someone a chance—" The words clamped her throat shut like a garrote. No one had been able to get to Ty in time. He'd died before the rescue crew could get there.

She knew the reason behind that too. And so did Cam.

Devon hastily took another sip of her beer, half-afraid it would come right back up. The bitter taste rolled over her tongue and lingered in her mouth.

"Dev. You know you—"

"Want another beer?"

"No."

She wouldn't look at him. She could barely look at herself in the mirror anymore. And she was facing another six-month-long deployment back to the place and job that haunted her every waking moment. Not to mention her dreams.

Forcing the thought away, she made herself focus on what Cam was feeling. She wasn't the only one hurting. This had to be really tough on him. "You okay? You must miss him."

"Yeah. I miss him like hell."

Her heart ached for him. He suffered through his grief stoically. "How long were you guys friends?"

"Almost four years. We went through The Pipeline together. Me and Ty and Ryan."

A sad smile formed on her lips. She was proud of every single one of them for getting through that grueling program. It wasn't called Superman School for nothing. "You know, if I was a guy and could qualify for Special Ops, I'd be a PJ too."

One side of Cam's delicious mouth turned up. "Yeah?"

A strange pressure began to build in her chest. Like a balloon being filled with helium. "I admire the hell out of all of you." She cradled the cold, damp bottle between her hands and managed to look at him. "What's it feel like to be a medic commando?"

"Nothing like it. I love what I do." He reached for his own beer and took a sip before offering her another smile. "What's it like to fly a Black Hawk on a night mission?"

She bit back a grin. "Pretty damn awesome."

"There you go, we're not all that different. Besides, you've got some medical training."

"Nothing like you guys." Some of the tension bled out of her tight shoulders. This was better. She could almost forget he was the reason for her discomfort when they talked easily like this. "Did Ryan want to be a Combat Controller right from the start?"

"Yeah. He wanted to be on the front lines with the SEALs and Delta boys. And he's good. It suits him."

Yeah, it did. Special Ops suited them all, but Ryan had that knife-edge to him. He was harder than the others. More suited to killing than saving lives like the PJs did. But Cam wasn't fooling her. "You work with 'mixed company' too, if you're stationed at Bagram. If you were working conventional missions, they'd have you based at Kandahar."

His eyes glinted with humor. "Yeah, but you're not supposed to know about that."

She had trouble envisioning him working with soldiers that hardened and deadly. "Have you worked with Ryan out there?"

"Couple of times."

She hated the thought of them going back into harm's way. She didn't want to bury any more of her friends. Or be the cause of more funerals.

"Can I ask you something?"

Something told her she wasn't going to like the question he had in mind. She tensed instinctively. "Sure."

"How come I make you nervous?"

She shot a startled glance at him. There was no amusement on his face, just a kind of puzzlement. And maybe a hint of disappointment. She looked away. "Why do you say that?"

He snorted like she'd just insulted him. "Because you're sitting over there as far away from me as you can get. Any further, and you'll fall off the end of the couch."

"That's not why. I've just…got a lot on my mind."

"You used to be comfortable with me," he pointed out. "But since Ty passed you keep giving me the cold shoulder. Have I done something?"

"No." Oh no, she'd done this to herself, and all on her own.

He was quiet a long time, scrutinizing her. "I wouldn't do anything, you know. Not unless you *wanted* me to."

Her gaze flew to his. "What?" She couldn't keep the alarm out of her voice.

His eyes held hers, direct and brutally honest. "You know I wouldn't."

So she hadn't misunderstood him.

*Oh, Jesus.* After all this time the awful truth was out, thrown into her face like a slap though he hadn't meant it that way. The blood rushed to her face so fast she felt dizzy. *This isn't happening.*

Had he known all along despite how hard she'd tried to hide it? Was he seriously telling her the forbidden attraction was mutual? It was too much. She jumped off the couch, looking anywhere but at him.

"Dev."

She held up a hand.

"Dev, it's okay."

No, damn it, it wasn't okay. None of this was okay, especially today. She felt exposed, like he'd invaded her mind and pried out her most private thoughts. "Jesus, Cam, we just buried him less than four hours ago." They probably hadn't even backfilled the grave yet.

"Yeah, and I'm due out in the morning, so when the hell else are we going to be able to finally have this conversation?" His eyes burned with frustration.

*How about never?* "I can't believe you'd say anything." He wasn't drunk—he'd only had two beers. She had no explanation for his behavior. "I'm not talking about this. It's completely inappropriate." No—it was *hideous*. Her lungs felt like they might explode.

"Just...stop for a second."

She shook her head.

"Look, all I'm saying is that you're overreacting."

She narrowed her eyes at him. "Like *hell* I am."

He came off the couch so fast she backed up. He stopped. In the awful silence the two of them squared off like adversaries. It made her want to cry.

Cam set his hands on his hips. "You're acting like you two were engaged or something, but you were only together a few weeks before he left." His expression was determined, implacable. "There's nothing wrong with the way we feel about each other."

"Yes there is." It would have killed Ty to find out

she had feelings for his best friend, let alone that they were reciprocated.

"No, there isn't. And ignoring it won't make it go away."

It had to. She couldn't handle the alternative. She retreated another step.

"Dev, just stop and look at me."

*Nope.*

Her back bumped into the wall. Embarrassed, she pushed away and stalked over to the table to clear the disposable plates. Anger crept in, taking away some of the shock, but she was still precariously close to tears. "Leave it alone, okay? Let's just forget this conversation ever happened." Or at least pretend to until he left. She couldn't face this now.

Before she could move, Cam's hand flashed out and caught her wrist. She swallowed a gasp as heat shot up her arm and pooled low in her belly. His long fingers curled around her bones, strong and protective, burning her skin. Yet gentle enough to remind her of all the reasons she was attracted to him. Part of her wanted to crawl into his lap and press up against his powerful frame to seek comfort, relief from the intense need he created in her. Torn between crippling shame and the strongest yearning she'd ever known, she turned her head away.

"Dev."

Not daring to look at him, she squeezed her eyes shut. "Please don't." She was afraid of what she might do if he pressed her about this. Right now she wasn't sure if she could fight her gut-deep desire for him. She felt weak, confused. Ready to shatter.

But he wouldn't let go. "I'm not coming on to you. I just want to set some things straight, and I don't want this lying between us." The warmth of his hand settled into her skin until she finally opened her eyes to glare at him. The intensity of his stare made her wish she hadn't. "Did you love him?" he asked quietly.

Her stomach seized up even harder. *Love* him? She and Ty had been together a short time before he'd deployed, but they'd been friends for months before that. The night he'd introduced her to Cam, however, everything had changed for her. "I cared about him," she said defensively. And the knowledge that she wasn't consumed with grief because he was lying in his grave made her feel horrible.

"I know you did. But you weren't in love with him."

Why was he pushing her so hard? She set her jaw, hating the betraying blush that stained her cheeks. "No." The worst part was she'd been ten times more attracted to Cam than she'd ever been to Ty.

"That's all I'm trying to point out. You've got nothing to feel guilty about," he finished, releasing her wrist.

She snatched her hand back as if he'd burned her, still feeling the imprint of his fingers. The paper plate wobbled in her grip.

"Hear me?"

"I think you should go."

The instant the words were out she went dead still. She couldn't believe she'd actually said that to him. Of all Ty's friends, Cam was the sweetest. Her favorite, for his personality alone. But he had no right to bring this up, let alone be insensitive enough to call her on it and keep insisting they talk about it. That hurt more than she'd ever thought possible.

Cam didn't move, but a flicker of anger showed in his eyes. "I probably should, but I'm not leaving until we clear the air."

She raised her chin. "Believe me, you've cleared it. And then some." Her cheeks still stung from it.

"That wasn't—" He ran a hand through his hair, his frustrated sigh loud in the quiet room. "I didn't mean to embarrass or upset you. I just don't want you to feel guilty anymore."

"Guilty?" she rasped, feeling like he'd sucker punched her. "What the hell do you know about the kind of guilt I feel?"

His jaw tightened. "Don't even go there, Dev."

"I'm already there, because guess what? I live with it every second!"

He took a step toward her, ignoring the way she drew back. "Yeah, we need to talk about this too." His eyes blazed down at her, full of conviction.

"No."

"Yes."

She shook all over. Had to wrap her arms around her body to hold herself together. "*Stop*."

He did, but she could tell he didn't want to let it go. "I don't want you to be uncomfortable around me," he said after a pause.

She almost laughed. "Like I won't be after this? God Cam, if you knew how I felt then everyone else had to." Including Ty.

Images formed in her mind like a slow motion movie. Of Ty in the barren mountains of Afghanistan, working on the other wounded despite the bullet wounds in his belly and legs and the sickening amount of blood he must have lost. Or the awful, relentless pain he must have been in. What if he'd been listening for the sound of the medevac's rotors while he lay dying? She wanted to throw up.

"He didn't know, Dev. Or if he did, he never said anything."

She fought the urge to cover her face. What if their relationship had meant much more to Ty than it had to her? Was it possible he'd fallen in love with her in such a short time? He'd never told her that. She hadn't seen their relationship as deep or permanent. In time it might have grown into something more, but not after Cam entered the picture.

"What…what did he say about me?" The words were almost a whisper.

"Just how great you were."

She flinched. Yeah, she was great all right. Fantasizing about his best friend instead of him when she went to bed at night.

In a way Cam was right, though. She *had* nothing to feel guilty about on that count. She and Ty had never talked about not seeing other people, or about being exclusive. She'd missed him when he'd deployed, but she'd also felt relieved because it meant she was free to move on. She'd planned to end their relationship once an acceptable amount of time had passed. And it wasn't as if she'd ever have acted on her feelings for Cam while she was with Ty. Hell, she wasn't going to act on them now that he was gone, but that didn't make her feel any better.

"And Ryan?" she challenged. God, did his flight really leave in two hours, or had he left to give them time alone, to...*console* each other? She wanted to cringe with shame. Is that how they all saw her? Some sort of Special Ops groupie? She pressed a hand to her churning stomach.

Cam shook his head in annoyance, the light picking out honey-gold highlights in his short hair. "You're reading too much into this." He folded his well-developed arms across his chest. It irritated her that she wanted to stare at the muscles stretching the cotton of his black T-shirt. "Look, I'm sorry I said anything."

That made two of them. "Why did you?"

His eyes tightened at the corners. Very un-Cam like. "You don't think I felt it? That I wasn't interested in you from day one?"

Had she recognized it? Maybe part of her had. The thing that frightened her most was her attraction to him wasn't just physical. What she truly wanted went far deeper than that. Cam wanting her wasn't enough, and pinning girlish romantic fantasies on him was as stupid as it was unrealistic. Even if she could give herself to him, losing him afterward would break her heart. "I'm going to clean up," she blurted, hating how off-balance she felt. She was always steady under pressure, always kept her emotions under control. Cam made her feel completely unhinged.

"Wait." He tried to stop her, but she brushed past him to pick up a few glasses and carried them to the kitchen. He followed her. Every second made her hyper aware of his presence. Being close to him was like having sandpaper rubbed over her raw skin.

By the time she finished, tears stung her eyes. She was a horrible, despicable person for wanting him this much, and so was he for adding to her misery.

"Hey."

The tenderness in his low voice nearly undid her. She bit her lip as she gathered the empty beer bottles, wishing she'd never invited him or Ryan back. Instead of saying goodbye to a good friend, she'd dishonored Ty's memory without meaning to.

"Dev?"

She bit down harder, wanting to cry, and shook her head.

He stepped up behind her, close enough that she could feel the heat of his body and catch the woodsy scent of his aftershave. "Hey. Ah, shit, honey, don't cry."

*Oh God, don't touch me.* She couldn't bear it. She looked over her shoulder and forced herself to meet his gaze. "Tell me the truth, Cam."

He set down the garbage bag he held. "Okay."

"Did I hurt him?"

His brows went up. "Hurt him? Jesus, no—never. You made him happy. The happiest I'd ever seen him."

A sob caught in her chest. She swallowed hard to dislodge the lump in her throat. "I never meant to hurt him." She sounded pathetic, but she was so confused.

"You didn't," Cam insisted. He ignored her flinch and laid a hand on her shoulder. The warmth of his palm felt good. She wanted to lean into his strength, but she couldn't allow him to know she was weakening. "He cared about you, but he knew it wasn't serious yet."

She hoped so. She would never have allowed it to get serious because her feelings for Cam made that impossible. Yet shouldn't she feel something more for Ty than a misty-eyed sadness? She'd slept with him, walked hand-in-hand with him, kissed him goodbye at the airport the day he left for Afghanistan. Instead of guilt, didn't she at least owe him more grief, regardless of how little time they'd been together?

"Stop doing this to yourself, Dev. Ty wouldn't have wanted this, and you know it."

"I can't *help* it."

Cam didn't argue. He pulled her against his solid chest before she could resist, his gentle insistence destroying the last of her control. His arms were strong around her, one big hand cradling the back of her head as she turned and pressed her cheek against his hard chest.

The tears leaked out, hot and silent. She cried for Ty, and because he'd died in the prime of his life, bleeding out in the desert waiting for the help that never reached him. She cried because such an incredible man was gone and no one would ever hear his infectious laugh again. She cried for his friends and family who were all grieving, whose lives would never be the same without him. She cried for her unintended betrayal of him.

And she cried for what could never be between her and the man holding her.

He wasn't making any advances on her. Right now he was back to Cam her buddy, there to shield and protect her. His embrace felt exactly right, no matter how much she wished it didn't. Yet for just a moment she allowed herself to savor the feel of him, tall and strong, his clean-shaven cheek resting against the crown of her head.

Forcing away the thought that she was somehow

cheating on Ty, she nestled closer, heart swelling at the way Cam's arms tightened. Enveloping her in security. His heartbeat drummed steady and strong beneath her. His clean, masculine scent was heaven. Her breathing slowed to match his, calming her, but she couldn't make herself pull away. He felt too good, and she'd imagined him holding her like this so many times...

Without warning, the heat began to build. Subtle at first, but quickly racing over her skin until her nipples peaked inside the lace cups of her bra. Clenching her teeth, it took all her will not to rub against his chest just to ease the ache in them. Between her thighs a hot glow throbbed, and when she shifted, the unmistakable ridge of his erection pressed against her abdomen. Sucking back a gasp, she stilled. The muscles in her aching core tightened, her mind already imagining what it would feel like to have him kiss her deep and hard while he pinned her to the bed with his powerful body and thrust in and out...

*No.* She couldn't think about that. Her hands pushed at his chest.

Cam's arms stayed locked around her. "I can't help it," he said softly, his tone irritatingly reasonable. "But like I said, I won't do anything unless you want me to. I know you're not ready."

She lifted her head to study his face. Did he mean he planned to wait until she was? It could never work between them. "Cam..."

"I know," he murmured, tucking her head back down to his chest. "Just pretend it's not there."

A soggy laugh bubbled up, but she didn't pull away. For her, this was a line she couldn't cross. Her conscience wouldn't let her. Besides, she was an officer and he was enlisted. Being caught in a relationship together could have serious consequences for both their careers, and though she might end up at Bagram too, she'd never be able to see him. Another reason why she'd let her relationship with Ty go when he'd deployed.

*But you might not get another chance with Cam,* a voice whispered. *He's heading back to the front lines in the morning. He might not make it back.*

She shook the words away. She couldn't think like that.

Cam respected her enough to honor her choice, and in light of her uncertainty she was grateful for that. Unless she told him otherwise, he wouldn't push her for more. She was as safe as she wanted to be.

Thing was, part of her didn't want to be safe at all with him.

Memorizing the feel of him, she stayed in his arms for a few precious minutes before carefully moving away. He didn't stop her, merely stroked her hair back from her damp cheek as he watched her. His eyes held so much hunger and regret it tore her up inside. He wanted her as badly as she wanted him. If she gave the word, he'd take her to bed here and now.

*Touch me.*

The words formed on her tongue, her body pleading for an end to this agonizing tension between them. She gritted her teeth to keep from blurting them out.

Standing this close, his body heat licked over her skin like a caress. His gaze never left hers. "Promise you'll keep in touch, and let me know if you're coming back to Bagram."

"I will." Her voice sounded husky, even to her. Partly hunger, partly the knowledge of what he would face once he went back there. Dangerous missions while Pashtun warlords like General Nasrallah prowled around looking for the opportunity to launch a guerrilla attack. "And you be careful out there."

He nodded, still staring down at her. His eyes wandered over her face and lingered on her mouth for a breathless moment. Before she could turn away, he threaded his hands in her short hair, gently controlling her head as he tipped it back and leaned in to press a slow, firm kiss against her forehead.

Devon gasped and grabbed his upper arms as her nerves went haywire. Her fingers dug into the hard swells of his biceps and held on tight. The air around them shimmered and crackled with explosive energy that begged for release. One spark. That's all it would take to make them both go up in flames. It would be easy to let it happen. Too easy to tilt her head back and lift onto her toes, find his deliciously full lips with hers and—

Cam abruptly let go and stepped back. She stumbled, wanting to weep at the loss of him, and he steadied her before moving away. Her body hummed with unfulfilled need, and her mind shrieked that this might be the last time she ever saw him. But she couldn't move. Couldn't take that final step over the invisible line between them.

His crooked smile was the saddest she'd ever seen. "Bye, Dev. Take care of yourself."

She choked back a sob. "You too."

Through tear blurred eyes, she watched him walk out

of her hotel room. When the door clicked shut behind him, a sense of panic welled up.

*Call him back.*

Her head came up, eyes fastening on the door knob only a few meters away. She could still stop him. All she had to do was throw the door open and call his name. He'd come back for her. She knew he would.

A car engine came to life.

*Open the door and call him!*

The muscles in her legs jerked, her body wanting to move toward the door. She had only moments left to change her mind. *It's not too late. Call him.*

"I *can't*," she cried in misery, heart racing beneath her too-tight ribs.

Headlights swung around through the windows and turned out of the parking lot, then faded as the car sped away. Her knees gave out.

She'd lost him.

Sinking to the carpeted floor, she wrapped her arms around her waist and rocked as the scalding tears fell.

# TWO

So THIS IS what a broken heart felt like. Cam rubbed a hand over his sternum as he drove down the I-95. Hurt like a son of a bitch under there. The tightness in his chest made it hard to draw a deep breath. Burying Ty and losing Devon in the same day was almost more than he could take.

He shifted in his seat and turned up the radio. To distract himself from the fact that each mile took him further away from Devon and closer to a warzone, he forced himself to sing along. Dammit, he still felt torn. Part of him was glad to be leaving, but the other part wanted to go back and stay with Devon so she wouldn't be alone. Even if she didn't want to talk to him again and it meant crashing on the couch in her hotel room. He couldn't stand seeing her sad, and knowing he'd inadvertently caused some of it made him feel like an asshole.

The flare of shock in her eyes when he'd not so subtly informed her he knew she wanted him. Had she really thought she'd been able to hide it from him? Or that it was one sided? The spark between them was undeniable, and she had to know it as well as he did. While he understood her reasons for trying to ignore the attraction, that didn't mean he liked them. It had taken every ounce of will to walk out of her hotel room. Holding her tight against him, feeling the tremor of arousal that ran through her delectable body had damn near killed him. He'd been dying to kiss her until she couldn't think, then carry her into the bedroom and stretch out on top of her. Make love to her until she cried out his name and came at least twice, then cradle her afterward while she slept.

He cranked the radio up higher, annoyed with himself. Man, he was a total sap over her, to be thinking like that. Maybe he should be glad she hadn't been ready to face the chemistry between them.

If he'd tried anything, he would have hurt her worse than she already had been. And he'd have irreparably damaged their friendship. Ultimately, that's what had stopped him. Devon meant a hell of a lot more to him than any other woman ever had. She understood what made him tick. She knew what his job meant to him, same as he knew what it meant to her to be a pilot.

Pounding drums and the scream of electric guitars came from the radio. He breathed a sigh of relief when the exit for the airport finally came into view. After he dealt with the paperwork at the rental car place, he shouldered his duffel and walked up to the check-in counter. By the time he cleared security and strode through the terminal, he was intent on getting to the nearest bar for a double scotch on the rocks.

*Christ, I should have just kept my mouth shut.*

Too late now. The damage was already done. He couldn't come up with a single reason why he'd thought talking to her about it would be a good idea. He blamed his upcoming flight for his frankness. Ordinarily he wouldn't have said anything—let alone on the day of his best friend's funeral—but knowing he only had hours

until a plane took him back to Afghanistan had shot
his common sense all to hell. Dev put on a brave face,
but he'd seen the vulnerability underneath it. At least
he'd always have the memory of holding her and having her melt in his arms. The woman had him tied in
more knots than a parachute rigging. She'd done that
to him since day one. How the hell had she never realized it before tonight?

His phone vibrated in his pocket. He yanked it out,
praying it was Devon. It was his mom. Pushing aside
the disappointment, he answered all her questions about
the funeral and did the best he could to soothe her fears
about him going back overseas. When he hung up, he
felt worse than ever.

Blowing out a breath, he spotted a bar and strode
over, dropping his bag and taking a high-top stool near
the bartender. He didn't drink much, normally. And he'd
already had two beers back at the hotel… The bartender
looked over at him and raised his brows.

The hell with it. "Two double scotches on the rocks."

"You got it."

Cam drummed his fingers on the polished wood surface and tried to get interested in the football highlights
playing on the TV mounted overhead. All that did was
remind him more of Devon, because the host was ana-
lyzing the Seahawks game. Her favorite team.

*Jesus, let her go already.*

Damned if he knew how, though. He knocked back
the first drink with one swallow and was reaching for
the second when a heavy hand landed on his shoulder.
He glanced up to find Ryan grinning at him. "What
the hell are you still doing here?" he said with a laugh.

"Flight got delayed." Ryan slid onto the stool next to him and ordered a beer. He glanced at the drinks Cam had lined up on the bar. "Guess I don't have to ask how it went with Dev."

"Nope." He picked up the next drink but sipped it this time. "Ah, shit, I don't know why I said anything to her about it in the first place."

"Yeah, you do." Ryan clapped him between the shoulder blades. "I'm only surprised you waited as long as you did."

Cam pretended to be interested in the Broncos recap. Damn, he couldn't get her face out of his head. A whole bottle of scotch couldn't do that.

"She'll come around. Just give her some time, buddy."

He didn't have much choice, did he? Cam reined in his thoughts. "You on the military transport to Andrews with me?"

"Yep. Kind of glad my other flight got canned."

In light of how depressing the whole day had been, Cam was damn glad to have the company. "Hard to believe we're going back already." On top of everything else, the heaviness in his heart reminded him they were leaving one buddy short.

"I know. It's the perfect ending to a shitty day." Ryan set his beer down and leaned his elbows on the bar. His gaze flicked from the TV to Cam, then back again. "So, uh… You ever hear what happened out there that night?"

His shoulders tensed. They'd never talked about it. Not even after the ramp ceremony when they'd escorted Ty's casket during that never-ending flight from Bagram to Andrews Air Force Base. The whole incident surrounding his death was still shrouded in secrecy like all Special Ops missions were. "Some. You?"

"Just what was in the after action report." Ryan fiddled with the label of his Budweiser. "I heard from some of the guys that he got cut off from the others."

"Yeah, I heard that too." Two other PJs had been out in that remote village with Ty, and neither of them knew what had happened to him after they'd taken the first casualties down the hillside for the evacuating choppers. Another firefight had broken out between them and the Taliban, and by the time they'd gone back into the village for him, he'd already been dead. "Visibility was the shits that night."

"I remember."

"It's possible the fog and wind played a part. I couldn't see fuck-all when we finally got in there." It was a miracle the pilot had gotten them to the LZ at all in those conditions.

Ryan nodded, still playing with his bottle. "Think he was maybe captured for a while? Would explain why nobody knew where he was until after the last air strike."

"Don't know, but he was still wearing his identifier on his sleeve when they found him. If he'd been at risk of being taken prisoner, he would've torn that off in a hell of a hurry no matter how badly he'd been wounded."

"Unless he was unconscious at the time."

Yeah. Cam shook his head. "If I'd been team leader that night, he would've been wearing plates in his body armor." A lot of guys took them out to lighten their load, but they might have saved Ty that night.

"Hindsight's twenty-twenty, man. He knew the risks."

Cam looked down at the melting ice cubes in his drink and managed a nod. It was hard to think of that happening to his best friend, dying out there alone, cut off from his PJ brothers. Harder still to know he'd arrived too late to do anything but zip Ty into a body bag. His fingers tightened around the tumbler. "Can we talk about something else?"

Ryan straightened. "Yeah. Sorry, man." He tipped his head back and drained the last of his beer. After a long pause he exhaled hard and signaled the bartender. Ryan indicated the empty scotch glasses with a nod. "Bring us two more of those, thanks."

Cam didn't argue. Some liquid anesthetic was welcome right now, especially if it meant he could get Ty and Devon out of his head for a little while. His phone went off again. His heart gave a hard thud when he saw the text message.

*Be safe. Dev.*

He stared at the tiny screen, the ache beneath his ribs growing worse. He could call her right now. Dial her number already programmed into his phone and try to smooth this whole thing over before he took off. The whole incident with her wasn't sitting well with him. *At all.* That sheen of tears in her eyes still cut him like a knife. She'd looked at him like he'd damn well kicked her in the gut, when all he'd done was tell her how he felt.

"Bad news?"

Yes and no. Her contacting him showed she cared and wasn't entirely pissed at him, but she'd texted instead of calling because she didn't want to talk to him. "It's Dev. Saying goodbye." He put the phone away. Calling her would only make things worse, and he'd already dealt with more than enough shit today.

For once, Ryan didn't have a snappy comeback. Or at least if he did, he kept it to himself. They sat in silence until the bartender set their drinks down. Turning toward his closest remaining buddy, Cam raised his glass. "To sleeping all the way to Bagram."

Ryan tapped his glass against Cam's. "Fucking A, brother."

*West of Peshawar, Pakistan*

SADIQ TOLD HIMSELF it was the bitter wind coming down the mountains that made his eyes sting. It had nothing to do with the fact he carried his beloved brother to an early grave. Grieving would mean he questioned Allah's divine will, and a devout Muslim would never do such a thing.

Yet a part of him did anyway. Hassan had meant everything to him. He'd been both father and mentor to him throughout his life, and his best friend. Now Sadiq was truly alone in the world.

A large group of farmers and their families watched the procession. Weathered faces and weary eyes followed him. The high-pitched wail of the women's cries lifted on the cold air and stoked his anger higher. He stopped them with a single, scathing glare. The awful caterwauling ended as quickly as if it had been cut with a blade, replaced by the eerie moan of the stiff wind.

As he walked he lowered his gaze to hide his contempt of the women who had made the offensive noise. Their bleating expression of grief was not welcome here.

Hassan had died a devout Muslim, unafraid of death because he'd known he would be welcomed into paradise. The peasant women's racket only drew attention to the fact they were burying a loved one and would make their enemies rejoice in the death of yet another innocent brother in Islam. Sadiq had no doubt some of them were watching right now.

A burning rage filled his heart. The front right pole of the litter he and three other men from the village carried dug into his shoulder, but he didn't adjust it. Concentrating on the pain in his muscles kept him from wanting to scream from the agony within.

The gathered crowd began a mournful dirge. Their voices rose into the clear air, rising and falling in eerie counterpoint to the constant wind. Fine dust blew into his face as he positioned his brother's body over the open grave and began lowering it. Sadiq clenched his jaw as it disappeared from view into the yawning hole. He alone had washed Hassan five times with camphor-scented water. He alone had carefully washed the right arm and hand twice, then the left, before ending with his brother's feet. He alone had wrapped him in the precious kafan their grandmother had made.

He set his back teeth as they settled his brother's corpse into its earthen cradle. The cleric's droning words of prayer drifted past him. All he could think about was holding Hassan's shrapnel-riddled body as he lay dying. No one had lifted a finger to help him or ease his pain, because his life had not been of value to the enemy. Sadiq's blistered hands balled into fists. He could still smell the warm blood mixing with the dust.

Mourners began filling the grave. They used their

hands as well as shovels, buckets and trowels. The only tools these poor farmers had. They lived in poverty, yet most of the extra money his brother had earned smuggling guns and opium had gone toward sending Sadiq to a better life in Europe. That's how much Hassan had loved him. His brother had not wanted him to suffer the same kind of bleak, harsh existence that he had been sentenced to. In the end, that same heroic effort had killed him.

Sadiq covered his brother with shovelfuls of the crumbling Pakistani soil he'd struggled to eke a living from. *Thank you, Hassan. May Allah bestow his blessings upon you.*

He made sure the earth was not packed too tightly, for Hassan would have to be able to sit up when the time came for him to undergo the angels' questioning. Sadiq had no doubt his brother would answer each question correctly and earn his swift passage into paradise. His body would then join his soul when Allah called all true Muslims home on the Day of Resurrection.

The raw blisters on Sadiq's palms burned from when he'd dug the grave. He ignored the pain and kept shoveling until he was satisfied he'd mounded the dirt high enough to deter any scavenging jackals. The crowd of mourners ended the final dirge as he finished, then one by one left the graveside. He stared at it, frozen, until his grandmother approached and laid her gnarled fingers on his sleeve. He did not protest her presence because she was a pure woman, many years past the chance of monthly bleeding that would have tainted Hassan's grave.

"Come," she whispered. He shook his head, watched

her give a final blessing to her dead grandson and hobble down the hill toward the tiny village where he had been born. She disappeared over the crest of the hill, her back bent over from a life of hard labor and birthing too many babies. It depressed him. Almost half of the children born here did not survive infancy.

Sadiq stayed long after she had gone. A deep hole remained inside him, as dark and empty as it had been the day of his brother's death. No. More so. Before that day he'd been a moderate living in the west among the unbelievers. Now he was hardened because of what the Americans had done to his family.

"I know what I have to do," he said to Hassan, for his brother's soul was still nearby. Sadiq hated the bitterness filling his heart. A worthy Muslim would not question the teachings in the Quran.

Death was predetermined by Allah, meant to be accepted without condition. Sadiq knew he could never accept Hassan's death. His brother had died unnaturally, shedding his life's blood into the soil of their homeland while the enemy stood by and watched. Retribution was necessary. Without it, Hassan's soul would forever wander between heaven and earth. Trapped as his mortal body was now trapped beneath the ground.

Sadiq would not let that happen.

With the wind whipping up more tears in his eyes, he knelt and laid a hand over the mounded soil. "I will make this right, brother," he vowed softly. Allah must have heard him, because the next gust that blew over him was warm as the spring rains.

# THREE

*Bagram Airfield, Afghanistan*
*Three weeks later*

DEVON HAD ALREADY served at Bagram, but it was still a shock to realize how big the remote base was when she landed. Stepping off the tail ramp of the C-17 Globemaster with all her gear, she looked around in awe at the small city before her.

"Home sweet home," Will said beside her, lugging his own duffel. "Looks a hell of a lot better than it did after the Russians used it."

"Does it ever." She scanned for her friend Candace, who'd been there for over a month on her own tour as an Air Force Spectre pilot.

She'd also contacted Ryan and Cam, but only a few hours before her flight to Germany so they wouldn't have a chance to reply. Almost a month had passed since Ty's funeral, but her feelings for Cam hadn't faded. She wasn't sure she was ready to see him again quite yet.

She thought of the emblem she was cross-stitching, tucked away safely with her gear. She had stitched Ty's name above the Pararescue angel with her spread wings surrounding the globe, and beneath, the words *That Others May Live*. She'd done almost half of it on the flight over, but she'd finish it on her down time between exercises and missions. Part of her wasn't ready to let him go yet.

Following the throng of fellow soldiers, she made her way into one of the large administrative buildings and waited in line to get squared away. Leaving Will to find his own quarters, she headed across the base to where the housing was located. Bagram was fully equipped to look after all the service members stationed there, and had all kinds of amenities, even a Burger King tractor-trailer. Anything was an improvement from what the first Americans had found here back at the start of the war on terror. Devon noted signs with red triangles that still lined the edge of the roads, warning people of un-cleared terrain outside the security fences.

Ahead of her, a group of women came out of another building. One was tall and blond, and her leggy stride had Devon craning her neck to make out the woman's distant profile. She caught the blonde's distinctively husky laugh as it floated through the air. "Ace!"

Candace stopped and whipped her head around. Her eyes opened in wide surprise and a huge smile broke over her pretty face. "Spike!" She ran across the pave-ment, and Devon had barely enough time to drop her bags before her friend all but tackled her.

Candace squeezed her tight before stepping back to look at her. "I didn't think you'd be in already! You look great, by the way. Love the short do," she said, ruffling Devon's inverted bob.

"Fits better under my helmet this way." Dev laughed. "I was just trying to get my bearings again. Wanna show me to my new digs?"

"And I happen to know just where they are." She

hefted a bag over her shoulder and put her free arm around Devon's waist. "I arranged it so we're roomies."

"How did you manage that?"

"It's no biggie. Two of the other girls in our hut are Army, so you'll be in good company. And there are your new best friends," she said, gesturing to the group she'd been walking with. "Come on, I'll introduce you."

Dragged along in the wake of her friend's longer legs, Devon smiled at the three women waiting on the road, watching them.

"Everybody, this is Devon Crawford. Dev, this is Maya Lopez, a Security Forces officer," she said, indicating a honey-skinned woman about Dev's height with dark straight hair and striking blue-green eyes. They shook hands. "This is Erin Kelly, an Army flight nurse."

"Hi," the brunette said softly. Her smile was a bit on the shy side, but she seemed friendly.

"And this is Honor Girard, the Army's best mechanic on this base."

"I try," Honor said with a grin, tossing her cap of strawberry blond hair.

Candace grabbed the dropped bag and took Devon's elbow. "Okay, pleasantries aside—let's get this girl squared away and get some chow into her."

Devon rolled her eyes as her friend dragged her along. "Some things never change, I guess. Ace likes to think she's my keeper."

"Yeah," Maya answered, her dry tone holding the faintest trace of a Latin accent. "We've noticed she's a bit bossy."

The group walked her to the forty by fifteen foot B-hut she was going to call home for the next few months. Eight iron-framed bunk-style beds filled the putty-colored room, four against each wall.

"Bathrooms and showers are across the way," Candace said, pointing out the window toward the narrow street.

Well, it was better than tenting. Devon took the bunk on the far end against the opposite wall. She stowed her gear, listening to the chatter of her new roommates before following them back past the huge Exchange building to the chow hall where they got in line. She picked out British, Canadian, Aussie and German uniforms in the crowd as she scanned the room, a lingering excitement fluttering in her belly that Cam might be there. Or was it nerves? They felt pretty much the same to her.

"So," Maya said beside her, "Ace tells us you fly Hawks."

"That's right. Medevacs mostly," she added, smiling at the female private who dished food onto their plates from the metal warming trays. "Your job sounds interesting. What got you into that line of work?"

Maya shrugged, her long dark hair rippling over her shoulders. "I always wanted to serve. I figured this might be my ticket to getting into the FBI or The Agency one day." She grabbed a dinner roll from a basket.

"I'll stick to flying, thanks." Balancing her tray of chicken, mashed potatoes and steamed veggies with one hand while she grabbed a bottle of water with the other, Devon made her way through the sea of long tables. The food was a bit on the bland side, but it was hot and nourishing. Finishing a mouthful, she glanced around her group. "Anyone bumped into any PJs here?"

Candace flicked an amused glance at Maya, who

scowled and stabbed a piece of carrot with her fork. "Yeah, there's one over there," Maya said, jerking her chin to the left and then muttering something in Spanish Devon couldn't make out.

Swiveling in her seat, Devon looked around and caught a well-built man with dark hair and even darker eyes gazing at them. He gave a polite smile when he saw her, then quickly looked away. She didn't recognize him, and there was no sign of Cam. The acute disappointment she felt took her aback. Forcing it from her mind, she switched her attention back to Maya, who still had a sour expression on her face. "What, you don't like him or something?"

Almond-shaped turquoise eyes focused on her. "He annoys me," she said with a wave of her fork. "Always staring but won't say a word. Besides, he's enlisted."

"She calls him Tweedle Dumb," Candace put in between bites, and the others snickered.

"His name's Jackson," Erin said. "I've met him a couple of times in the hospital. He's really nice, just quiet," she added in his defense, sending Maya a hard look.

Maya shrugged. "Then you tell him to stop staring at me. He's not my type."

"You have a type?" Honor asked from across the table.

Maya shot her a withering look. "Yes, and apart from not being a creepy stalker, he has to at least be able to string a few words together."

Wow. The woman was more prickly than Ace, and that was saying something. Devon wasn't sure what to think of her.

Candace bumped her with an elbow, though her eyes

held a note of empathy. "Why'd you ask about the PJs, anyhow?"

"Oh, it's just that a friend of mine is doing another tour here."

"What's his name?" Erin asked.

"Tech Sergeant Cam Munro."

Erin frowned as she thought for a moment. "Is he tall and built, with light brown hair—"

"Dark blond." The picture the other woman's words painted of him sent a shockwave of heat rushing through her. Warm, hard muscle and a killer lopsided smile that had the power to make her weak in the knees. Her throat went so dry she almost couldn't swallow her food. "But, yes," she managed to croak.

Candace set down her silverware and grinned at her like an evil cat. "Really? Well now, this is interesting. How good a *friend* is he?"

Her cheeks flushed as she lowered her eyes and forked up another bite of chicken. "It's not like that. He's just a friend. I met him through Ty."

Candace immediately lost her cocky attitude. "I heard about what happened. I'm sorry."

Devon nodded but didn't answer.

"Ty as in Tyler Bradshaw? Wasn't he a PJ as well?" Erin asked.

*PJ groupie,* an inner voice accused. She cleared her throat. "Yes. I dated him for a short while before he deployed here." And now they were naming a street after him here on the base. So everyone would remember him and the sacrifice he'd made.

"Under the radar, obviously," Candace said.

"Very under the radar." She still felt conflicted about

that. She should have broken things off cleanly, and way sooner than she had. Instead, she'd waited until he'd gone overseas to let things fizzle out. Her lame attempt not to hurt him.

"I'm sorry." Erin's clear green eyes were full of sincerity. "I didn't know him well, but everyone seemed to like him. I heard he was really brave out there."

"Yeah. I heard that too." And she knew he had been. Without a doubt Ty would have given his all to protect the others. Just as Cam would if it came to that. All part of the Pararescue code of conduct. Devon pushed her plate away, suddenly unable to eat another bite.

"I saw your friend the other day," Erin put in. "He was going out as I was coming in with a patient."

Stupid of her stomach to clench up, but Devon couldn't stop worrying about him and Ryan. "I'm sure I'll cross paths with him eventually." And she dreaded that moment almost as much as she was dying for it.

"Well," said Maya as she raised her bottle of water toward her lips, "if you do see him, maybe you could ask him to get his PJ pal to keep his eyes to himself."

"I'll try to remember," Devon promised, sharing a grin with Erin.

As she was getting up to clear her place, she spotted a familiar face at the next table over. "Liam!" she called, setting her tray down to wave.

His dark head turned and a big grin broke over his hard face when he saw her. Laughing, Devon rounded the end of her table and rushed over to hug him. He squeezed her tight. "What the hell are you doing back over here, Spike?"

"Following orders, Major." She eyed his flight suit. "Just coming in, or going out?"

"In. Thought I'd grab a bite before I hit the rack."

"They still got you flying Chinooks?"

"Yep, and I know you're jealous." His blue eyes twinkled. "You on the 60?"

She nodded. "With Will. Have you seen him by the way? We're supposed to be at a briefing at nineteen hundred."

"Sorry, haven't seen him." His eyes flickered to the table she'd just vacated, but then he looked away fast, some indiscernible expression crossing his face. "They've got me out pretty much every night, but maybe I'll bump into you at the Exchange sometime. You owe me a game of pool as I recall."

She cocked a brow. "You want your ass handed to you in front of all your buddies?"

Liam laughed. "Good to see the flight from Germany didn't slow your mouth down." He tweaked her nose. "See you around, kid."

The others watched her silently as she made her way back to the table. "That was Liam," she explained when they all kept staring at her. "He's with the Night Stalkers, flying Chinooks." They still stared. What, like they didn't know about the fabled Night Stalkers?

Maya arched a dark brow. "You sure know a lot of guys around here for someone that just got in."

"I met Liam a few years back," Devon answered evenly, wondering what the sudden tension was about. "He's based out of Fort Lewis. I was up there for a training exercise."

"What's really happening," Candace interjected, "is

that Devon's got a lot of male buddies, because she considers herself to be one of the guys. And somehow she's still completely oblivious to the fact that they see her as anything but."

Dev rolled her eyes. "Oh, please. That's why I've got a swarm of men following me around, right?" And why she'd only ever dated a handful of them in her whole life. "Anyway, you know Liam too," she accused her friend. "You were with me the night we stayed out at the bar shooting pool because his fiancée had just dumped him, were you not?"

Candace winced and gave a nearly imperceptible shake of her head. Her eyes darted toward Honor.

"What?" Devon demanded, glancing over at her new roommate. Anything else she might have said evaporated when she saw the pinched look on Honor's face. Her eyes were downcast. The sweep of her strawberry blond hair obscured some of her profile, but what Devon could see of her skin had gone pale except for the rosy blush staining her porcelain cheeks.

Then it hit her. Honor. Not a common name. Couldn't be merely a coincidence that Liam had been engaged to someone in the Air Force named Honor.

"Oh, shit," she breathed, then bit her lip. "Sorry. I didn't know…"

Honor shook her head and forced a smile. "Don't worry about it. It's fine."

Devon looked to Candace for help, but her friend merely sighed and stood as she gathered her tray. "Well that was an interesting meal. Thanks, Dev."

Contrite, Devon followed in the wake of the suddenly quiet group as they left the chow hall. Honor made a point of patting her shoulder and smiling on the way back to their barracks, and Devon relaxed. Six months was a damn long time to live with four other women if they didn't get along. Grudges, cattiness...*ick*. No wonder she felt more comfortable hanging with the guys.

A cool wind picked up, blowing dust around them, but the sound of it was drowned by the sudden roar of an incoming Chinook's engines. Heart beating fast, Devon raised her head to watch it descend, a hulking mass of metal silhouetted by the twilit sky, its dual rotors tearing through the air with a thunderous noise. The rotor wash hit them even from where they stood far from the runway. Once its wheels set down, the pitch of the engines dropped as the pilots cut power. Adrenaline flooded her veins. She couldn't wait to get up in the air and do her part for the mission.

"Getting itchy, huh?" Candace asked.

"*So* itchy," she agreed, unable to wipe the grin off her face. Was there any better job in the world than being a helo pilot?

"Hey, Dev, is that you?"

She whipped around at the male shout and squinted through the cloud of dust raised by the Chinook's blades. The man was big, decked out in his BDUs and full combat gear.

Something about his stance was familiar. Then the dust cleared a bit, and she let out a squeal. "Ryan!" Throwing protocol aside, she ran over.

He dropped his massive ruck and opened his arms, catching her when she flew into them. His deep familiar laugh almost made her tear up. "Hey, Dev."

"Hi." She squeezed him tight before stepping back. "It's good to see you."

"You too."

She glanced around, heart rate increasing, but other than her roommates, nobody was staring at them. "Is Cam with you?"

"No, he's crashed. Had a long night last night."

She tensed. "Is he okay?"

"Yeah, he's fine. Lost a couple of guys, though."

*Oh.* Cam was tough, but he was a softie inside. Losing men would be hard on him. She imagined him wiped out, crawling under the sheets and throwing a muscular arm across his eyes. It made her want to find him just to make sure he was all right.

And then crawl in beside him to hold him against her, skin to skin.

She shook the thought away. "You heading out?" she asked Ryan.

"In a few minutes, yeah." His gaze fell unerringly on the group of women waiting for her. "Those your friends?"

"Roomies. Not sure they like me much, though. I've already managed to put my foot in my mouth."

He glanced down at her. "What, you? Come on."

"Trust me. I can still taste the dirt from the bottom of my boots. And that was before I scandalized them by running over to hug a non-com. But you're charming—maybe you can smooth this whole thing over for me, regardless of your inferior rank." She winked, then dragged him over by the hand. He went willingly enough, and it made her grin. There was no way she could've made him budge if he didn't want to, but he was a shameless flirt. "Ryan Wentworth, meet Maya, Honor, Erin and Candace."

Ryan shook their hands as she introduced them, but held Candace's hand a moment longer than was necessary—or polite—as he took in her flight suit. "You a pilot?" Devon winced. Poor guy had no idea he'd just inadvertently hit Ace's hot button.

Candace withdrew her hand and actually wiped it on her thigh as she gave him a contemptuous look from down the length of her nose, even though he was at least six inches taller. "That's right. Got a problem with that, Sergeant?"

Ryan's eyes lit with amusement, as though he got a kick out of her defensiveness. "No ma'am."

"Good. I take it you're a CCT?"

"Yes ma'am."

"Then you might need my services out there one day. And even though I am female, I still outrank you. Plus I'd hate for there to be any confusion as to whether you're talking to the right aircraft if you heard my voice during an operation."

He chuckled. Actually snickered, and Candace's dark eyes flashed as he spoke. "I'll keep that in mind, but I'm not real worried. I'd recognize your voice instantly if it came through my radio."

*Okay...* Before things could get more uncomfortable, Devon stepped in. "How long will you be out this time?"

Ryan deliberately held Candace's glare for another moment before looking at Devon. "Not sure. Day or two maybe. Depends on how quick the SEALs are with their hunting."

Going after Taliban and al Qaeda chiefs. Or warlords.

like Nasrallah. "Be careful. And say hi to Cam for me when you see him."

He smiled. "Trust me, Dev, you'll see him long before I do."

He picked up his ruck and walked away. Devon stared after him, thinking about that cryptic comment. Was Cam going to come looking for her? Her stomach flipped. God, she wasn't ready yet.

"Dev, let's go."

Falling into step with her friend, she glanced at her watch. Only forty minutes until her briefing, and she still had to find Will.

"By the way," Candace began, "about you rooming with us...know why a bunk suddenly became available in our hut?"

"No, why?"

Her friend's eyes were full of censure. "The lieutenant that used to be in it is up on charges for fraternizing with an enlisted airman."

Devon's stomach dropped. "Seriously?"

"Yep. Happened last week. Granted she wasn't being very discreet about her relationship, but...something you should be aware of."

"Thanks for the heads up." She shoved her hands into her pockets. "It'd be weird to not talk to them, though, Ace. They're my friends."

Candace shrugged. "Just warning you to be careful." A few beats passed before she spoke again. "I realize they're your pals, but you know what?"

Devon could tell by the hard tone that it was a rhetorical question. She raised her eyebrows in silent reply, and didn't have to wait long for the answer.

Her friend's mouth pressed into a tight line. "So far, I don't think any of us like them very much."

Yeah, Devon thought with a sigh. She was getting that message loud and clear.

# FOUR

*Peshawar, Pakistan*

SADIQ CLOSED THE Holy Quran he always carried with him, and listened to the footsteps approach the living quarters of the modest, middle class house. He rose as the door pushed open, revealing a solidly built man in his early fifties with a thick sable beard sprinkled with gray and eyes the color of caramel. His face was weathered and lined from spending his life exposed to the harsh elements of the Afghan climate, and his skin was brown as tanned leather.

Sadiq greeted his host with a polite nod. "General Nasrallah."

The general smiled and clapped a fatherly hand on his shoulder, his grip strong despite the arthritis distorting his joints.

"I understand you have been quite busy helping to boost our ranks these past few weeks. Did you recruit any new men during your travels yesterday?"

"Yes," Sadiq replied. "Two from the second village."

The older man's gaze lit with amusement. He switched from Pashto to English. "All this time back in your homeland, yet you still carry an accent."

Sadiq fought the flush staining his cheeks. "I spent

many years in the UK, as you know. I suspect I will always carry it to some extent."

The general waved his concern away. "I was not criticizing you, Sadiq. On the contrary, your education makes you invaluable to me, as few others speak English as well as you do."

"I only completed my first two years at Cambridge, sir."

"Two years studying physics is much more than most of my men could ever dream of." The general tilted his head, that shrewd gaze lingering on Sadiq's face. "Tell me, why did you abandon your studies?"

A tightness spread in his chest. "My brother asked me to. He needed help on the farm." Sadiq couldn't say no to the brother that had half killed himself working to provide Sadiq with a life and post-secondary education in London. Sadiq had been shocked by how much Hassan had aged in his absence. Twenty years instead of ten. His back had already been bent like an old man's. All because of his sacrifice to give his younger brother a better life.

"Your loyalty to your brother is to be commended. But about your work here. How many men does that make this week?"

"Six."

"And all together?"

"One hundred and six."

"That almost doubles the size of my force." The older man's eyes gleamed with appreciation. "You have been an invaluable asset to me."

Sadiq ducked his head, though his heart filled with pride. "I only wish I could do more." Like get into the fight firsthand rather than working behind the scenes recruiting.

"And you will." Nasrallah squeezed his shoulder once more before releasing him. "Come. Have tea with me."

Honored by the request, Sadiq followed him to a comfortable living room where a low table in the center of a rich, red woven carpet was already laden with bread and steaming cups of chai. They sat opposite each other and Sadiq waited while his commander said a short prayer before picking up his cup and taking a sip. Few people were allowed private meetings with the general. That he was granted such an audience proved just how important the great leader considered him to be.

Nasrallah's eyes crinkled at the corners as he smiled. "You have surpassed my expectations, Sadiq. I thought at first you would not be able to control your anger, but you have proved me wrong. You have taken your brother's death and used it to hone your discipline, and I am extremely impressed with you thus far."

Sadiq felt like a little boy earning hard-won praise from a stern father. He straightened his spine, determined not to show how much the general's words meant. He was not a child. He was a grown man ready to accept his destiny and join the fight he fervently believed in. "Allah guides me well."

"He guides all of us well, if we are willing to listen," the older man agreed. "My commanders tell me you have become an expert shot with your rifle, and that you are one of their best trainees. I was pleased to receive this report, because I need more good men I can count on in my new operations."

Sipping his tea, Sadiq tried not to seem too eager,

though his heart pounded at the thought of going out into the field and taking part in the war that had already cost him so much. "I will help any way I can, sir."

As though his words amused him, Nasrallah leaned back and regarded him over the rim of his cup with smiling eyes. "You must have heard the talk by now."

"Some."

"I intend to move my army into the foothills for the next phase of operations. As you are aware the Americans are moving farther and farther out of their base to conduct their patrols. You know my philosophy about how to strike them when they are most vulnerable?"

"Yes. Hit them when they are the farthest away from their base, and have an ambush in place, ready for when they try to escape."

"Why?"

It irritated Sadiq that Nasrallah would test him like this. If he was pleased with his progress and considered him such an asset, then surely he was aware Sadiq knew all of this inside and out. He pushed aside his annoyance. "Because our aim is to create chaos and inflict the most casualties possible to draw more forces in. And because the Air Force will send in aircraft to assist."

"Exactly." His gaze hardened into shards of amber. Focused and predatory, like a wolf's. "We turned the Russians into whimpering babies by destroying their aircraft one by one. The Americans and their allies are far too powerful for us to meet them head on in a fight. We must organize and maintain discipline in order to fight them effectively. Our tactics and willpower have to outweigh their superior numbers and weapons. The aircraft are vulnerable to the very missiles they gave us to get rid of the Communists, and every time we shoot one down it guarantees they send in more. Think of the damage we could inflict if the right opportunity arose."

Sadiq sensed the fire burning in the warrior's soul. It blazed out of his sharp eyes, contagious in its power.

"The Presidential elections are next year. If we inflict enough damage and kill enough soldiers, the American people will elect the new president on the basis of pulling out of Afghanistan." He gave a hard smile. "Then we will have defeated yet another superpower."

An excited shiver tingled down Sadiq's spine. This was why he admired the general above any of the other leaders he'd met. The man understood the way things were, and he made his goals both finite and attainable. Both of those qualities ensured his men had higher morale than most of the other forces in the area. Other leaders foamed at the mouth about killing all the infidels and pushing them out of the Middle East entirely, and a select few were bent on expanding the Islamic empire until it encompassed the globe. Others terrorized their own people in that cause. Like the Taliban, prowling the tribal region to enforce their interpretation of Shari'a law on the villages they took.

"And the Taliban? They are nothing more than archaic bullies." He hated them almost as much as the occupiers.

"Perhaps," Nasrallah allowed. "But still a formidable enemy. More so than when our Northern Alliance defeated them. The Americans were our allies at the start of this war but I can no longer support their continued occupation."

"None of us do. But that fight is here, on our soil, not in North America. Too many zealots get that wrong."

"I couldn't agree more, which is why my men support al Qaeda's efforts only in this region."

"I understand." Sadiq didn't care one way or the other about what the Americans did in their den of iniquity on the other side of the world. For all he cared they could wallow in their own moral filth until the Final Judgment when Allah would wipe them all away with a cleansing fire. What he wanted was vengeance, plain and simple. And he wanted the western soldiers out of his country once and for all. When that happened, he would return to the UK and finish his studies, fulfilling his brother's dream of seeing him earn a university degree and making something of himself in the world. But first they must win the war.

Excitement and determination rushed through his veins. "When do you need me and the others?"

The general's lips curled in the midst of his salt-and-pepper beard. "Tonight. Can you be ready?"

"I'm ready now."

He let out a rumbling laugh. "Have the new men here at sunset. We have a long way to travel in the next few days."

"We will be waiting, sir."

Nasrallah set his cup on the table and rose, signaling the meeting was over. Sadiq pushed to his feet and gathered his Quran, his brother's most cherished possession. He never went anywhere without the leather bound heirloom.

"Your brother would be proud of you."

Halfway through the door when the general spoke,

Sadiq stopped and looked over his shoulder. "I pray that's true."

Leaving the comfortable house, he stepped into the cold mountain air and pulled in a deep breath, letting the purity of it sweep through him. The wind cut through the woolen scarf he wrapped tightly around his face and neck, but he barely noticed the cold. His resolve kept his inner fire burning hot enough to counteract the coldest night.

He pulled out the battered photograph he always carried in the shirt pocket over his heart. He kept it there as a daily reminder of his earthly purpose since that terrible day two months earlier. Like the Quran, it went with him everywhere. The familiar faces, one male, one female, stared back at him. He knew every line of them now, so well that they often haunted his dreams. He stroked a thumb over the smooth surface, thinking of his brother, and sent up a prayer.

*God willing, I will do what must be done.*

*Bagram Airfield, Afghanistan*

CAM WALKED INTO the pool hall at the Exchange and stopped short. Still a bit groggy from the short but deep sleep he'd pulled himself out of, he fought the urge to rub his eyes.

Holy shit, she was there. Right in front of him.

The room was crowded and noisy, but all his senses focused on the slim woman in the center of the room. What was it about her that made his pulse pound in his ears and the blood rush from his head to pool between his legs?

Leaning against the pool table as she chalked her cue, Devon chatted to that Night Stalker pilot, Liam. Her camo cargo pants and snug T-shirt did little to hide the trim curves that featured in every erotic dream and fantasy he'd had over the past three months. Already she had a crowd of men surrounding her, eating up her every word. A bass chorus of male laughter followed whatever she'd said. Jesus Christ, she was like Scarlett O'Hara holding court over her suitors, only Devon didn't have a fucking clue about the effect she had on men.

It always made him shake his head because any man with a pulse would be attracted to her.

Cam didn't know exactly what it was about her that drew him so strongly. She wasn't beautiful. Not in the classic sense, anyhow. Her features were too sharp, her eyes almost too big for her face. She wasn't his usual type, either. Not even close.

He usually went for ultra-feminine women. The kind that spent hours doing their long, carefully styled hair and even more carefully applied cosmetics. The last woman he'd dated had freaked if she chipped an acrylic fingernail. She hadn't known a thing about the military and wouldn't have wanted to, beyond what he looked like in his BDUs. Or rather, without them. And he was just fine with that.

By contrast, Devon made all the other women he'd been with look like simpering prima donnas. And whatever it was he felt for her, it wasn't casual like all the others had been. He'd never felt this protective of a woman before. Only she brought that out in him. That powerful, odd mixture of independence and vulnerability completely melted him.

The fact that she flew a Black Hawk and could talk shop with the best of them? Hot as hell. And her laugh. God, she had the dirtiest laugh he'd ever heard. Every time he heard it he thought of sex. Hot, sweaty sex, the kind that left a man exhausted and weak and his partner unable to move.

He shoved his hands into his pockets, admiring the shape of her butt when she leaned down to adjust her pool cue. Her shirt pulled taut along the lean plane of her back as she lined her shot up and executed a perfect bank shot. Almost a month had passed since Ty's funeral. That made it almost four months since she'd have last seen him alive. A long time considering they'd only been casually dating before he deployed.

Cam didn't believe for a moment it was coincidence that she'd sent the e-mail about her arrival at Bagram only hours before showing up.

Couldn't be solely guilt over Ty, though. Not at this point. Maybe she was still avoiding other relationships?

Namely with him.

Something else was still hanging her up. The difference in their ranks put a definite wrench in the works. If that wasn't the problem, then damned if he knew what it was.

What other woman could talk to him about forward-looking radar and Egress training, let alone because she understood them first hand? He remembered Ty's smug grin the night he'd introduced her. Devon had been describing a midair refueling when he'd walked up to say hello, and his eyebrows had shot up in shock. Then she'd turned her bright smile on him, and in that instant he'd felt some sort of primal recognition deep inside. Like his body knew she belonged with him and not Ty. At the time, it had shocked the shit out of him. Not anymore.

Since then he'd admired her from afar, content to be one of her buddies. The awareness in her eyes when she looked at him made it damn hard. So hard he'd wanted to tell her how he felt long before Ty's death. He thanked God he hadn't stooped to poaching.

Maybe Devon did still feel conflicted about wanting him, but Cam's conscience was clear. If he could've talked to Ty about it, he knew his friend would approve of them being together as long as he treated her right. And if anything did happen between them, it wouldn't be short term or casual. With her, Cam intended to play for keeps.

Another rumble of laughter rose around the pool table, and Cam caught Devon's saucy grin. She had every cell in his body standing up and paying attention to her. Him and all the other men around her. Horny bastards.

From out of nowhere, an unprecedented surge of possessiveness streaked through him. The hair on his nape stood up in primitive reaction, his body demanding he go over and claim her in front of the others. She was *his*.

As though sensing his stare, she straightened. When she turned her head with a swish of her shiny hair and focused her storm-gray eyes on him, he almost forgot to breathe. She seemed to glow under the overhead fluorescent lighting. Her skin was like pale cream, her inky brows and lashes emphasizing the unusual color of her irises.

She stilled, eyes widening a fraction, and a telltale flush crept into her cheeks. Attraction? Or nerves? She had nothing to worry about, though. He knew or at least recognized all of the guys in the room. None of them would rat them out to a superior. And he'd never do anything to jeopardize her reputation or career. Didn't she realize that?

Her lips twitched nervously for a moment before breaking into a quick grin, dazzling despite the fact that one of her front teeth overlapped the other. Yet another detail he found irresistibly charming about her.

Coming out of his paralysis, he moved through the crowd. She set down her cue and took a few steps to close the distance between them. "Hey!"

"Hi, Dev," he said when he reached her, pulling her into his arms for a hug. She hesitated the tiniest instant before wrapping her arms around his neck and returning the embrace. He bit back a groan at the feel of her. Sweet God she felt good. The light floral scent that rose from her skin and hair drove him crazy. Delicate and understated, just like her. Subtle enough that he had to get up close to smell it, but once he did it went to his head faster than a half-bottle of tequila.

Her body was strong and supple, and all too feminine. Her small, firm breasts pressed against his chest. He wanted more, so much more of her. His dreams were haunted by images of her spread out beneath him as he moved in and out of her clinging body, those soft lips parted on a desperate moan of pleasure while she stared up into his face. Every inch of him got hard thinking about it, and he set her away before she noticed.

Her eyes were anxious as they scanned his face. "You okay? I saw Ryan—he said you had a tough night."

He brushed a lock of hair away from her smooth

cheek, touched by her concern. "Yeah, it wasn't my best. But I'm okay."

She studied him for another moment, her smile saying she didn't believe him. "Shouldn't you be sleeping?"

*Not if it means going without seeing you.* "I got a few hours already." The painful politeness of the conversation bothered him. If things deteriorated to the point where they talked about the weather, he'd lose it. "What about you? All settled in?"

"Yep. Co-pilot and I had our briefing, and as of morning we'll be on standby."

He laughed at the excitement in her voice. "You realize that being called out means somebody's in real bad shape on the other end of your flight."

She winced. "I know. But think of how fast I'll get to them, and how quick they'll get to a medical facility. And if I've got a PJ like you on board, their chances are even better."

The earnestness in her eyes made him want to kiss her so bad he almost gave into the temptation. "Much as I'd love to go up with you, I don't think that's gonna happen. They've got me doing insertion and extraction runs in case they need CASEVAC during the missions." She was smart enough to fill in the blanks he'd left. The men the helo crews delivered could get into serious trouble out there. Tough as they were, the bad-ass SEALs and Delta operators still bled like everyone else when they got shot up. So did the Rangers and Green Berets. If they were hurt bad enough, they died like every other mortal being, despite every effort to keep them alive.

And sometimes a PJ died defending those same

wounded, because it was his duty to make sure he got them out alive, no matter the risk to their own safety.

They were both thinking about Ty now, he could tell from the shadows in her eyes. The knowledge of his slow, painful death lay between them and Cam didn't want that. "You guys got room for one more?" he asked, nodding at the table.

"Sure." She moved back and picked up her cue, flashing him another smile as he rounded the table to wait his turn.

Liam handed him his cue. "You're just in time. I need to crash for a while." He threw him a rueful grin. "Actually you'd be doing me a favor, because she's a sniper with that thing."

"I'll take one for the team and stand in for you, then." Liam waved and headed for the door, leaving Cam alone with Devon at the table. He noted the subtle difference in her posture as she faced him. A stiffening in her shoulders. "Mind if I rack 'em up again?"

"Go ahead."

He got the balls into place, casting a glance around the room. No one was paying any attention to them. "As I recall you beat me last time we did this. Guess I've got to defend my honor tonight."

"You can try."

He grinned at the amused twinkle in her gray eyes. "Ever occur to you I took it easy on you last time?"

"Nope. You might be sweet, but you're still alpha enough to not like losing."

"You think I'm sweet?"

A light flush spread over her cheekbones. "Most of the time."

Except for what had happened in her hotel room. He needed to fix that somehow. But sweet was good, right? He hung the rack up on the wall. "Don't expect me to show my softer side in the next ten minutes."

"Wouldn't dream of it." She leaned over the table and executed a perfect break, sinking two solids. Her cocky smile taunted him playfully. "Watch and learn, Cameron."

God, when she said his name like that he could hardly think. "I'm watching." *Oh baby, I'm definitely watching.*

She sunk two more balls before narrowly missing her next shot and sidled past him with a negligent shrug. "All right. Let's see what you've got."

The challenge made him meet her eyes for a moment. She thought he was sweet? If they'd been alone he would have upped the stakes between them and stroked his thumb over that pouty lower lip of hers, but she knew damn well he wouldn't touch her in front of anyone. Instead he gave her a slow, wicked grin, pleased when her flush deepened. If she thought he was giving up on them, she had another thing coming.

Before she could say anything, he leaned in and lined up a shot. He executed it perfectly, then rounded the table to move in next to her. Devon moved a step to the side, but she didn't have much room to maneuver and couldn't go far. He took advantage of that and stretched out for his next shot, making sure his hip almost brushed hers. Close enough that he could feel her warmth. Every cell in his body was aware of the way she watched him set up. He could feel her eyes on his face, almost like a caress. She made it damn hard to concentrate. The sharp crack of the cue against the ball broke the subtle tension between them.

On her next turn she went to the other side of the table. She didn't line anything up, though. Instead she chalked her cue, a slight frown creasing her brow.

"Something on your mind?"

She met his gaze. "Yeah, kind of."

"Okay, let's hear it."

She shifted her weight and focused once again on her pool cue. "I've been hearing conflicting bits and pieces of information since I got here." Her gaze darted to the side as if she was making sure no one was listening.

"What about?"

"Nasrallah."

Whoa. Of all the things she might have said, he hadn't expected that one. Cam leaned a hip against the table and gave her his full attention. "What about him?"

"Some people said he's still in the area planning more attacks and that his army's even bigger than it was a few months ago. Others told me he's disappeared into the mountains and no one knows where he is."

He waited for her to continue.

"Which is it?" Her eyes searched his, challenging him to tell her the truth.

"Bit of both."

She set her cue down. "What's that mean exactly? Or can't you tell me?"

As bad as he wanted to tell her everything he knew about the situation with the warlord, most of it was classified. He couldn't tell her much, but he wasn't going to lie to her, either. "He's still out there with some of his former Northern Alliance pals. Intel says he's probably in Pakistan fundraising and recruiting."

"And the men he's already recruited?"

Cam sensed the buried unease in her, but he refused to lie. "Could be anywhere, but more than likely there are still some groups in the surrounding area."

She blew out a breath and nodded. "That's what I figured."

"The chances of you coming into contact with any of them on a mission is pretty remote."

Her eyes flashed up to his. "Maybe. But not for you."

*Ah, honey.* "I'll be okay, Dev." He smiled to make it clear he wasn't trying to placate her. "What about you? You okay with flying again so soon?"

"Yeah, I'm fine."

He wasn't sure about that. She was putting on one hell of a brave front, but he knew she was battling her own demons. He understood that perfectly. "Okay."

Giving him a tight smile, she set the chalk cube down and took up a position for a shot.

She wasn't fooling him. He knew damn well her mind was still working overtime about Nasrallah, because of all the hype about the threat level he and his followers posed. And because they were the ones who'd killed Ty. The truth was in the way her knuckles turned white around the pool cue. "You want to go for a walk or something?"

She straightened. "A walk?"

"Yeah. We can find somewhere quiet to talk." And once he did what he could to dispel her fears about Nasrallah, he might finally be able to get her to open up about the night Ty died. He'd bet his life she'd never talked about it to anyone. But she definitely needed to, and he was more than willing to listen.

Her black hair shone under the lights as she shook her head. "Thanks, but maybe some other time."

The shutdown was his fault. Hell, the way their last conversation had gone, he was lucky she was speaking to him at all. "You sure?" He wanted to ease her. He could feel the stress she was trying hard to hide. "I'm a good listener."

She smiled at him, an unguarded charming smile that made him want to wrap her up in his arms and squeeze her. "See? You are a sweetheart."

He cringed. "Not so loud," he admonished, looking around to see if anyone had overheard her.

Her husky laugh slid through him like silk. She was so damn beautiful and proud and brave. After what happened the night Ty died she could easily have made a case with her superiors for taking a stress leave. But here she was, back at Bagram without complaint, facing doubts and fears that would cripple most people. He could kiss her for that alone.

Walking around the table to get ready for his next shot, he stopped when Dev straightened to reposition, bumping her hip into his thigh. Her eyes flew up to meet his, but she didn't step away. The hunger simmering inside him turned molten. Cam's fingers clenched around his cue as heat rocketed up his leg to his groin. Blood pooled between his legs, swelled his growing erection. He wanted to touch her. Take her face between his hands and kiss her the way he'd dreamed of. Feel her gasp into his mouth, then tremble and melt for him.

Devon stared up into his face as she finally stepped

back, her cheeks stained a wild rose pink. Cam broke eye contact and cleared his throat.

"Sorry about that." He wasn't, but he had to say something to break the tension.

"It's okay." She looked away and made a show of chalking her cue. When she glanced up and smiled at him, his heart did a slow somersault.

"Come on," she said with a wink, the familiar gesture erasing any trace of lingering awkwardness between them. "You're not getting out of this that easy. Take your medicine like a man."

His heart squeezed. There she was. The old Dev that loved to joke around and was comfortable hanging around with him. The one he'd been teetering on the brink of falling in love with for months. "Don't let your mouth write checks your body can't cash, sweetheart."

She raised a pitch black brow. "I resent that remark. Want to put a friendly wager on this game?"

"Sounds good to me." Because no way in hell was he losing this time.

# FIVE

CAM PICKED UP the last of the bloody bandages off the Pave Hawk's deck and stuffed them into a trash bag. The three badly wounded Afghan Security Forces personnel they'd just brought in were already in surgery. "Bring that hose over here, will you?" he said to Jackson. He stepped aside when the other PJ came back with it and climbed into the belly of the helo. Cam took one last look around to make sure he hadn't missed anything, and his eyes caught on something near the back lying on the steel floor. He crouched down and picked up the severed thumb.

"Oops. That's my guy's," Jackson said. "Must have gotten lost in all the blankets."

"Jesus, Thatcher, you're never getting near me with a pair of scissors."

Jackson grinned and turned on the hose as Cam hopped out of the aircraft. Seconds later, a rush of bloodstained water cascaded out the open door. Cam took the thumb to the hospital, then headed back to the PJ area in the control tower's base to clean up.

He'd been thinking about Devon all day during the resupply runs to and from Kandahar before the rescue call had come in. Now that he was done for the night, he could finally meet up with her to collect on their bet. He thought he'd made good headway repairing any damage to their relationship last night, and couldn't wait to see her. He hoped she wanted to see him too.

After stowing his gear and grabbing a quick shower, he wolfed down a Power Bar instead of stopping at the chow hall and headed over to the Exchange. There he found Devon methodically clearing the pool table while Liam shook his head in good natured disgust. Cam shoved his hands into his pockets and watched her for a minute, admiring every beautiful line of her face. When she sank another combo, he finally spoke up. "You about finished embarrassing that pilot yet?"

Her pretty gray eyes flashed up to his, and her quick smile made his heart thud. "Hey."

"I believe I kicked your butt last night, so pay up. You owe me a walk, lady."

She hesitated then glanced over her shoulder at Liam. "Are you sufficiently embarrassed?"

"Humiliated," he deadpanned. "Go ahead. I'll find someone less lethal with that cue to play." He gave Cam a nod of acknowledgement, eyes brimming with amusement. "Get out of here. I'll cover your sixes."

"Thanks, man." Devon might still be a bit leery, but Cam intended to get past the awkwardness he'd caused once and for all.

Since there were no superior officers around to worry about, he walked over and slid an arm around her shoulders, both as a friendly gesture and one meant to warn anyone watching that she was off limits as of now. His own actions caught him off guard. He'd had no idea he was that territorial.

Devon glanced up at him but didn't say anything. It didn't surprise him that she scooted out from under his arm the moment they stepped outside, and he didn't try to stop her. He might want her so badly he could taste her, but he wasn't going to cross the line into dominant asshole and send her running from him again.

The idea of taking control had its merits, though. Many times he'd fantasized about backing her up against the nearest wall and kissing her, hands wrapped in her hair and his body pressed tight against hers with his hips wedged between her toned thighs until she trembled and moaned for more. He knew exactly what she'd feel like, her body soft and firm at the same time, tense with anticipation and need. He knew the way her pupils would expand until they all but swallowed the nimbus of gray ringing them, and the husky note of her soft cry of submission once she let herself trust that she was meant to be with him.

He hid a grimace as his dick hit the back of his zipper. He shifted to discreetly relieve the pressure, but it didn't help. Beside him, Devon looked straight ahead, presumably to avoid eye contact with him, which was just as well. He wasn't sure how much longer he could hold back his true feelings. He was known for his patience, but she tested him to his limits.

If he hadn't been absolutely sure she wanted him as badly as he wanted her... But he'd seen the answering hunger in her eyes when he'd held her in that hotel room. He'd felt it in the taut lines of her body. She'd been thinking about going to bed with him, fighting it.

"How long until you go out?"

Her voice brought him back to the present. "Isolation starts at twenty-two hundred."

She nodded, still avoiding his gaze. "They keep you pretty busy, I guess."

"Yeah. There aren't very many of us around, so we're spread kind of thin." That was something he was proud of, actually. There were thousands of SEALs and Rangers, but less than three hundred active duty PJs in the military. The Pipeline took care of that. And he wouldn't have it any other way. In the field they all needed to be able to trust the man next to them.

"Erin said you fill in at the hospital sometimes."

"Now and again. All of us pitch in from time to time if they need us and we're not on rotation."

Her head turned, lips curving in a gentle smile. She was fresh and beautiful, without a trace of makeup. It made him ache. "I love it that you're trained to save lives instead of taking them. I mean, I know you're trained to kill when you have to, but I admire the fact you wanted to become a PJ instead of a SEAL." She frowned up at him. "Am I making sense?"

"Perfect sense. And I accept your compliment with pleasure." Pleasure. The word made him think of her stretched out beneath him, head thrown back, eyes squeezed shut, her mouth open on a cry of ecstasy while he moved inside of her, giving her all she could handle and then some. He swallowed. "You settling in here okay?"

"Pretty well. My internal clock's a bit off, but not too bad. I just can't believe I'd forgotten how noisy it is here all the time."

"It is that." No matter what time of day or night, something was always happening at Bagram.

"Guess we won't be seeing much of each other," she

said, her eyes fixed on an approaching C-130 coming in to land. "You'll be out for long stretches or working at night and I'll be operating mostly during daylight hours." Was he imagining that wistful note in her voice?

"We'll still see each other." He was going to make damned sure of that, just as he was going to ensure she knew what he wanted from her. What she meant to him. "It just means we'll have to be a bit more creative."

She raised a brow. "Creative as in how?"

He shrugged. "We'll make it work." He had plenty of ideas, and they kept him awake in the middle of the day when he should have been sleeping.

She fell silent and this time the lapse in conversation grew until it was uncomfortable. He wouldn't allow that. "Any place you haven't seen yet around here that you want to?"

"Actually, I'd kind of like to just find a spot to watch the aircraft land and take off."

Of course she would. "Right this way." He put his arm back over her shoulders and turned her, and this time she didn't move away. She fit against him nicely. Just the right height to fit under his arm without making him lean over. The imprint of her body felt perfect, soft yet firm. Torturing him.

He led her over to a bench at a somewhat quiet spot along the end of the main runway. The whap of rotors rose near one of the hangars as an old Huey came to life, and blended with the roar of a C-130 tanker beginning its run for takeoff.

Careful not to crowd her, he settled back in a casual pose and laid his arm across the back of the bench. Close enough that he could feel her warmth, but not quite touching her. They watched the aircraft come and go for a few minutes, until he got tired of waiting for her to initiate the conversation. "How you doing, Dev? Really."

"I'm good. Looking forward to going out the first time."

She meant on her bird, of course, not with him. And probably because she needed to prove to herself she could do it again. "That's not what I meant." And she knew it, because she wasn't looking at him.

Devon stared down at her hands, fidgeting in her lap. "I'm doing okay. You?"

"Yeah." Enough with the polite banter. He didn't want to scare her, but he needed to start moving this forward. "Still miss him?"

She stiffened for a second, then relaxed. "In some ways. He had a great sense of humor."

"He did. And so do you."

"I try."

As the silence stretched between them, he was tempted to play with the ends of her hair sweeping against her jaw. He searched for a neutral topic. "I've been wondering about what you told me. You said you wanted to learn to fly because you were afraid of crashing."

She nodded, gazing out at the parked aircraft.

There was a story here. He wanted to know what it was. "Why's that?"

Right away her fingers began toying with the bottom of her jacket zipper and her expression tightened. He mentally cursed himself. Making her uncomfortable was the last thing he wanted to do. "You don't have to tell me if—"

"No, it's fine." She shifted on the bench, still not looking at him. He wished he could see her eyes. "It was my dad."

His guts knotted as a horrible suspicion formed. "Your dad?"

"He'd been training to get his pilot's license for his fortieth birthday. Flying fixed wings."

Cam waited in silence. He could see the shadows of hurt in her eyes, remembered Ty saying something about this.

"He...he was doing his first solo in a Cessna. We all came out to the airport to watch." Her gaze remained fixed out on the tarmac. "My mom and brothers and I were there to watch him take off. We were excited for him, but later we got a call that the tower lost contact with him." She fidgeted with her coat again, her throat working as she swallowed. "Mom couldn't find a baby-sitter for all of us so she took us to the crash site."

"Jesus, Dev, I—"

"I still remember the smell of the jet fuel and the burnt metal."

"I'm sorry." And sorrier still that he'd brought up something so painful.

"It's okay. It was a long time ago." She exhaled. "Anyway, I couldn't get on a plane after that."

No fucking wonder.

"After some therapy in my late teens I made up my mind to get my own license after college. The Army seemed like a good idea, plus they paid for the training. Flying a helo instead of a fixed wing made me feel that much safer." She shrugged. "And here I am."

If he'd admired her before, now he was in awe of her. "That was incredibly brave of you."

She ducked her head. "Nah. Just got tired of being afraid, that's all."

Cam let his hand move down to cradle her shoulder. "I'm sorry about your dad."

"Thanks."

He curled his other hand into a fist to keep from touching her face. "So what did your mom and brothers think of you signing up?"

"They thought I was crazy, of course," she said with a laugh.

He smiled. "Well you gotta admit, it is a little unorthodox."

"That's what you get when you're the youngest of three and the only girl."

"Is that how you wound up with the call sign Spike? Was it a nickname?" He'd always gotten a kick out of it.

"Happened in flight school. My classmates thought I needed something scary sounding to make up for my less than intimidating size and looks."

He laughed, because she looked about as scary as a Labrador retriever. "You close with your family?"

"Very. My oldest brother kind of took over as man of the house after dad died." She tossed him a rueful grin and settled back against the bench, seeming more comfortable now with his arm being around her. "What about you?"

"I've got a sister that's two years younger than me. My parents divorced when I was in high school, and my mom's remarried." Without thinking he started sliding his hand up and down her shoulder.

It wasn't quite a caress, but she moved restlessly on the seat, pink creeping into her cheeks. "Cam…" she began.

"Yeah?"

Her uncertain gaze cut over to him before she dropped her eyes to her lap. "I wanted to talk to you about something that's been bothering me."

This wasn't going to be good, he could tell that much. "Sure."

She fiddled with her coat some more before finding her voice. "About what happened in the hotel…"

He remained silent, watching her. Another awkward pause followed, but he wasn't going to fill it and make this easy for her. She was the one that had to wrestle with her feelings, and he'd be damned if he'd make it okay for her to hide from them.

Devon glanced up into his face, and when their gazes locked she stared at him helplessly a moment before looking away. "I uh…I don't know what Ty said to you about me or what you've heard, but…" She shook her head, making blue highlights stand out in the wash of the lights along the security fence.

"But what?" he asked quietly.

She huffed out a breath. "I don't sleep around."

After the initial shock passed, her clipped statement pissed him off. "I know that, and I never thought you did." He removed his arm from the back of the bench and sat up straight as he faced her. "Is that why you've been avoiding me?"

"I just got here, so how could I be avoiding you?"

"Don't play dumb. You're way too smart to pull it off convincingly."

She folded her arms across her chest. "I just don't want to build that kind of a reputation. There are very few female pilots here, and the last thing I need is for people to talk about me like that behind my back."

What the hell? "So military protocol aside, getting involved with me would still be bad for your reputation."

"Don't twist my words," she said defensively. "Even though we kept it quiet so my command wouldn't find out, everyone knows I dated Ty off base. If I was with you, they'd talk."

"What makes you think they'd talk, assuming they ever found out?" He'd never embarrass her that way.

"Trust me, they'll talk. My roommates already think I'm way too friendly with a lot of the guys here, and someone from my unit has already been put up on fraternization charges."

He stared at her. "I would never put you in that position."

"I know you'd try to protect me, Cam, but people will notice no matter how much we tried to hide it or you tried to protect me."

He couldn't believe what she was telling him. "You'll fly a Black Hawk at night nap-of-the-earth, but you won't be with me because you're afraid of what other people will *think*?"

The blush in her cheeks darkened. "I don't expect you to understand."

Good, because he didn't. What kind of fucked-up reasoning was that? But then another thought occurred to him. "Let's back up a minute then. When you say 'sleep around', do you mean one-night stands?"

Her eyes darted up to his, wide and full of alarm. "No! I've never done that—is that what you heard?"

"I haven't heard anything but how much people like and respect you."

She seemed to relax a bit, but then shook her head like she was disappointed. Or hurt. "So then, you mean you want *us* to be a one-night stand?"

He cursed mentally. "Jesus, Dev, no." Not even close.

Her brow furrowed as she looked at him. "Then... what do you want?"

He arched an eyebrow. "Sure you want me to tell you?" Something was bound to get lost in the translation, and he didn't want to spook her. He'd much rather show her what he wanted from her instead.

"I hate talking about this."

"I noticed." He couldn't keep the sarcasm out of his voice.

She glanced away. "Look, I haven't dated very many men, despite what you might think."

Why the hell was she hung up on this? He'd never guessed she might have low self esteem, or that she much cared what others thought of her.

Rather than argue, he changed tactics and reached out a hand to tuck her hair behind her ear. As he'd expected, she froze, her eyes locked on him. He let one finger trail gently across her flushed cheek. When he was sure he had her full attention, he leaned in until their faces were inches apart. Still caressing her skin, he deliberately dropped his eyes to her luscious mouth, lingering there for a moment until he caught her quick intake of breath.

Lifting his gaze, he stared deep into her stormy eyes.

"For the record? It doesn't matter to me how many men you've dated."

It was true. He didn't care. Without a doubt she'd be faithful to whoever she was with. It was one of the things he admired most about her. "What matters is how I feel about you." His gaze dropped to her mouth imagining the feel of those petal soft lips beneath his. With effort he dragged his eyes back to her face.

"How do you feel about me?" she whispered, her eyes locked with his. The hope he read there turned him into mush.

"Pretty damn serious."

Heat whipped through his body at the banked need he saw mirrored in her eyes. She definitely wanted him to kiss her, and he wanted nothing more than to oblige her. He wanted to tip her head back and settle his lips over hers, kiss her until she moaned and opened for the slow caress of his tongue. But he didn't. Instead he clamped down on the rising sexual need inside him and opened his clenched hand to cradle her face in his palm. The innocent touch sizzled straight up his arm. "I would never do anything to hurt you. You know that, right?"

Staring back at him, she managed a nod. Her gaze flicked to his lips, then back up. Her pink tongue darted out and swept over her bottom lip, as if she was thinking about how he would taste.

Before he could over think it, he leaned in and kissed the soft skin next to her mouth. Soft and slow, less than an inch from her tempting lips. The muscles in her shoulder tensed beneath his hand. He itched to tighten his hold there, slide his other hand into her hair to hold her still. Take away the control she loved so much. He paused there, a breath from her mouth. And waited.

Devon pulled in a sharp breath and closed her eyes. The tension thrummed through him like an electrical current, sparking over every nerve ending. She didn't turn her head, but she leaned into his kiss, adding subtle pressure. Silently asking for more, but afraid to take it.

He kissed her there again and angled his head to brush his lips over hers. Once, twice. Asking. Coaxing. Her hand came up to plant against his chest and a tiny whimper escaped, but she didn't shove him away. Her fingers curled into his jacket. So hungry. So torn.

*Dammit.*

Done with torturing himself for the night, he dropped his hand and stood. Devon gazed up at him in surprise, and he thought he caught a flicker of disappointment in her expression. "Come on. I'll walk you to your barracks."

She got up, watching him with an odd mixture of hunger and regret. Then she surprised the hell out of him by snagging his hand. He stopped and turned to face her, vividly aware of how small her hand was compared to his. Her slim fingers were cold, but whether from nerves or the nip of the fall air, he couldn't say.

She stared at him for the longest time before speaking. "Cam, you must know how I feel about you."

Yeah, he was pretty sure he did. And that made it damn hard to keep his hands to himself.

"I really care about you, but it's not…" She seemed to struggle to find the words. "It's not the right time or place. And it's not just physical for me."

His heart squeezed. "Not for me, either."

A startled, almost shy smile spread across her face. "Oh."

Yeah, *oh*. Damn, how had she missed that part? Had he said or done anything to make her think otherwise?

Before he could change his mind and resort to physical coercion to make her take the next step, he began walking, keeping her slender fingers entwined with his. By the time they reached her B-hut, he felt like a teenager suffering from the most painful crush in the world. It felt like his chest was in a damn vise.

At the door he let go of her hand and stepped back. Stuffing his hands in his pockets, he smiled down at her upturned face. "Sweet dreams."

But she grabbed his arm when he turned to go. "Hey…"

He stilled, taken by surprise again when she threw her arms around his shoulders and burrowed tight against him. His body responded instantly, but he didn't try to hide the growing erection pressing into her stomach, allowing himself to hold her full length against him. She felt damn *good*.

Tightening his arms, he dropped his head and pressed his face against the side of her neck to inhale her delicate scent. The instant he did, a sharp gasp tore out of her, her slender body rippling with a shiver as the sexual energy arced between them. Cam couldn't help but groan and gather her closer, nuzzling the velvety skin beneath her ear.

She lifted her face, and took him off guard by kissing him full on the lips. Hard and fast, the gesture so full of hunger it made him ache. Before he had the chance to respond, she drew back. Her fingers clenched in his jacket, and her face buried against his chest. "Cam…" The stark desire in her voice twisted his guts. He could feel her fighting with herself, and didn't want to push her for anything she wasn't willing to give without hesitation.

*Baby…*

He smoothed one hand over the back of her head in reassurance, praying for strength. He'd never wanted a woman like this. Not to the point where his chest ached and it hurt to breathe. If he read her right, she was hurting too. The rapid tremor of her body betrayed her unrelieved hunger.

He'd have given damn near anything for the chance to ease their pain in the closest bunk he could find. All night long, until she finally understood how he felt about her.

Brushing the lightest of kisses against her jaw, he released her. Slowly, her hands lowered from their death grip on the back of his jacket. Her eyes were dazed as she looked up at him. "You mean a lot to me, Cam. I don't want to lose you."

"You won't lose me." Whatever happened—or didn't happen between them—he'd always be there for her. He'd made that promise to himself and to Ty before their deployment.

"I just need some time," she whispered, her voice hoarse with suppressed longing.

"Okay," he whispered back, unable to keep from rubbing his thumb over her full lower lip. It trembled slightly beneath his touch. "But promise you'll come to me when you're ready."

He was to the second row of B-huts when she called out his name. He looked back at her over his shoulder.

She stood in the pool of lamplight outside her barracks with her arms wrapped around her waist, her eyes haunted. "Be careful out there. I'd hate to answer a call and find out I'm transporting you to a hospital."

If she understood how precious the time was between them, why wasn't that enough to make her take the next step with him? "I will. And you too." He *hated* the thought that she was now in harm's way, but there was nothing he could do about it.

Dev nodded at him and forced a smile, then disappeared into the hut. Rubbing a hand over his face, Cam blew out a breath. He walked away, his footsteps hollow thuds that echoed in the darkness.

He was attached to her in so many ways, and every time he saw her the ties around his heart tightened a little further. At least he had another mission tonight to keep his mind off her for a few hours.

# SIX

LOOKING THROUGH THE left chin bubble below her feet, Devon gently guided the Black Hawk onto the tarmac. The aircraft hovered over its landing spot for a moment before the fixed wheels beneath the fuselage touched the ground. She and Will powered everything down, and the on-board medic jumped out to brief the medical team standing by.

Watching them unload her two passengers, Devon fought to suppress her emotions. The mission had gone well enough, but she was glad to have the flight behind her. The stretchers held a six-year-old girl and her ten-year-old brother who'd wandered into an uncleared mine field and suffered severe damage to their legs.

Someone helped the children's grandfather down from the open bay door. He instinctively crouched beneath the spinning rotors, one gnarled hand clutching his wool cap on his head as he followed the two stretchers into the hospital.

"You okay?"

She looked over at Will. His eyes held sadness and understanding. "Yeah. You?" He had two girls back home.

"Let's just say this is one mission I'll never forget. It was a great flight, though. One of the smoothest I've ever been on."

She flushed at the praise. The medic and crew chief had stabilized the boy during the flight, but his sister was critical. She'd heard them talking with the flight surgeon over the radio during the flight back. The girl's chances were slim.

"What about some coffee?"

She frowned, unsure her stomach was up for that yet, but she could use the distraction of some company. "Sure. I'll meet you over at the Exchange once I file the log." As Will climbed out, she pulled off her helmet and glanced in the back. Her breath stuck in her throat.

Amidst the blood stains and soiled bandages, a doll lay face-up near the open bay door. Devon's fingers shook as she picked it up. Its cloth face was smudged with dirt and the brown wool hair was ragged. The well-worn appearance told her how precious it was to its owner, and now it was tragically spattered with blood. The metallic scent of it rose around Devon, warm and thick in the air.

Her stomach rolled as she exited the bird and stepped out into the bright late afternoon sunlight. Minutes counted for the wounded children. Had she done everything she could to get to them as quickly as possible? Had she taken the fastest, most direct route?

*You know you did.*

She took a few deep, bracing breaths of clean air before trusting her feet to carry her into the Tactical Operations Center to fill out the required paperwork. After that she stopped by the hospital to return the doll to its owner in the hopes it would help pull the little girl through her surgery and recovery. On her way over to the Exchange to meet Will, she thought of Cam.

Had he responded to calls involving children before? Probably. He must have dealt with kids at some point when he'd volunteered at the hospital. She bet he'd be great with them. Calm and kind and reassuring. His warmth would register even with the most frightened child.

What she wouldn't have given to feel some of it right now.

*You could have felt it last night if you hadn't been so damned scared. You're the one that shut him down.*

She sighed, but it didn't ease the pressure in her chest. She'd barely slept at all last night, and had purposely not worn earplugs so she could hear the outbound and incoming aircraft. Each time she'd heard a Chinook taking off she'd wondered it was him going out. She didn't think she could handle it if anything happened to Cam.

Damn, why *was* she fighting her attraction to him so hard? She hated to think it was because she was afraid of what people would say if they got together. And it was stupid to stay away because she was scared he might die out there. She had no control over any of that. Why couldn't she live for the moment, wring every ounce of happiness she could out of life? God, the way he held her…like he was fighting every instinct he had not to lay her out on the nearest bed and get inside her as fast as he could.

*Cut it out.*

Forcing Cam from her mind, she entered the Exchange. She found Will in a lounge area watching a sports show on a plasma flat screen TV mounted on the wall.

"Hey," he said. "Got you a cup, but it's cold now. Better go get a fresh one."

"Yeah, sorry. Paperwork took longer than usual." Thanks in part to her unsteady hands.

"You checked on the kids, huh."

She gave him a sardonic smile. "Yup. Didn't find out anything, though."

He patted the seat next to him. "Come on. Watch the highlights with me."

She did, letting her brain idle. Liam joined them, sighing as he sank into the cushions of the easy chair beside her.

"Long night?" she asked.

"Hell yeah. I'm beat. You?"

"Just got in, but I'm not that tired."

"Yet," he mumbled. "You guys see any trouble out there?"

She exchanged a frown with Will, then looked back at Liam. "No, why?"

His green eyes grew serious. "Group of SEALs I just talked to heard Nasrallah and his al Qaeda buddies might target the base again."

Devon frowned at the mention of the local warlord's name. One of the most dangerous men in all of Afghanistan. "I didn't see anything out there." She glanced at Will for confirmation, but he shook his head.

Obviously what the SEALs had heard wasn't classified, or they wouldn't have said anything to Liam. "Where'd they hear that?" she pressed. No one had mentioned any specific threats against them during the premission briefing.

"Didn't say," Liam answered. "Just keep your eyes

open for enemy movement when you're out there. His
men love to take pot-shots at our aircraft with RPGs.
But don't worry—there hasn't been a rocket attack here
on the base in weeks."

Gee, she felt so much better now.

Liam stayed and ate dinner with them in the chow
hall, but she didn't spot any of her roommates in the
crowd. Or Cam, for that matter. She didn't want to ask if
anyone had seen him because that would make her look
pathetic and create suspicion that there was something
going on between them. But damn, with every passing
minute she regretted turning him away.

CAM GLANCED UP from the dinner he was eating for
breakfast when Ryan slid into the seat across from him
at the mess hall table. "You just getting up now? Lazy
bugger."

Ryan scowled and pursed his lips. "Up yours." He
sat and pulled his metal tray closer to him. "How come
roast beef doesn't taste as good when it's your breakfast?" he asked before popping his fork into his mouth.
"Grub's not as bad as I remember," he said between
bites.

"It's hot, and it beats the hell out of MREs."

"That it does." He stabbed another piece of roast beef
and shoveled it into his mouth, frowning as he chewed.
"Hear you guys haven't had much action lately."

Cam shrugged and reached for his bottled water. "I
keep busy enough." He loved what he did, but this time
he was glad he hadn't been embedded with a SEAL or
A-Team yet, because that would mean living in the field
for days on end until they completed their mission. He

didn't want to be away from Devon that long. "I've been volunteering at the hospital when I've got time."

"In other words, you're restless as shit."

He grinned. "Pretty much." They were all varying degrees of adrenaline junkies. He liked to be active, and hanging around waiting to be called out usually drove him nuts. Being mostly segregated from the rest of the base was harder this time, too, because it meant he had few opportunities to see Devon. "Who knows—maybe I'll be going out with you one of these days."

"Love to have you, man." Ryan chugged some of his water. "I hear Dev flew her first mission this afternoon."

He set his fork down. "She did? How'd it go?"

"Fine. Evacuated some kids that got too close to a land mine."

His hand tightened around the plastic bottle until it dented with a crinkling sound. "Have you seen her?"

"No. Just woke up. Heard it from another pilot on the way over."

Cam took his last bite of mashed potato, wondering how Devon had reacted. She'd been worried about her first mission back, but to transport critically injured kids would have been even harder for her.

"So," Ryan said, watching him with interest. "You two official yet?"

"No." He didn't mind Ryan asking. "Don't know when it's going to happen." Or if. The rules and regulations made it damn near impossible to make it happen on base. Hard to hide a relationship in a place like Bagram.

"Why not?"

"She's not ready." Not her conscience, anyway.

"Bullshit."

Cam cracked a grin. "All right, I haven't figured out how to get around the fraternization with an enlisted rule yet."

"What's to figure out?"

Cam swallowed a chuckle. For a moment he'd forgotten he was talking to the king of rule breaking. "You know you're going to land up at a court-martial someday, right?"

Ryan's lips turned up in a cocky smile. "Probably. But think of all the fun I'll have before then. Some rules were made to be broken, buddy. Maybe you should learn to bend them more often."

*Yeah, right.* If he gave Devon the full court press right now, she'd never face him again. Not an option. With her he had to be more subtle, and find a way around the rules. Build the trust and anticipation until she couldn't handle staying away from him. To do that, he had to prove she could trust him, and that he wouldn't bully her into making a decision she wasn't willing to face.

Ryan wasn't through giving advice, though. "Seriously, man. You have to step up and take charge. I've seen the way she looks at you."

That was exactly the problem. On top of guilt over Ty, her deep-seated fear of everyone finding out about them and what it would do to her career was a major stumbling block. Cam sighed and shook his head. "I have no idea what's really going on in her head."

Ryan snorted and set down his water. "No shit, buddy, she's a woman. Better not even go there. We're not meant to understand how they think."

"I can totally see why women are crawling all over you," Cam said dryly.

His friend shrugged his broad shoulders. "It's the truth, man. And the ladies love me because I'm straight up with them. What you see is what you get." He turned his head as Jackson sat down next to him. "What about you, Thatcher? You figured out how a woman's mind works?"

"Sure I have."

Ryan's nonplussed expression was almost comical. "No shit?"

Jackson frowned. "What's to figure out? All you have to do is listen to them, read their body language. Every woman's different, but it's just a matter of hearing what she's telling you."

Ryan's brows hiked upward and Cam smirked in amusement. Jackson didn't say much, but when he did it was always worth paying attention to.

"What makes you such an expert?" Ryan demanded.

"I was raised by three older sisters and a single mother. What can I say? I just get women." He shrugged as if it was no big deal.

"That would make you the first man that's ever happened to," Ryan muttered, taking another swig of water. "And you're full of shit," he added, thrusting a finger at him. "I've seen that security forces hottie you've been watching. She throws poison darts at you with her eyes, man. I think you're grossly overestimating your secret powers."

"Okay." Jackson gave him a mysterious smile and dug into his meal.

Cam stood and picked his tray up before Ryan could

drag Jackson into his dilemma with Devon. "See you guys. I'm going to head back and hit the gym for a while or something—" His words died the instant Devon stepped into the building.

She was with her friend, the tall blonde pilot. Dev's low laugh drifted over the noise of the crowded mess hall. Every muscle in his body tightened. God, that laugh of hers was raw sex.

"For Christ's sake, don't just stand there stripping her with your eyes," Ryan said in exasperation. "Go get her."

Cam tamped down his irritation. Yeah, he was just going to march over there and fraternize with her in front of everyone. That'd win her over for *sure*.

"Better yet, take me or the woman whisperer with you," he said, gesturing to Jackson. "I'd like to see his self proclaimed mojo put into action."

"I don't need help," Cam said crisply. "And if anyone's full of shit, it's you. You think I don't know the real reason you want to go over there?"

"What?" Ryan asked, all innocence. "Spike's my friend too."

*Uh-huh.* "If you want to hit on the blonde, then do it without me standing there."

Ryan gave a lazy smile. "Okay, fine, I'll stay put. Go work your magic without me, then."

Damn right he would. Cam strode over to the trolley and set his tray on it, his eyes focused on Devon. As if she felt it, her head turned, and the moment she saw him she stilled, her beautiful smile freezing. He gave her a friendly grin, though what he felt was far more possessive, and sauntered over.

The blonde followed Dev's gaze to him, then looked back at Dev with a worried expression as she bent her head to say something. Devon glanced up at her for a moment before turning her attention back to Cam, a light flush staining her cheeks. The subtle tension around her mouth put the match to his temper. Did she really think he would jeopardize her in any way, let alone strike up a conversation with her in front of this crowd?

Her lips compressed, the muscles around them tightening further. Her fingers clenched around the edges of her meal tray. Her gray eyes were wide and guarded.

When was she finally going to trust him?

Cam held her stare, letting her see what he felt for her. She didn't look away, didn't move, just watched him. The blonde stayed right at her shoulder, disapproval stamped all over her face. Cam barely spared a glance at her. His eyes were all for Devon, and he made sure she knew it.

Nearing her, he smiled again, and because it was the only thing he could do to reassure her, he raised a salute. "Ma'am," he said, and dropped his hand.

In the blink of an eye her expression went from wary to surprised, and he could have sworn he saw guilt there too. She gave him a tentative smile and nodded at him as he passed by.

Walking outside, he pulled in a deep breath. Dammit, he hated this. Every cell in his body wanted to march back in there and stand right in front of her until she couldn't ignore him anymore. Scowling, he stalked off to the Special Ops part of the compound. Being at Bagram with her was going to be the death of him.

DEVON'S HEART POUNDED. Her fingers curled around the rim of her tray so hard the edges bit into her skin. She wasn't sure what she'd expected from him when he'd walked up, but it hadn't been that. My God, he'd just *ma'amed* her and walked away.

"Come on," Candace said, patting her back. "Let's grab some food."

Funny, but she'd just lost her appetite. Her stomach was clenched up too tight to hold any food.

"Let's go. You have to eat." Candace dragged her toward the chow line-up by the elbow.

Dev glanced over her shoulder, but no one stood outside the mess hall doors. Cam was gone.

"What was he supposed to do, Dev?" Candace said in her practical way. "Waltz over and start chatting you up? Not only was he polite, he showed you respect. He did you a huge favor by not trying to talk to you. Personally, I'm impressed."

Didn't feel that way to her. It felt like he'd deserted her. A hollow sensation lay in the pit of her belly. "Yeah."

But ignoring him wasn't okay with her, her conscience pointed out. She couldn't leave things like this between them. The distance was killing her. After filling her tray she followed Ace over to a table and sat down. She pushed some veggies around with her fork. "I need to talk to him, Ace."

Candace studied her shrewdly while she chewed a bite of her dinner.

Devon didn't know how to explain her feelings. Hell, she didn't *understand* her feelings, except they were real and getting more intense every day. "I can't stop thinking about him."

Candace's eyes filled with empathy. "You're really into him, aren't you?"

She nodded, exhaling to dispel the tension in her chest.

"As much as you were with Ty?"

Devon forced out another slow breath before answering. "More. Way, way more than that." She peered up at her friend and let her expression speak for itself.

Candace's eyes widened. "Oh crap, really?"

"Does that make me an awful person?"

"Not at all. But back to your earlier comment, is that what you want? To have time alone to talk with him?"

"Yes. I need to…clear some things up with him."

"Then we'll find a way to make it happen."

"Easier said than done around here," she muttered.

Candace shrugged. "But not impossible."

"What's not impossible?"

They both turned their heads as Ryan swung one long leg over the seat beside her and parked it, leaning a thick forearm on the table. Candace dismissed him with a slight frown and looked down at her plate to stab a bite of chicken.

"Just…something we're trying to figure out," Devon replied, scanning around her surreptitiously for higher ranking officers that might be watching. As an NCO, technically Ryan shouldn't be talking to them either, but nobody appeared to be paying attention.

"What, you mean you and Cam?"

"Shhh!" Devon laid her fork down and cast a hurried glance around in case anyone had overheard them.

Ryan rolled his eyes. "You think they'd arrest you or something if you got caught talking to me or him in public?"

"I—"

"That's exactly right," Candace interjected, glaring at him. "Some of us are concerned about protecting our careers."

"Oh, come on. Like non-coms and officers don't get together all the time in the military? And medevac is a hell of a lot more relaxed than the Marine Corps or regular Army."

The muscles in Candace's jaw flexed. "Devon's command isn't, but maybe you don't care. She's worked her whole life to get where she is. You think it's easy for a woman to make it to Captain in the military? I don't blame her for not risking it all over a possible misconduct charge."

Ryan turned incredulous eyes on Devon. "Is that what's holding you back? Because if it is, then I don't know you as well as I thought I did."

Dev sighed. The last thing she needed right now was to have a black mark next to her name. She'd earned the right to be here, and she would perform her duty to the best of her ability. "It's not just that. It's complicated."

"It's not that complicated. There're ways around the rules when you want something bad enough."

She knew he was right. She just hadn't figured out what those "ways" were around her problem. Popping the last piece of her dinner roll into her mouth, she cleared her place and pushed her chair back. She really didn't want to hear any more. "I'm done. See you guys."

"He's gone back to the compound," Ryan said.

She paused for a second, then stood. "That's okay, I've got stuff to do." Like plan what the hell she was going to do about this thing between her and Cam. She glanced at Candace, but her friend's eyes were full of unspoken support. "You all right if I take off?"

Ace flicked a cool look at Ryan, then back at her. "Yep."

Devon held back a grin. Candace could definitely take care of herself. Ryan was in for the surprise of his life if he thought he could work his considerable charm on her.

"I'm just gonna say one more thing."

She threw a hard look at him. "What?"

"Don't make him wait too long, Dev."

She didn't need Ryan's soft warning. That's what her gut said too.

Like their relationship had an expiry date and the sand was running faster and faster through the neck of the hourglass. "See you later," she replied and walked away.

RYAN STARED AFTER Devon for a moment, admiring her confident stride as she moved to the exit and disappeared through it. He'd never met anyone like her. Talented. Cute. Sweet. Not to mention a huge NFL fan too. If he didn't love her like a buddy, he might have made a move on her a long time ago. Though he had to admit, it'd been damn good entertainment watching her and Cam tap-dancing around each other these past few months. Lucky for him, he had something else to entertain him at the moment.

Switching his attention back to his reluctant dinner companion, Ryan hid a smile. Candace's shoulders were set, and she kept her eyes downcast to avoid looking at him.

He couldn't say no to a challenge, especially when it was packaged like *that*. The woman was hot, and built. She was tall, at least five-ten, with deep curves that made him itch to grab hold of them. Her body was flat out sexy, yet everything about her spoke of tightly-held control, from her rigid posture and her limited eye contact to the mass of thick, honey-blond hair she kept restrained in a bun at the back of her head. He'd love nothing more than to have the chance to unravel her, inch by inch, and muss her up a little. There was fire underneath that cool exterior. He could feel it.

"Can I help you with something?" The words held a definite edge.

He grinned at the bite in her tone. "Am I bothering you?"

"Yes, actually."

"Why's that? I'm on my best behavior, here."

Candace gave him a frosty look. "*This* is your best? I'd hate to see your worst."

"Hey, I'm being a total gentleman."

"And I'm being a lady by tolerating you. But I don't like living dangerously as you so obviously do."

"Sure you do. You're a military pilot, aren't you?"

She impaled him with her deep brown gaze and stabbed another bite of chicken, hard enough that the tines hit the plate with a sharp crack. Her message to fuck off wasn't lost on him, but it was all he could do to keep from grinning.

"Trying to push Devon and Cam together is not a good idea," she said stiffly.

"I'm not pushing. Mother Nature is taking care of that all by herself. But I think they'd be good together."

"Maybe. But it can't happen here."

"Why not? As long as they keep their mouths shut, command won't give them any grief." God knew he'd never let something as trivial as that get in his way if he wanted a woman.

"Her command will." Candace scooped up the last of her salad, and Ryan couldn't help but stare at the way her pink tongue swept across her full lower lip to catch a drop of dressing. Her lips were full and soft-looking. The exact opposite of her flinty stare when he raised his eyes to hers. "Excuse me, *Sergeant*. I have some repairs to make in my barracks."

He got up with her, unaffected by her dig about the difference in their ranks. "Why, what do you need fixed?"

She shot him a haughty glare. "I can handle it myself, thanks."

He ignored the dismissal and followed her anyway. "What's broken?"

Candace sighed in irritation, her lips pursing. "My bunk."

Shoving his hands into his pocket, he couldn't help himself. "Why, what've you been doing in it?"

Without breaking stride, she threw him a look of total disgust. "It was broken when I got here. One of the slats under the mattress is loose, and the frame wobbles." She lifted a hand and shook her head as she looked up at the ceiling. "God, why am I even telling you this?"

"I'll fix it for you if you want."

Her expression turned wary, as if she was suspicious of his motive. "Out of the goodness of your heart, no doubt."

"Hey, I'm not looking for anything in return. I'm just offering to help. I'm good with my hands."

She stopped and folded her arms across her ample chest, and the gesture was so distracting he had trouble maintaining eye contact. Somehow he managed to keep his eyes on her face.

"I'll bet."

He held up his palms. "That came out wrong."

"I'm sure it did." She considered him with those semi-sweet chocolate eyes for a moment before continuing. "So you're offering to help me out just to be a nice guy."

He shrugged. "I'm pretty handy. And besides, you're a friend of Devon's, and I'd hate for one of our pilots to go without sleep because of something I could have fixed."

She eyed him suspiciously for another few seconds, then turned and walked away. "Fine," she called over her shoulder. "But don't talk to me, and don't walk next to me."

Jesus, was she uptight or what? Walking behind her worked fine for him though, because it gave him an awesome view of her shapely ass on the way over to her barracks. She marched up the wooden steps with her head held high and her bun perfectly in place, and didn't so much as look back to see whether he'd followed her. Not that there was any question about that.

The place was empty, and she stood on one side of

her bunk, watching him. The hut was laid out the same as his, but somehow it seemed homier. Feminine touches were sprinkled throughout the room. A few framed pictures, what looked like a handmade quilt on one of the bunks, and a lingering scent of some sort of fruity lotion or shampoo hung in the air. "Tools are over here," she said, gesturing with a nod to the small toolbox beside her bed.

Next to her bunk he spotted Devon's cross-stitch bag, and the half-finished PJ emblem she'd been working on before Ty's funeral. Didn't bode well for her being ready to move on with Cam, now did it?

Going down on one knee next to Candace's bed, he saw the loose slat, and gripped the frame with one hand to give it a shake. Jesus, it was more than loose. "You're lucky this hasn't collapsed on you."

She stiffened, and a flush rose to her peaches-and-cream skin. "Is that your not-so-subtle way of pointing out I'm not a size four?"

"No," he said quickly, mentally smacking himself on the forehead. "I'm saying the bed's not sturdy enough for anyone. And trust me, there's *nothing* wrong with the way you're built."

The flush deepened, and a small frown creased her forehead. "Thanks. I think."

"You're welcome." He might not have Jackson's gift of understanding a woman's mind, but he wasn't stupid. Underneath all that remote armor she wore, for some fucked-up reason this gorgeous creature was insecure about her body image. Probably some dipshit in her past had caused that.

Before he could blurt out his suspicion, he grabbed

a wrench and tightened the bolt holding the loose slat, but soon saw the real problem. "See here? It's bent." He moved aside a bit so she could lean down and see for herself. The scent of strawberries hit him, light, not too strong, and he leaned in a fraction of an inch closer. The skin on her nape looked smooth and soft beneath the tightly coiled bun. He almost bent his head to nuzzle her there and pull more of that delicious smell into his lungs.

"It's really bent." Her frown deepened.

"Looks like whoever used this bunk before you was having a whole lot more fun in it than you are."

She pushed to her feet and stepped back, staring at the bed like it was contaminated with some contagious disease. She eyed him doubtfully. "Can you still fix it?"

"Yeah. I'll just bang it. Out, that is."

Her gaze flicked to his, and he winked. She rolled her eyes. "Uh-huh. I can tell you love to bang things, but as long as all you want to bang is my bed frame, go ahead."

He put a hand to his heart as though she'd wounded him. "I already told you, I'm being a gentleman."

"Good, then we won't have a problem."

Chuckling, he picked up a hammer and put her blanket between it and the slat to muffle the noise. It took a while to straighten it out, but finally he was able to get it into proper position and tighten the bolts in place. He tightened a few on the frame itself, then checked the whole thing over to make sure he hadn't missed anything. Tossing the wrench back into the toolbox with a clang, he looked back at her. "There you go. Good as new."

She eyed the bunk with distaste, making him think

she was going to douse the works with Lysol before she remade the bed. "Thanks."

"Want to test it?"

Her eyes flew to his. "Pardon?"

She was so much fun to tease. "Climb on, and see how it does."

"No thanks. I'm sure it's fine. I appreciate your help."

"Might as well check it while I'm still here. Want me to get on?"

"No," she said with tried patience, "it'll be fine now. Thanks."

Ryan smothered a grin. He'd pushed her far enough for now. She intrigued him, though. There was a lot of heat inside her that she went to every effort to hide. Her expressive eyes told him that much. "Let me know if you need any more help," he said, climbing to his feet and dusting off his hands.

"Thanks, I will."

He knew she was lying. At the door, he paused and looked back at her. She hadn't moved, just stood in the same spot with her perfect posture and perfectly coiffed hair, her melting eyes meeting his warily. He shrugged. "If you change your mind about testing it out…"

He could have sworn those delectable lips twitched for a fraction of a second before they thinned out into a disapproving line. "I know where to find you," she finished. "Thanks again." As in, *'See ya, and don't let the door hit you in the ass on the way out'*.

"Anytime." He flicked her a negligent, two-fingered salute. "Have a good evening, ma'am."

Her eyes hardened. "You too, *Sergeant*."

# SEVEN

"EVERYONE QUIET!"

The sharp whisper silenced all chatter among the ranks. Heart thudding, Sadiq stopped and raised his AK-47, ready for trouble. Up ahead General Nasrallah moved out front, his broad shoulders even wider with the heavy coat he wore.

The light wind whistled through the rocks as it blew down the narrow canyon they traveled through. Despite the chill, his feet grew clammy in his heavy boots. He kept his eyes on the general, watching for any sign that the enemy might be close by.

"I don't see anything," Khalid scoffed behind him in heavily accented English. He spoke it when he didn't want anyone but Sadiq to know what he was saying.

"Shut up," Sadiq snapped. Idiot could get them killed if an enemy patrol heard him.

"What's the matter? Afraid to die, brother?"

*I'm not your brother*, he wanted to snarl, but bit his tongue. If he ignored him long enough, Khalid would eventually lose interest and find someone else to irritate. Brothers in Islam they might be, but Sadiq didn't trust him. There was something almost sinister about him. A deep seated rage that bordered on maniacal was embedded in his dead eyes. The topaz color looked unnatural with his dark complexion and black hair, but the emptiness in them was enough to send a shiver of warning up a man's spine.

"Are you?"

Sadiq's jaw hardened. Stupid git wouldn't leave him alone until he got satisfaction.

The all clear sounded. Letting out the breath he'd been holding, Sadiq slung his rifle and resumed the march, keeping pace with the man in front of him. He was near the end of the column, the rear guard in an army of nearly two hundred men. He'd recruited many of them himself, mostly boys in their mid to late teens from farming villages scattered throughout the valleys near the Pakistan-Afghan border. All of them uneducated, and all of them itching for the chance to spill American blood. They wanted the chance to become martyrs for Allah. Sadiq understood that, but it's not what he wanted. If he was going to die, he intended to take as many Americans with him as possible.

"Answer me."

The menace in the other man's voice made Sadiq look over his shoulder. Khalid's eyes were narrowed, glowing that unearthly shade of yellow that reminded him of a hungry lion. "Shut up and march," he snapped.

Khalid's mouth curled into a smirk. "You *are* afraid."

"The only thing I'm afraid of is you getting us killed before we can attack the enemy."

Those odd eyes glittered. "Is that all? Or perhaps you are uneasy because you know I'm behind you with my weapon."

Rather than answer, Sadiq picked up his pace and moved closer to the others. Khalid was a bully that loved picking on individuals he considered weak or beneath him. That wasn't the problem between them, because Sadiq was far from weak. Theirs was more a struggle for authority and power over the other men in the ranks. While he wasn't afraid of Khalid, he was smart enough to watch his back. He made a point of never being alone with him, just in case.

This time, Khalid wouldn't let it go. He came up behind him again, close enough for Sadiq to smell his stale body odor and feel the heat of his breath. "You think you are so much better than the rest of us. That just because the general trusts you and you have been educated in the west that you are somehow superior to us. But you're not." Sadiq didn't have to see the expression on the other man's face to know he was sneering. "Those expensive clothes and warm boots won't keep you alive out here, and neither will your useless education. *We* are your only protection now. Your brothers. You had best remember that or none of them will follow you anywhere."

Sadiq ground his back teeth together. The sodding idiot deserved to be punched in the throat for speaking to him like that, but he would not lower himself to fighting a fellow soldier. "Then I would urge you, *brother*, to remember that we are fighting the same enemy. Leave your quarrel with me out of it."

A sly laugh was the only reply.

Sadiq pulled his woolen scarf around his face to cut the wind. His hands and toes were numb despite the waterproof Gore-Tex jacket and boots he'd bought back in London. The other men were in much worse shape. Most had only wool or cloth wrapped around their feet and hands to protect them from the cold, and some were barefoot in their sandals. Poor bastards must be freezing already, and the weather was only going to get colder as the days wore on.

He trudged onward through the mountain pass, the temperature dropping as they climbed. The sun momentarily broke through the thick clouds overhead and reflected off the light skiff of snow covering the ground. Squinting in the glare, he saw a dark shape circling high above among the clouds. He paused, trying to make out the shape and decide whether or not it might be a threat. Was it a bird? Or an unmanned drone?

Nasrallah called out a halt again. Everyone hunkered down in position. Sadiq's heart beat fast as he stared up into the sky. The bitterness he carried with him rose up swift and potent. Those bloody drones killed more innocents than soldiers in these mountains. They carried infra-red cameras linked to satellites and powerful missiles that could blow up an entire village. He'd seen it happen.

His cherished Quran lay inside his jacket against his chest. He'd be damned if he died because of some military toy operated by a desk jockey back in the States like a sodding video game. He wanted to laugh. No one back in England would recognize him as the mild-mannered student they'd known at Cambridge. Well, none of them had seen what he had. The attack had forever changed him into a hardened warrior, prepared to die to defend his people and homeland. And, if nothing else, avenge his murdered brother.

"Sadiq!"

He glanced up the line at one of the other commanders, who beckoned to him. When he reached the front of the column to meet with General Nasrallah and the others, he saw the reason for the abrupt halt.

It wasn't a drone up there. It was a vulture. Its next meal lay spread out on the side of the trail ahead. Two bodies and a donkey carcass were sprawled in the snow a hundred yards or so up the trial. The men were covered with a light dusting of last night's snow, but their partially eaten remains suggested they had been dead for a while longer than that.

"Casualties from the fighting here three days ago," the general told them. "Americans could be close by."

"Shall we bury them?" someone asked.

"No."

The gravity of their situation struck Sadiq. Leaving the bodies of dead Muslims to the animals instead of burying them went against the teachings of the Quran.

"They could be booby-trapped, and even if they're not, burying them would take valuable time and make it easier for the enemy to spot us. We will alert the people at the next village to come out and bury the dead. For now we must keep moving."

The men seemed uncomfortable with the decision, but no one argued. Before he could leave, Nasrallah stopped Sadiq with a hand on his shoulder. "I understand there is some friction between you and Khalid."

Sadiq scowled. He would not be intimidated by a bully who should be with the Taliban. He couldn't figure out why Khalid hadn't joined up with them already. The scary bastard would get off beating women and old men that refused to obey the Taliban's strict interpretation of Shari'a law. "There is no problem, sir. We just don't like each other."

The older man's eyes crinkled. "I know how he is. But he is a good fighter." He switched to English so no one overhearing them would understand. "Beggars can't be choosers, my son. Keep clear of him if you can."

Everyone got back into line and moved out.

Eyeing the decomposing remains as they passed, Sadiq said a prayer for their souls and repressed a shiver. The thought of Americans in the area put him on edge. What really made him nervous was the knowledge that Special Forces were in these mountains waiting for nightfall to begin their hunt.

WITH NO HOPE of seeing Cam, Devon turned down a seat in a poker game and headed back to her barracks for the night. Slipping inside the hut, the strong smell of lemon disinfectant hit her. Somebody had given the place a good scrubbing while she was out.

She spotted Maya sound asleep in her bunk against the far wall, but the other beds were empty. Candace would be at a briefing or out on the flight line getting ready for her night's mission, Honor was probably taking care of the helos in the hangar, and Erin had to be at the hospital. Maybe she knew how the children were doing, because when Devon had checked at the hospital one last time, nobody would tell her anything.

As for Cam…he'd be either waiting to deploy with the Quick Reaction Force, or onboard an outgoing Chinook for an infil or extraction with a Special Ops group.

Slipping under the covers still dressed in her pants and T-shirt, she said a silent prayer for him and the children, then closed her eyes and let herself drift off.

It seemed like she'd barely shut her eyes when a loud

explosion jolted her from sleep. Sitting bolt upright, she barely heard Maya's low curse over the sound of her heart thundering in her ears. "What was that?" Devon demanded, gaze swinging around the darkened room, all her muscles tensed.

"Dunno. Rocket attack, maybe," Maya replied, scrambling out of her bunk.

Rocket attack? Throwing back the covers, Devon shoved her feet into her boots, grabbed a jacket and followed Maya out the door. The outside lights illuminated the M-4 held in her roomie's hands. *Well Jesus, you should have a weapon, too, since the freaking* base *might be under attack.* Without a word she darted back inside to grab her sidearm.

Following Maya, she ran to the end of the row of B-huts. As she cleared the last one, a faint whiff of jet fuel carried on the wind hit her nostrils. People shouted in the distance, running around in the semi-darkness. Amidst the confusion, she looked toward the airstrip and let out a gasp. A few hundred meters short of the runway, a wall of flame shot into the night sky, rising from the wreckage of an aircraft lying stricken on the ground.

"Shit," Maya said, running toward the scene. "I think it's a Spectre."

Oh my God, it was. Devon recognized the distinctive shape of the nose and the four propellers. Her heart was in her throat as she kept pace with Maya. *Please don't let it be Ace. Please God, not Ace.*

Crews were already on scene battling the fire, and a group of men were hauling two stretchers away from the wreckage, running flat out to a waiting vehicle. The smell of the smoke and burning jet fuel was suffocating. The sharpness stung her nostrils and made her eyes water.

"What the hell happened?" she shouted to one of the bystanders when she reached the fence. She clutched the chain link with white-knuckled fingers. It couldn't be Candace. Just couldn't.

"Don't know," he answered, shaking his head as he stared at the spectacle. "I was in the hangar when I heard a bang. I ran outside and next thing I knew the plane was on fire. It tried to make an emergency landing, but didn't make it."

Devon put her hands over her mouth. Christ. The aircraft held a crew of eleven plus two pilots. She dropped her arms, wrapping them around her waist. "Anybody else get out besides the two crewmen?"

"Don't think so."

With the raging heat hitting her this far away from the runway, she knew nobody could survive the fire and suffocating smoke.

She was still staring in horror when Maya walked up, her pretty face grim in the orange wash of light from the flames. "Some guys I talked to think it took a direct hit from an RPG."

Devon shook her head slowly, thinking of Liam's comment. Was it possible Nasrallah's men had acted so soon? Watching the fire devour the wreckage, she tightened her arms around her body to combat the shivers rolling through her. She was staring at her darkest nightmare. Images of her father's smoldering plane filled her head.

For years the fear of being in a crash had all but paralyzed her when she'd stepped on an aircraft. Yet now all she could think about was what the doomed Spectre crew had felt in the final moments before the crash. What must have gone on in her father's head before impact.

She imagined the shrill scream of the turbo-prop engines, master alarms blaring in the cockpit. The pilots desperately calling out a mayday and the rest of the crew bracing in crash positions. Those final, terrifying seconds when they still hoped for a miracle. Their hearts slamming against their ribs, every muscle tight with denial. They must have felt a painful surge of hope once the airfield came into view out the cockpit window.

Devon bit her lip. God, the terror those poor people must have suffered when they realized they weren't going to make it. And then the terrible, bone crushing impact. The shriek of tearing metal, and the instant explosion of the fireball. Had they been conscious after the crash? Had they suffered the unimaginable agony of the flames blistering their skin?

*Her father had been so badly burned they hadn't let her mother see his body.*

The gathered crowd was silent while the crews fought the fire. It must have been visible for miles out on the Shomali Plain. Nasrallah's men were probably watching right now, laughing, celebrating the death of the American servicemen aboard the burning Spectre. Maybe the warlord himself was listening to their jubilation from the other side of the border in Pakistan. The thought galvanized her into action.

Unable to watch another second, Devon spun away and headed for the main buildings.

"Hey, wait up!" Maya jogged up behind her, still toting her rifle like it was second nature to her. Which it probably was, considering what she did in the service. "Where're you going?"

"To find out where Ace is."

Keeping step beside her, Maya laid a hand on her shoulder. "I'm sure she's okay."

Devon couldn't answer for the lump in her throat. She kept thinking of Candace at the controls, trying to guide the plane in despite the terror flooding her veins.

She started running. At least eleven people were dead, and the other two would likely die. All because a handful of brainwashed assholes got lucky with an RPG. Fury burned through her fear, making her heart race. "Think someone's already gone out to look for the bastards that did this?"

"Oh yeah," Maya said. "The assholes won't be around for morning prayers, I promise you that. But damn, I wish I was part of the team going after them."

"Well, you can be part of my hunter team. Help me find out about Ace. I'll meet you back here in fifteen minutes."

"Sure."

Devon made a beeline for the Exchange in the hopes that someone would know where her friend was. But the crowd in front of the building was too thick to get through, and the few people she asked weren't any help. She doubled back and took a different route, frustrated at the time slipping by. *Somebody* had to know where the hell Candace was.

"Spike!"

She whirled at the feminine shout, searching around her. Out of the crowd, a figure emerged, and when the overhead lights revealed a head of blond hair, her knees went weak. "Ace!"

Candace rushed over and threw her arms around her. "I'm okay," she said, squeezing hard.

"Oh, God." Suppressing a shudder, Devon held on tight and closed her eyes. "I think I lost twenty years off my life when Maya said it was a Spectre."

Candace pulled away and smiled. "Yeah." She ruffled Dev's hair. "Thanks for caring so much."

Her throat was too tight to respond right away. She looked back at the fireball and swallowed. "Do you know them?"

"Not sure yet. Nobody seems to know anything."

Now that she knew her friend was okay, her head started spinning. "I think I need to sit down."

"Come on." Candace dragged her to the wall of the building and sat her down. "Need some water?"

"No." She already felt like a wimp. But her skin wouldn't stop crawling. "Good thing I fly helos, because this would've set me back years if I flew fixed wings."

"Yeah, have to say I'm not feeling great about my choice of vocation at the moment."

Devon pulled in a deep breath, the air heavy with the harsh smell of burning jet fuel. Once someone smelled it, they never forgot it. What had just happened served as a pointed reminder she was in the middle of a war zone. No one was safe here. An RPG could hit a slower moving, lower altitude helo way easier than a fixed wing aircraft. She pushed the thought away. She couldn't think like that, because she had a job to do and a crew that relied on her. Fear wasn't going to help anything, let alone keep her safe.

Candace craned her neck to see through the crowd. "Hey, there's Maya. Maya!" she shouted.

Maya's eyes closed in relief for a moment when she spotted them. "Good to see you, chica," she said as she reached Candace, giving her a quick hug.

Candace eyed the M4 warily. "Going someplace with that?"

"I'd love to, but unfortunately not." Reaching down, she grasped Devon's hand and pulled her to her feet. The hard glint in her eyes left no doubt she'd rather be using her weapon on the men that shot down the plane, instead of hanging around the base. Then her gaze fastened on something behind Devon, and her expression soured. "Great. Here comes Tweedle Dumb."

Devon and Candace swiveled their heads. Sure enough, Jackson exited the hospital and strode toward them, his black eyes running over Maya and the rifle she held. "Yeah, keep staring at me, buddy, and see what happens," she muttered darkly, shifting the weapon in her grip.

"Jesus, Maya, don't shoot him," Candace laughed under her breath.

Devon ignored the undercurrent of hostility radiating from Maya and walked up to him. "It's Jackson, right?"

"That's right," he answered, his deep voice holding a distinct southern drawl. "You must be Devon."

"Yes, nice to meet you," she said, distractedly accepting his handshake. "I was wondering if you'd seen a PJ friend of mine tonight. Tech Sergeant Munro."

His eyes flicked to Ace and then Maya, lingering for a moment before coming back to Devon. "Cam's inside."

Her eyes shot to his, "In the hospital?"

He nodded, black gaze steady and somber. "He was one of the first on scene to evacuate the wounded."

*And the dead.* Jackson didn't say it, but he didn't have to.

"Oh." He was safe, then. She swallowed, nearly overcome with the need to see him. "I just wanted to make sure he was…" *Okay.*

"He's just finishing up," Jackson put in. "You can probably still catch him."

She cast a quick glance over her shoulder at Candace and Maya. "Maybe I'll just…say hi."

"Go ahead," Candace answered with a sarcastic edge. "I think it's safe to say everyone's too busy to notice you guys right now."

"I'm going back to the hut," Maya announced, flashing a warning glance at Jackson before whirling away. Candace shrugged and followed.

Devon smiled at Jackson to cover the awkward lapse, but his eyes still tracked Maya's retreating figure. "Thanks for your help."

He met her gaze with a smile. "Anytime, ma'am."

Devon walked toward the hospital, her heart thudding against her ribs. She just had to see Cam. Then she'd feel better. Once she saw him and reassured herself he was okay, she could go back to her barracks and try to get some sleep. Entering the sliding doors and rounding the corner, she came to a sudden stop. He stood in the brightly lit hallway, removing a surgical mask and gloves. Her heart turned over at the sight of him. "Cam." His name came out rough.

His head snapped around and his mouth lifted in a tired version of the lopsided smile she loved. "Ma'am."

It was all she could do not to run into his arms as he walked over, but his proper greeting held her in place. Her throat was tight, choked with emotion. She couldn't stay away from him anymore.

But he didn't touch her when he got to her, just stood before her when all she wanted was his arms around her. She almost reached for him instead, but checked the impulse. They didn't have any privacy here, and these were his co-workers and colleagues. She didn't want to embarrass him in any way. The lingering awkwardness felt all wrong.

"You okay?" he asked, fathomless eyes delving into hers.

She nodded, swallowing the lump wedged in her throat. "You?"

He shrugged. "Yeah, I'm fine."

Staff burst out of the room behind her and rushed past them down the hallway. When she looked back at Cam, he was watching her expectantly. Clearing her throat, she found her voice. "The impact woke me up, and Maya and I ran out because we thought it might be a rocket attack. When I saw the plane I thought it might be Ace, but she's okay." She was babbling, but didn't care. "Did you…see any of the crew?"

"Yeah."

When he didn't elaborate, her stomach clenched. "Any survivors?"

"One, but he won't make it."

Oh, God. Thirteen crewmen, dead. Cam's face said it all. Lines of strain bracketed his mouth and eyes. Tired, angry, but hiding it well. "I'm sorry."

"Yeah, me too. And I'm sorry you saw it. Must have brought back some ugly memories for you."

"The smell was the same. I'll never forget the smell." She wanted his arms around her, this instant so she could feel safe and banish the ghostly wisps of fear creeping into her subconscious. But of course it wasn't going to happen.

He blew out a breath and glanced over her head at something. "Heard you brought in some wounded earlier. Tough thing, seeing kids critically injured."

*Terrible.* "When I talked to the nurses last they said the boy was critical but stable. They wouldn't tell me anything else."

"Want me to find out for you?"

She tilted her head back to look into his eyes, so clear and full of understanding her heart ached. He wanted to help, and this was all he could do for now. "Would you?"

Without replying he took her elbow and led her to a plastic chair across the hall. "Here, sit down and wait for me. I'll see what I can do."

Devon watched him walk away with a painful mix of longing and hope. Seeing him made her question what the hell she was waiting for. Life was fleeting, fragile. She knew that better than anyone. Was she really going to risk losing him because of fear? She didn't want that. She was stronger, braver than that. But how could they possibly make a relationship work here? It would be nearly impossible to spend time together without asking for trouble, not to mention they wouldn't have any privacy.

It didn't matter. She wanted him, cared about him, and thought he felt the same for her. She'd make it work.

But first, she had to take the leap and accept what he was offering.

Footsteps approached. She lifted her head and watched until Cam appeared around the corner. One look at his face and the flame of hope in her chest snuffed out. On shaky legs she stood and faced him, though she already knew what he was going to say.

This time he took her stiff hand when he reached her. "The little girl died about an hour after arrival," he told her, his palm shockingly warm against hers. "She'd lost too much blood."

She nodded woodenly, staring at the center of his wide chest. So the on-board transfusions hadn't been enough. The trip to the base had taken too long. Her first mission back and though she'd gone right away without any delays, it hadn't been enough.

She went over the mission in her mind, going over every detail. Maybe she could have pushed the twin turbine engines harder and shaved a few minutes off the flight. Would that have made the difference?

"Don't."

"Don't what?"

"Second guess yourself. There was nothing they could've done for her, Dev, even if she'd come in sooner."

She remembered the pale little face, and the long strands of dark hair whipping in the rotor wash when they carried her away from the Hawk on the stretcher. "And the boy?" she managed.

"Made it through his surgery. He's still stable and all his vitals are good. He'll be okay."

Yeah. He'd be okay, but he'd return home without

his little sister. She closed her eyes and shook her head, erasing the picture of the morgue where she'd sat with Ty's remains. Such a waste. Another young, innocent life taken by her own people, and for what?

"Come on," Cam murmured, tugging on her hand. "I'm done for now. Let's get out of here."

Gripping his fingers tight, she followed, but stopped when she saw the children's grandfather in the waiting room. All alone, head bent so his chin rested on his sunken chest, his worn, frayed wool hat held between his gnarled hands. She didn't know what to say to him, but felt she had to say something. "Do you speak Pashto?" she asked Cam.

"A bit. Why, you want to say something to him?"

"Yes."

He searched her eyes for a moment as though judging whether or not she was up to it. "Hang on, I'll get someone."

A minute later he returned with a young Afghan man. "This is Saiid. He'll translate for you."

Devon wiped her hands on her pants and followed the man into the waiting room. The grandfather looked up at them, his dark eyes time-worn and weary in his weathered face. Full of sorrows she couldn't even begin to comprehend. The instant he focused on her, he stiffened. He looked so shocked that she stopped, his wide-eyed gaze making her uneasy.

She hesitated inside the doorway. Did he find her presence offensive because she was a woman? He stared at her like she was a ghost. Almost like he recognized her, but that was impossible. Even if he'd seen her through the rotor wash in the cockpit earlier, there was no way he could have seen her face through the visor. Still, the look on his face was unnerving.

Saiid bowed slightly and addressed the elder. The old man nodded, looking at her with that strangely intense expression in his eyes. When Saiid finished and gave her an encouraging smile she cleared her throat and spoke. "Sir, I flew the helicopter you came in on today." The old man held her gaze steadily while Saiid translated. Something in his expression still bothered her. He watched her closely, as though she either fascinated or horrified him. "I'm very sorry for your loss," she added quietly. That was inadequate, but what else could she say to comfort him?

She paused for a moment, uncertain, wanting to ease the terrible burden of loss he must be suffering. "Please know my thoughts and prayers are with you and your family." She hoped he wasn't offended by her message. Considering her mere presence had shocked him, the idea of an infidel praying for him might be a complete insult. "If I can help in any way, please let me know."

Saiid finished relaying her message and she nodded solemnly. The old man nodded back, staring at her with unblinking black eyes. Having done all she could, she left the room. "Thank you," she said to Saiid.

"Of course, Captain."

"Did it seem odd to you that he kept staring at me like that?"

Saiid laughed. "I don't think it ever occurred to him that a woman would be a pilot."

Devon wasn't sure that was the reason. With a tired sigh she let it go and went to find Cam.

He was leaning against the wall waiting for her when she came out. "Okay?"

She nodded. As okay as she was going to be for the time being.

He held out a hand and she took it gratefully, comforted by the strength and warmth of his grip. The instant they stepped outside the smell of burning fuel hit her again. In the distance the flames were almost out in the blackened carcass of the aircraft, but the smoke rose in a roiling black mass. The crowd of onlookers had thinned, most people having returned to their huts or back to their posts. Tearing her eyes away from the smoldering hull of the plane, Devon suppressed a shiver.

Cam gently rubbed her cold fingers with his as they walked toward the barracks. She was very aware of the heavy beat of her blood in her veins, every cell attuned to him. She needed to tell him how she felt before they lost any more time together, but she couldn't find the courage.

But as they approached the second group of B-huts, she stopped walking. Cam glanced down at her questioningly. The memories of her father's and Ty's deaths were fresh in her mind. Cam could make them disappear.

She battled with herself. No way could she go into her bunk and sleep now, and if she didn't tell Cam what was on her mind she'd never forgive herself. She tugged on his hand and led him down a darkened alley and behind a storage building to give them some privacy.

Facing him, her heart pounded so hard she was sure he could hear it. His face was in shadow, but she could feel his eyes on her. Watching. Waiting. Because the next step was up to her. He wasn't going to do it for her. And she wanted this, so badly she burned. The urgency hummed through her veins, impossible to ignore.

"Cam…"

"Be sure, Dev," he warned, settling his hands on her waist.

Gathering her courage, she stepped closer, close enough that her breasts almost brushed his chest and she could feel the incredible heat emanating from his body. Before she could lose her nerve she slid her hands up his arms, following the hard swells of muscle to his shoulders and neck. Her fingers threaded into his thick, soft hair. In answer he bent his head and leaned into her touch, and even in the semi-darkness she saw his lids drop in pleasure. Heat speared through her lower belly.

Her hands were unsteady as she brought them to his stubbled cheeks, stroking the strong lines of his cheekbones. He turned his head and gently kissed her hand, his lips sinfully warm against her palm. She saw the silent message in his eyes. No going back if she took this step.

"I'm sure," she whispered back, then leaned up on tiptoe to find his mouth with hers. He angled his head and met her part way. A gasp tore out of her at the velvety feel of his lips.

He groaned in response and moved in closer. His amazing hands smoothed up her back before he wrapped his heavy arms around her and kissed her deeper. She wound her fingers through his hair and opened her mouth under his. The soft, erotic glide of his tongue against her lower lip sent a spear of heat between her thighs. His body was warm and hard, and he held her so tight.

She lifted her head. His eyes were almost black, and raging with need. He was rock hard, and hot against her, even through the layers of cloth separating them. Without thinking she pressed tight against him and found his lips again, gently stroking her tongue into his mouth. He made a rough sound and held her face as he kissed her in return, and she lost herself in the feel and taste of him. The heat built steadily, enveloping her in the sensual experience of being locked in his arms while he kissed her with a lingering thoroughness that weakened her knees. She was drowning in sensation, blind to everything but the feel of his mouth and the hard press of the powerful muscles that caged her.

*Oh my God...*

She felt hot and dizzy. Weak yet hungry. Time slowed and expanded, setting her adrift. He was gentle with her. She knew how turned on he was by the feel of his erection prodding her, but his kisses were tender and slow. The most seductive she'd ever experienced. Combined with the way he cradled her, she melted in his hold and would have slid to the ground in a puddle without his arms wrapped around her.

With a quiet sigh she stroked his shoulders and the back of his neck, reveling in the way he sighed and nuzzled at her lips and jaw. Her body trembled with the knowledge of how incredible it was going to be when they finally got each other naked. She was thinking about sliding her hands under his shirt to feel the sculpted muscles of his chest when he released her mouth with a slow suction on her bottom lip. Nibbling for another moment, he lifted his head.

She was breathless, staring up into his face. The hunger was there in his eyes, unquenched and vivid, but tempered with the tenderness he'd shown her. A slow smile spread across her face, and he answered with one of his own.

He stroked a thumb across her cheek. "What, baby?"

The tenderness in his voice made her throat clench. She couldn't say it. She was going to have to show him instead.

A jumble of emotions tumbled through her. Tears threatened. She squeezed her eyes shut to stem the burn in them, but her breath hitched on a half sob.

Cam tucked her face against his chest, surrounding her with his arms. "Don't cry," he whispered against her temple. "It kills me when you cry."

She gave a tight shake of her head, fighting to get hold of herself. "I need you."

"You've got me." His hands stroked over the length of her back. "You've always had me."

Her heart cracked wide open, a sudden rending pain that tore into her chest.

"That help?" he whispered, tracing the curve of her cheek with an index finger.

Devon wrapped her arms around his shoulders and laid her head against his chest, snuggling in tight. "Yes," she sighed, eating up every second of the embrace. "I could stay like this forever."

He kissed her temple. "I love holding you."

"Good." She planned on taking advantage of that at every opportunity from now on.

Cam bent and kissed her gently again. She looped her arms around his neck to deepen it, but he gently set her away with a wry grin. "Much as I'd love to keep kissing you, it's only a matter of time before someone comes this way. And I promised to protect you."

"Even if it's from myself," she teased.

"Yep. Or from me." He slid his arms around her for one last hug, lifting her from the ground with a deep groan. "But Christ you feel good."

"You too," she whispered against his ear, nipping the lobe.

Cam jolted and set her down, giving her a playful glare as he put some space between them. "I'll remember that, Spike."

# EIGHT

"You got somewhere more important to be?" Will asked her from across the table.

Devon set down her cards and glanced up at him with a frown. "Pardon?"

"You keep checking your watch every ten minutes, and you're playing hell on my ego. Am I that boring?"

*Ah, jeez.* "No, it's not you. Sorry." She was distracted. Restless and edgy waiting around for the call to go out, and because she hadn't seen Cam or Ryan all day. Nobody she'd asked had seen them, so they must have gone out on another mission, or were in isolation.

"And it *would* be the one time I'm beating you," he muttered, tossing his hand onto the table and gathering up all the cards.

"I was thinking about going over to watch some football if you're interested."

Will snagged his coat from the back of his chair. "Nah, but thanks. Think I'll spend some quality time with my e-mail account."

Dev smiled. "Tell your wife I said hello, and to give the girls a hug from me." She followed him outside, and quickly tucked her hands into her pockets. The sky was already dark, and the air was cold enough that she could see her breath as she headed over to the Exchange.

Halfway there, she ran into Candace.

"Hey," Devon said. "You were up early. I didn't even hear you come in or leave. Were you out last night?"

"No. Had a meeting. Then when I got back I couldn't sleep worth a damn."

"Your bunk still bugging you?"

Rather than answer, Candace looked around as if to check they couldn't be overheard. "Not really."

"You fixed it, then?"

"No. Your friend Ryan did."

Devon tucked her tongue into her cheek. "Oh, really?"

"Oh, stop. You know nothing happened." A dark scowl marred her pretty face. "He's a bad-ass."

"Yeah, I can see why you'd think that, but he's really a sweetheart once you get to know him." Once people got past his enormous ego, that is.

"That's exactly my point, Dev. I don't want to get to know him, let alone *here*. If he keeps being all palsy-walsy like that he's going to get us written up."

She thought about it. "All right, I'll talk to him."

"No, I didn't mean I wanted you t—" She paused and pursed her lips. "I already made it clear I don't want to fraternize with him."

*I bet you did.* Devon had to work really hard not to not smile, imagining Ryan alone with Candace in the B-hut, needling her every chance he got.

"And *you* shouldn't either."

Probably not, but she wasn't going to cut a friend off like that. "So, is the uh…bunk fixed?"

"Yeah," she said grudgingly.

"Did he test it out for you before he left?"

Candace turned shocked eyes on her. "Christ, you're

just as bad as he is! You need to stop hanging around with him before I stop liking you too."

Devon laughed. "Damn, I wish I'd been a fly on the wall for that little interlude yesterday."

"Shut up," she said without heat. "I handled it just fine."

"I don't doubt that for a second."

Candace blew out a breath, the puff of vapor rising into the cold air. "Where are you going, anyway?"

"I don't feel like going to the gym or taking a run. I thought I'd find some football on TV or something."

"God, you're a piece of work. How the hell are the rest of us supposed to compete with you around? You're like every man's fantasy come to life."

"That's kind of a backward compliment, but I'll take it. But I'm not everyone's fantasy. I can't cook worth a damn." Dev grinned at her. "Why so hostile, Ace?" she joked.

"I'm not trying to be hostile with anyone. I just want to be taken seriously around here, and I don't appreciate some…*people* that think it's okay to throw military law out the window whenever it suits their libido."

"I hear you."

"Not criticizing you, by the way."

"No, of course not."

"Hey, I'm serious." Candace poked her in the shoulder. "You and Cam are a different matter entirely. For one thing you've been friends for months, and you think he might be 'the one', so that's different."

Devon smirked. "Thanks for your blessing."

There was a game on the big screen TV, and though Candace made it clear she couldn't care less about football, they sat down with a group of male officers and watched until half time. When Devon glanced over, Candace was practically asleep in her chair, her head propped up on one fist, eyes at half-mast.

Dev nudged her knee. "You don't have to stay."

Candace sat up, her face brightening, one cheek bearing red marks from where her knuckles had dug into her skin. "Is it over?"

"No. Another half to go yet."

"God." She collapsed back with a groan. "Do you really like this stuff, or do you just tolerate it to hang with the guys?"

"Sorry to disappoint, but I really like it. I'm a die-hard Seahawks fan."

Candace stood, stretching her arms over her head. The move earned her several interested stares, but as always, she seemed oblivious to the attention.

Dev grinned and swatted her behind. "Get out of here and get some sleep."

When the game ended, she was too edgy to go back to her hut. She accompanied Liam to the hangar instead. "You sure you don't mind a tag along?"

"Don't mind at all," he replied with a smile. "Just checking the hydraulic system on my bird. The Chinooks are old. They keep the maintenance crews busy around here."

She knew better than to ask if he was going out for the night, because he wouldn't be able to answer her. She thought of asking him about Cam's whereabouts, but held off on that too. Nearing the hangar, the sounds of hammers and wrenches clanging and banging against metal filled the air. As she stepped inside the brightly lit building, the smells of oil and hydraulic fluid filled her nostrils.

"Have to admit, those are pretty amazing machines." Devon stared up at the hulking Chinook.

"They're not as pretty as the 60, but they're my favorite bird to fly."

They walked over, and Liam approached the closest mechanic. "How's she look?"

"She's holding her own. Want a status report?"

"I'd appreciate it."

"Hang on." The younger man turned his head and hollered, "Hey, Girard!"

Devon's gaze swung to Liam, whose face went rigid at the mention of the surname. She winced inside when Honor poked her strawberry-blonde head out the back of the cabin. Seeing them, Honor froze.

"Hi," Liam managed. The awkward tension hanging thick in the air made Devon look elsewhere.

"Hi," Honor replied. The word was soft, laced with uncertainty.

Oh, shit. Devon wanted no part of this, but she couldn't make her escape without further embarrassing Liam.

"I was just checking on the old girl's status," he said, standing stiffly with his hands clasped behind his back.

To her credit, Honor never looked away from him. "She's fine. Had a slow leak in one of the hydraulic lines, but it's all fixed up now."

Liam shoved his hands in the pockets of his flight suit. "Good. That's good."

"You need her now?"

"Shortly, yeah."

"She's ready when you are."

"Okay." He stared at her like she was water and he was a man dying of thirst.

Devon bit the inside of her lip and was about to make some excuse to leave when Honor spoke.

"We're all done here." She wiped her hands on a rag and bent to gather some tools. "Let's go, boys," she called, and her crew followed suit. She hopped down from the belly of the Chinook and spared a smile at Devon before nodding politely to Liam. "Have a safe flight, Major."

"Thanks." He followed her progress with haunted eyes as she walked away.

Devon cleared her throat, bringing his attention back to her, and the raw pain in his eyes shocked her. "Do you want me to, uh…" She gestured toward Honor's retreating back.

"No, it's fine." He checked his watch. "I've got some stuff to get done before the briefing. See you later."

"Sure." After he left she let out the breath she'd been holding. Well, that had been fun. Certainly put things in perspective for her. She might well end up in Liam's position if things didn't work out with Cam.

Wandering around, her gaze landed on a lone Black Hawk over at the end of the hangar. She walked over, taking in its sleek lines as the crew worked on the main rotor. Beautiful machine. Like a black panther coiled and ready to run.

Staring at the fuselage, a niggling unease took root. Mostly she'd avoided examining this fear too closely since coming back, but all of a sudden she couldn't shake off the doubt. *Oh, perfect, just what I need. Only thing that could cap this night off is—*

"Hey. Glad I caught you," said a low, sexy voice.

She whipped around. Cam stood at the hangar entrance in his combat uniform, that heart-melting crooked smile on his face. She couldn't move as he strode toward her, tall and strong and looking so damn heroic he broke her heart without even trying. Her throat tightened.

He came up beside her. Along with the uniform, the absence of the delectable scents of soap and cologne she associated with him confirmed he was about to embark on a mission. "One of the guys at the Exchange told me you left with Liam. I just missed you by a few minutes."

Being this close to him made her system go haywire, her body remembering with vivid clarity the things they'd done the night before. She licked her lips, staying the impulse to look around and make sure no one was staring at them. At this point, she didn't much care. "I thought you were out somewhere."

"No. Isolation starts in twenty-five minutes."

And sometime after that if the intelligence and weather reports held up, the mission he'd been prepping for would get the green light.

He glanced over at the Hawk. "What are you looking for?"

"Nothing. I was just thinking."

His vivid blue eyes assessed her knowingly. "About what?"

She shifted her stance and looked away. "The usual."

"We need to talk about it, Dev. We should have had this conversation a long time ago."

She didn't even know where to start. How much did he know?

Cam was silent a moment, watching her. "You made the right call that night. Deep down you know that, don't you?"

An ache settled in her throat. She clenched her fingers together and twisted them.

"You had the responsibility of safeguarding your crew and your helo first. Their safety was paramount to anything else, and the weather was the shits that night. I remember how bad it was because I could hear the wind howling outside my hut when I was trying to get to sleep."

She almost choked on the lump in her throat. "He might have lived if I'd gone."

Cam's gaze never wavered from her face. His body heat curled around her like an inviting blanket. "You might have crashed on the way out there, too, and you knew it. That's why you made the call not to go, and every other sane pilot would have done the same."

"Not Liam, or any one of the pilots that fly you guys." Any of the Night Stalkers would have gone. Why hadn't command sent one of them instead of her?

"You're not being fair to yourself, Dev. You can't even compare your training to theirs." He paused a moment. "Look, it's bizarre Ty was even in that village, since he was stationed at K2 up in Uzbekistan. It's weirder yet that you got the medevac call. It should have been a CSAR mission right from word go."

Maybe. But the fact remained Ty had died because she hadn't made it to the target area that night. "If I'd known it was him, I would have gone." She looked up at Cam. "I swear to God, I would have gone no matter how bad it was out there."

"And you might have died trying to get to him," he said quietly. "Sorry, babe, but you can't solely take the blame for what happened. You would have gone if there'd been any chance of getting there in one piece. I know you, and I know you'd do damn near anything to get your wounded out. But you're forgetting something else. Ty knew the score, Dev. We all do when we earn the right to wear the maroon beret. He knew what his job was, even when he was out there wounded. And he wouldn't have blamed you for scrubbing the mission, let alone for his death. If you don't believe that, then you didn't know Ty."

Devon swallowed the tears threatening to erupt. "All I can think about is him dying alone out there, listening for the sound of rotors. And then you having to bring his body home."

He took her hand, noticing the clenched knuckles. "You and I did what we had to, and so did he. All any of us can do is do our duty, and yours was to protect your crew and your aircraft. You did the responsible thing, Dev. The only thing you could have done in that situation."

Responsible, yes. But at the cost of the lives of the wounded she'd inadvertently left stranded. When she'd later found out just how much her decision had cost, she'd made a vow to herself not to make the same mistake again. And she wouldn't. Unless conditions were bad enough for takeoff to guarantee suicide, she was never scrubbing a mission again. "It's…hard for me to live with," she admitted in a strained whisper.

He squeezed her hand, giving her his reassurance and warming her cold skin. "I understand. I wish I knew what else to say, but in the end it doesn't matter what I think. You're going to have to forgive yourself if you're ever going to get past this. You can't keep holding on to this, or it'll destroy you."

Keeping her fist clenched, she looked down at the concrete floor. He was right, she knew that in her heart. But she wasn't ready to forgive herself yet. She didn't know if she ever could.

"Devon?" a soft voice called out.

Through swimming eyes she looked over her shoulder at Honor as she approached. The other woman gave her an apologetic smile and stood near the Chinook the crew was moving out of the hangar. "Sorry, but someone's coming, and…" She let it trail off, her expression uncertain.

"It's okay. Thanks." Hating to sever the link, she pulled her hand free of Cam's grasp.

"Guess I should get going," he said, taking a step away. Her need to reach out for him was strong and she had to fight to keep her arm at her side.

There were so many things she needed to say to him, but this was the wrong time and place. Once again she'd have to wait and pray she got another chance to tell him how she felt. "Be careful out there."

He gave her a gentle smile. "I will." His hand came up, and he wiped at the tears gathered on her lower lashes. "Stay safe and warm, baby."

Her throat was too tight to speak. She nodded. But when he started walking away, a bolt of fear sliced through her. "Wait!"

He turned back to her, and without thinking she took off her necklace and ran up to him. "Here." She pressed the quarter she'd had soldered to the chain into his palm. Cam stared at it, unmoving, and she knew he understood that he held the twin of the coin he'd placed on Ty's casket. "He gave it to me before he deployed," she told him. "I think you should have it now."

"I don't know if I want it." More than the words, the reluctance in his voice told her how uneasy he was about this.

"Please take it."

He met her eyes. "You sure?"

"Yes. I'd feel better knowing you had it."

"All right. Put it on for me, then."

She took it from him, and fastened it around his sturdy neck with unsteady hands. Helpless to stop herself, she laid her hand over it, pressing it into the thick muscle beneath his desert camo uniform. "Now we'll both be watching over you, to make sure you stay safe."

Something flashed in his eyes. "Dev."

She shook her head. "Just come back, okay?"

"I'll be fine. Be back before you know it."

She prayed he was right. "There's one more thing."

"Yeah?" That trademark crooked smile curved his lips. "What's that?"

Gathering her courage, she swallowed past the lump in her throat and held his gaze. It wasn't how she'd envisioned telling him, but she couldn't let him go without saying the words. "I'm falling in love with you."

The smile died, his amused expression dissolving into shock. "What?"

"Yeah. So you have to come back so I can finish the job."

A jumble of emotions swirled in the blue depths of his eyes as he stared at her. Then he broke into a wide smile and brought a hand up to cradle her cheek. "I'm coming back, sweetheart. I wouldn't miss that chance for the world."

Shoot, now she was on the verge of crying. "Honor?" she called.

"Yeah?" Her friend answered from somewhere near the doors.

"Look away for a minute, will you?"

"Uh...sure."

Cam grinned as she lifted on her toes to kiss him. His wonderful arms surrounded her. The few days' worth of stubble on his face rasped against her skin, adding to the heat. She gripped the back of his head with both hands to hold him close as she kissed him, losing more of herself with every second. All too soon he pulled away. The fire burned like banked flames in his eyes.

"I'm glad you told me." His long fingers slipped around her nape and squeezed gently. "Because honestly? I think I fell a long time ago."

Was he saying he loved her? Before she could even form the words to respond he dropped a tender kiss on her parted lips and pulled away. "See you soon." He disappeared out the hangar doors.

Devon watched him go, jumping when Honor put a consoling arm across her shoulders. "It's been a hell of a long day for all of us." Her voice was soft, full of warmth. "And before I go back to the hut, I just thought I'd mention I happen to have a key to one of the storage sheds." The silver key winked in the lights when she held it up.

Frowning, Devon took it from her. "What—"

She lowered her voice to a whisper. "Unless there's an emergency, everyone's done in here for the night. You'd have some privacy if you wanted it." She added a conspiratorial wink.

A hot blush stole up Devon's cheeks. "Oh." She cast a glance at the doors Cam had just disappeared through. He had probably less than twenty minutes now.

"I know how hard it is. Go. Catch him before it's too late."

Sparing Honor an appreciative smile, Devon squeezed her hand. "I owe you one."

"Nah. I'm just happy to help. Now go get him."

Damn right she would.

HE HATED WALKING away from her with so much unsaid between them. This last time had felt like he was ripping off his own skin. Cam glanced up at the night sky and the few stars twinkling between cracks in the cloud deck. Who knew what the next mission had in store for him?

"Cam!"

He stopped in midstride at the sound of Devon's voice and turned around. She ran through the hangar doors and straight toward him. Hiding his surprise, he walked back and met her partway. "What's wrong?"

"Nothing," she said breathlessly, staring up at him. "But I need you to come with me for a few minutes."

He sighed and checked his watch. "I'd love to honey, but—"

"Please?"

He had less than twenty five minutes until isolation started, but he couldn't say no when she was gazing up at him like that. "All right. Where to?"

She grabbed his hand and towed him past the hangar to a storage facility. He didn't protest, but he kept an eye out for anyone wandering around and prepared to pull his hand away. His eyebrows went up when he saw the key in her hand. She had it in the lock and a second later the door swung open. Without a word she dragged him inside and shut the door. The place was crowded with aircraft parts and smelled like axel grease and hydraulic fluid. Though his body pulsed with sudden arousal, he couldn't help but chuckle. "This is romantic."

"Works for me."

"God I love how low maintenance you are."

She reached up to thread her hands into his hair, and he stopped laughing.

Cam's heart pounded against his ribs when her lips settled on his. He couldn't hold back the groan of need at the feel of her warm mouth trembling slightly beneath his. His hands coasted up the narrow line of her back and then he wrapped his arms around her to bring her up flush against him. Her lips parted on a gasp and he gently ran his tongue over them. His body tightened painfully when she opened and let him inside.

He explored gently, savoring the velvet softness of her tongue against his, loving the desperate tension that gripped her, the bite of her hands on his shoulders. She pushed closer against him, flattening her breasts against his chest, wringing another groan out of him. He threaded his hands in her beautiful hair and closed his fingers around fistfuls of it, holding her still as he settled in deeper. Her answering moan was full of hunger and need and it rocked him to his core.

He turned them and pressed her back against the plywood wall, one hand moving between her shoulder blades to cushion her as he moved a thigh between hers and leaned in close. She gasped into his mouth and shivered in his arms.

"Cam," she whispered shakily, clutching him tighter. Fighting to get closer.

He lifted her, settling her astride his thigh, swallowing the soft whimper she made, angling his head to get deeper. His fingers sought the smooth skin of her throat, trailing down the side to the neckline of her T-shirt, following the path with his mouth, his tongue. He nibbled and licked his way to the sensitive spot where her neck joined her shoulder, then scraped his teeth over it. She rewarded him with a soft cry of pleasure, igniting every possessive instinct in him.

Gently gripping the nape of her neck with one hand, he slid the other upward over her belly to brush his fingers against the curve of her breast. She lifted into his touch, spine curling to bring his hand closer to where she needed it. "There. Touch me, please."

Steeling himself, he cupped the soft mound of her breast with his palm and lightly stroked his thumb across her rigid nipple. Devon jerked in his arms and whimpered, attacking his mouth with hers. Holding her steady as he kissed her, Cam caressed back and forth over her nipple, swallowing her cries while he rubbed the length of his cock between her open thighs. He could come right now, just from doing this. Just from the incredible heat and feel of her, and knowing she wanted him so much. She was so goddamn soft and responsive. He'd always known it would be like this with her. Hot and explosive and so damn good it ripped away the civilized part of him to expose the raw, dominant hunger inside.

He wanted to pull her shirt up and shove her bra out of the way so he could pleasure her taut nipples with his mouth. He wanted to lick and suck them until she was mindless, writhing against the length of his cock and begging for release. Wanted to slide her pants down, rip open his fly and enter her with one smooth thrust, watching her eyes go hazy and blind from pleasure. Wanted to move slow and deep while he stroked her wet clit, and make her scream into his mouth when she came.

*Fuck.*

He pulled back, breathing hard, and stared down into her flushed face. Her eyes were dilated, lips swollen, her fingers digging into his shoulders. She moved her hips against his, a throaty moan escaping as another shiver rippled through her taut body. "Don't stop," she whispered.

Cam shook his head, jaw clenched so hard it ached. "No."

She stilled and stared up at him, eyes searching his. "W-what?"

He released the back of her neck and settled his hands on her hips to hold her still. "No," he repeated, dying with the need to push into her. Inches from losing control. "I'm not taking you out here against a fucking wall, Devon." Not here where anyone might walk in on them, where anyone could hear her cries of release. And not with only a twenty minute window to work with. She deserved a hell of a lot better than that. "Look at me."

He waited until her dazed eyes focused on his before continuing. "When I take you it'll be in a big, soft bed with no time limit and enough privacy so I can take my time touching and tasting every inch of you. Got that?"

Devon shuddered at his words, blinking fast as though fighting tears. Tears of frustration, because she was hurting as badly from the need for release as he was. "But I don't... How? When?"

He wrapped himself around her and held her close, absorbing the tremors running through her muscles. "Soon." He'd damned well find a way to make it happen if it killed him, but right now he was pissed off at himself for letting things get out of hand.

Her breathing was still choppy. "I don't... I can't wait that long."

"Baby," he whispered, cuddling her close, cradling the back of her head as she buried her face in his neck. He should be shot for tormenting her when he'd known from the outset he could never finish this. He could at least give her some relief before walking away. He could slide his hands into her pants, ease his fingers into the wet folds between her thighs and make her come to relieve the desperate trembling of her body. Dropping a tender kiss on the side of her neck, he smoothed a hand over the curve of her bottom and ruthlessly ignored how badly he hurt as he prepared to take the sharp edge off for her.

Devon bit her lip when his fingers slid beneath the hem of her shirt to stroke across the velvety skin of her belly, then closed her eyes on a gasp when he caressed beneath her waistband. She was so warm. He couldn't wait to cup her in his palm. "Cam, please…"

"It's all right, baby, I'll take care of you."

"But what about y—"

"Shh," he whispered against her lips, stealing inside while his fingers played over her soft skin. He'd just undone the button at the top of her fly when voices brought his head up. At least three men, coming toward the hut. Their footsteps got louder with each passing second. *Shit.*

Devon made a rough sound and hid her face against his shoulder, and he automatically turned her, shielding her from view with his body in case anyone opened the door. He gathered her up into a tight hug, passing a hand over the crown of her head so the embrace didn't appear sexual, and the men walked past. The moment they turned the corner and kept going, another group approached, and Cam knew their brief interlude had come to an end. He sighed in regret and kissed her temple. "Damn, I'm sorry, Dev."

She took a deep breath and let it out slowly, nuzzling her cheek against his chest. "Me too. I thought we might have enough time, but…"

He could feel her unfulfilled need in the heat rising from her skin and the unnatural tension in her body. Setting her away from him finally as the other people walked up, he gave her a rueful grin. "Think of this as the best foreplay you've ever had."

Snickering, she pushed at his shoulder and stepped back to run a hand over her face. "God, I've never felt this frustrated in my whole life."

"I'll make it up to you."

Her answering smile turned his heart over. "You'd better. And soon."

"Very soon," he agreed. "I promise I'll be worth the wait." Cupping her petal-soft cheek in one hand, he kissed her tenderly. The hunger wouldn't let go, and he couldn't stop himself from giving her something else to think about after he walked away. "When you touch yourself later," he whispered, "imagine me going down on you."

She flushed, floundering for a moment, then narrowed her eyes at him. "Yeah? Then next time you're taking care of business in the shower you have to imagine me doing the same to you."

He smiled against her lips and kissed her one last time. "I always do, sweetheart."

# NINE

Shifting around to get comfortable on her bunk, Devon squinted at the fabric in her hand and pushed the tip of the needle through a tiny square in the Pararescue angel's wings. The compact reading light attached to her bed frame barely gave enough light to let her see what she was doing, but the cross stitching relaxed her and gave her something else to do besides worry about Cam. She wasn't going to be able to sleep with him going out on this sort of a mission, and besides, she was on call.

The metallic gold thread glimmered in the light. Her mind wouldn't shut off even with the methodical stitching. She kept shifting around, thinking of what Cam had said. She'd told him she was falling in love with him, but who was she kidding? If she was honest she'd given her heart to him a long time ago. And the feel of his hands on her body…God, she was still so revved up it drove her insane.

The glowing hands on her watch read a few minutes after midnight. The briefing must have finished long ago. Was he waiting for word on whether the op was a go? She imagined him sitting around with all his gear packed and stowed away, rifle at the ready, his fingers thoughtfully toying with Ty's quarter. With a sigh she set aside her work and switched off the useless light, but soon realized what a mistake it was. All the darkness did was make the memory of Cam's touch more vivid.

After another half hour of lying there she gave up any hope of sleeping and grabbed her heavy jacket from the end of her bed. Tiptoeing out of the barracks, she walked across to the service buildings and hitched a ride over to the Special Ops area of the airstrip. The driver let her out at a vantage point near the runway. Huddling deep into the warm folds of her coat, she stood by the chain-link fence and watched as a crew—maybe Liam's—fired up a Chinook. The twin rotors began to turn, slowly at first, then speeding up until they were a blur against the airstrip lights.

The building door opened, and a line of big, heavily equipped men came out. She stepped closer to the fence, twining her fingers through it. She couldn't tell at this distance what branch they were, but when only eight men came out, she assumed they were a SEAL squad, or maybe Delta. Then three more soldiers came out. Devon peered harder at the last two. Her breath caught. She instantly recognized Cam's silhouette and easy stride, and Ryan following him. Cam's name crowded her throat, but she didn't bother calling out because he'd never hear her at this distance.

Her friends disappeared up the tail ramp with the others, then the engines powered up for taxi clearance. The thought that Liam might be at the controls eased her, but a lingering apprehension nagged at her.

She tightened her fingers around the cold chain link while the wind and rotor wash beat at her face. Right now she was more worried for Cam than Ryan, though they were going on the same mission. It should console her to know they had each other out there, but it didn't. The tail ramp began to close. "I love you," she murmured under the roar of the rotors. "Be safe out there."

CAM DITCHED HIS heavy ruck and sat against the starboard side of the Chinook next to Ryan. The helo vibrated as the pitch of the engines rose, and the pilots began to close the tail ramp.

"Hey, we've got an audience out there," one of the SEALs remarked.

At this hour? Cam craned his neck with Ryan, looking toward the fence. Someone was standing there in the freezing cold, he guessed to watch them take off. Why in hell anyone would want to do that was beyond him, especially when it was so cold out.

Ryan tensed and came part way out of his seat. "It's Spike," he said incredulously.

"What?" Before he realized what he was doing, Cam stood up and peered past him out the closing ramp. Shit, it *was* Devon. She had to be goddamn freezing, because he was feeling the cold already despite all his layers and gear. He lifted a hand and she didn't react, but then, he was standing in shadow inside the aircraft. The ramp shut and he sat back down with a sigh.

The SEAL squad leader looked at him and arched a caustic brow in the midst of his camouflaged face. "That your girlfriend?"

Cam met his questioning stare for a moment, but didn't answer.

"Pretty dedicated chick, standing out there at this time of the morning in the cold."

"Yeah." Over the intercom the pilots received clearance for takeoff. When the bird lifted off the tarmac, he swiveled in his seat to get a better look out the small window behind him. She was still there, her jaw-length hair whipping in the rotor wash as she stared up at the aircraft. *Ah, honey, go inside and get warm.* He hated the thought of her being cold and uncomfortable, standing outside at this time of the morning to see him off. How long had she been waiting there? She could be called out at any time for a medevac run. She should be sleeping. His heart twisted when she wrapped her arms around her body and huddled deeper into her coat. "Ah, hell, Dev, you're killing me. Go in."

Ryan pressed a hand to the wall and peered out with him. "She won't. You know how she is."

Yeah. She was the most incredible woman he'd ever met, and she'd admitted she was falling in love with him. He could hardly keep from grinning like the lucky bastard he was. He felt like he'd just won the biggest lottery prize in history. And yet an unsettling disquiet wouldn't let him enjoy it completely.

"Don't worry about her," Ryan said. "We'll be gone in no time, and then she'll go in."

"I *am* worried about her."

"Why, what's up?"

"She's still torn up over what happened to Ty. It's going to make her push the envelope on the next risky call she gets, no matter how dangerous it is."

Ryan snorted. "Come on. Spike?"

"I'm serious. Maybe it's not completely obvious to everyone else, but it's there." Before Ty's death she'd been ultra cautious. Cautious about keeping her relationship with him a secret, and cautious with her aircraft and crew. But she'd changed. More and more he could see her pushing through the boundaries that used to hold her in check. Like tonight. Her telling him she was falling in love with him and kissing him in front of anyone that happened to walk by. Then later in the storage hut. If he hadn't stopped them, she would have let him take her there against the wall and not care about the consequences. He'd loved every second of it, but that kind of behavior wasn't the Devon he knew.

It seemed like she was becoming more daring every day, and now she almost bordered on the edge of reckless. It scared the hell out of him that she might take risks on a mission she wouldn't have before.

"She'll be okay," Ryan said, settling back for the ride. "She's got to work through her stuff in her own way, that's all. Don't worry, man. She's got a good head on her shoulders, and she can take care of herself."

They began cruising forward. Cam lost sight of her but knew without a doubt she would stand against the fence until she couldn't see them anymore and the noise of the rotors faded into stillness.

Ryan slapped him on the back a couple of times. "Look at the bright side. Guess this clears up how she feels about you."

Letting his unease go, a smile tugged at his mouth. "Maybe. But she might have come to see both of us off."

"True. I am better looking and more charismatic than you. But don't worry—I'll try to remember to tone it down around Dev so she won't be tempted to go after me."

Grinning, Cam laid his head back against the wall and closed his eyes, thinking of Devon's soft weight pressing against him with her tongue in his mouth. He couldn't wait for this mission to be over. Once he got back to base, he intended to make her his once and for all.

They cruised out toward the mountains through the thickening fog and were only a few minutes away from the base when the pilot's voice came through the headsets. "We've got an A-team member down about nineteen miles from our target LZ with what appears to be appendicitis. The area's not hot at this time, and he needs transport back to base. Any takers back there, PJs?"

Cam exchanged a look with Jackson. "I'll take care of it." He was PJ leader for this mission anyhow.

"I'll go with you."

He felt better having a partner with him, just in case. "We'll both handle it," Cam told the pilot.

The SEAL leader leaned forward. "We're not going to wait around for you guys. You'll both have to infil afterward and link back up with us on your own." He made it clear he wouldn't be heartbroken if they didn't rejoin them.

Cam didn't resent the guy's attitude. He didn't expect any preferential treatment, and he was looking forward to proving how valuable PJs were on a joint mission. "Yep, that's the plan."

"Uh-huh. Let us know when you're in position." The SEAL's dry tone and expression said they both knew most well-laid plans went to shit out in the field.

# TEN

CHILLED AND LONELY, Devon crawled into her bunk dressed in her flight suit. Determined to sleep, she shut her eyes and willed away the memory of being in Cam's heavenly arms. She'd never known such exquisite torment. The images in her head were a great distraction from worrying about him, but it didn't help quiet her busy mind. She tossed and turned, but finally exhaustion pulled her under.

A hand landed on her shoulder. Her eyes flew open, blinking to adjust in the darkness. "What?" she whispered, staring up into Candace's shadowed face.

"Your radio's going off."

It was? Devon sat up and groped beneath her pillow. Sure enough, a message came through telling her to get to the hangar ASAP. "God," she muttered, fighting the cobwebs in her brain.

"Apparently you're first up crew now."

"Okay." The original first up crew must have been called out. If not for Candace, she would have slept right through and maybe missed a mission. Yanking on her boots, she ran her fingers through her hair and grabbed her sidearm. She shoved it into a shoulder holster and pulled it on over her flight suit. "Thanks for waking me," she said to Candace on her way to the door.

"You bet. Be careful out there if you get called out," she said over a yawn.

"Will do."

The instant she opened the door, a shroud of gray surrounded her. She stilled on the top step, her heart starting a painful thud against her chest wall. The fog was so thick she could barely see the next row of B-huts where Will was lodged. Was he up already? He'd be worried about the fog too. Dread snaked up her spine. It was like walking back two months in time to the night Ty died. Would the visibility be as bad out there now if she had to fly?

Forcing her legs into motion, she left the hut, shivering beneath her jacket in the cold pre-dawn air as she jogged over to the ready room. *Relax. It's not like you've been called out. You're just on standby—*

The radio crackled. "Nine-line, nine-line, nine-line."

"Shit," she breathed, and ran. This was it. She was going out in a few minutes.

Somewhere above the fog the sky was still dark, but soon it would turn from inky black to a rich indigo as the sun crept up toward the horizon. She wanted to be back before the sun came up to avoid any unfriendly troops on the ground.

Inside, Will was already suiting up and looked over his shoulder with a grin. "Hey, sleeping beauty."

"Hey, sorry. I was out like a light." She donned her Escape and Evasion vest, checking to make sure she had her flares and mini flashlight, and that her hand-held radio had fresh batteries. "Know what's up?"

"I'm just the co-pilot," he pointed out. "They don't tell me jack."

She checked her watch. "Any word on the visibility?"

Will met her gaze, his guarded expression telling her he was thinking the same thing she was. "It's bad out there."

Didn't matter how bad it was this time. They were going. "Okay, I'll find out what the scoop is."

"Meet you on the bird."

"See you in a few."

Grabbing her knee board and helmet, she hurried from the room fastening her survival vest. A flight commander was waiting for her when she reached the ready room, but there were no other pilots. Was she the only aircraft going out? Feeling like an idiot, she nodded to the commander. "Crawford here, sir." She glanced between him and the brown-haired man dressed in a flight suit seated at the table. She could feel his intensity from across the room. Was he a pilot? She didn't see any wings on his suit, and she didn't recognize him.

He wasn't as tall as her commander, but he was broader through the chest and shoulders, his forearms thick with muscle beneath his rolled-up sleeves. His features were almost harsh, and his pale blue eyes regarded her carefully. Like he was sizing her up. Or questioning her ability to handle a flight in reduced visibility. A moment's unease gripped her. Had he read her file? He held her gaze for a moment longer, then finally gave her a half smile.

"Do you know Master Sergeant McCall?" her commander asked.

"No, sir."

"We were short, so he's volunteered to be your medic

for this mission. And you're lucky to have him because he's with the 160th."

A Night Stalker. That would explain the laser-like intensity of his stare. "Sir," she said to McCall with a respectful nod. He returned the courtesy. What kind of mission was important enough to warrant a Night Stalker medic going with her? Her heart beat a little faster. The commander handed her the printed nine-line to read. Target location, call signs and radio frequencies. Number of patients and their status. Equipment needed.

"A group of Marines got into trouble during a night-time reconnaissance operation," the Major explained as she read. "Their lead vehicle hit an IED on a road in the middle of a gulley, and they got ambushed from all sides. They've got seven wounded, four that need a lift out. Three of those are critical. None are ambulatory. They've established a secure perimeter for now, but those three boys need to come out now, and more like yesterday."

"Yes sir. We'll be using a carousel then?"

"Yes."

She glanced at McCall. "Can you work back there with a full carousel?"

"I'll make do." He didn't sound happy about it, and she wasn't surprised. Crews hated the cumbersome equipment because it left them no room to work.

Her commander pulled out a map and together they went over possible waypoints. "Intel reports enemy activity to the northwest of your LZ," he added. "As of fifteen minutes ago visibility was poor, but the winds should clear the fog enough for you to see the ground by the time you arrive. Your armed escort is being re-routed to meet you there."

"Yes sir." She made notes about the terrain and co-ordinates, and possible landing sites if they ran into bad weather. Armed with the info she needed, Devon and the medic ran out to the Black Hawk. Less than ten minutes had passed since she'd heard the nine-line call. Parked out on the tarmac, Will already had the bird's rotors turning. "Where's my crew chief?" she shouted over the noise of the engines.

McCall nodded over her left shoulder. "Right there."

Devon glanced over and saw the soldier sticking his head out of the cabin. "Morning, Sergeant," she called out.

"Ma'am." He nodded at McCall, who was lifting a cooler into the cabin. Knowing they were carry-ing whole blood on the mission told her how dire the situation was. If she didn't make it in to evacuate the wounded, they would probably die. She would not let that happen.

The young crew chief's eyes were warm as he smiled at her. She was glad he'd dropped the stilted formality. "Got a message from someone named Cam through the grapevine. He said to take extra good care of you."

"Did he?" She forced a smile and strapped on her helmet as she climbed into the left-hand seat and took her position as pilot commander. Whatever happened from here out, it was her responsibility.

SADIQ COULD BARELY make out the man ahead of him through the encroaching fog. It was more oppressive than the snow that had obscured their vision at the start

of the march. And twice as eerie. He shivered beneath
the folds of his coat and shifted his rifle higher up on
his back.

"Is it true?" a voice rasped behind him.

He fought the urge to turn around and shove Khalid away from him. Bastard had an irritating habit of
sneaking up on him, and he moved like a predator. Swift
and silent on his feet. Sadiq prayed for patience. "Is
what true?"

"That a group of Marines got themselves blown up?"

"Yes." The night before, some of the men had laid
pressure sensitive explosives in the only road leading
out of the small valley ahead.

"And we're going to finish the rest of them off?"

What a freaking idiot. "No," he said, trying not to
grind his molars together. "We'll probably set up an ambush and wait for the reinforcements to arrive."

"Is that your educated Cambridge opinion? Or do
you know something the rest of us don't?"

"You should know by now that's the general's pre-
ferred method of attack. We have to coordinate our
forces carefully to offset the enemy's superior firepower."

Khalid's laugh was low and full of evil delight. It
skittered down Sadiq's spine like fingernails scraped
over a blackboard, raising the hair on the backs of his
arms. "Must be nice to be included in the general's
trusted circle. Makes me wonder what you did to earn
your place there."

*Ignore him. Sooner or later he'll get bored and walk
away.* But it was damn hard to keep the bugger from
getting under his skin.

Khalid dropped his voice to a low, oily murmur. "It's said the general has a taste for handsome young men, especially if they're educated. Perhaps that's the secret behind why he favors you."

"Sod off," Sadiq snapped. He could ignore the moral smear to his own name, but how dare Khalid insult the general in such a way? Nasrallah was a man of God, and a devout Muslim. He would never engage in such filth. "Spreading disgusting rumors like that might get you killed."

"Why so defensive?" he purred. "Have I hit too close to the truth?"

It was Sadiq's own fault that he'd let the bastard know he'd hit a nerve. "Shut up and spend the rest of the march preparing yourself for what we're going to do."

He almost stumbled when he felt the unmistakable shape of Khalid's rifle muzzle pressed into his spine. "You should heed your own advice. While we march you might want to prepare yourself for the next life, my brother. Battles can get confusing. Shots can go astray even in the middle of the clearest day. But with this fog…" He tutted softly.

The implied threat made the bottom of Sadiq's stomach drop out, but he didn't respond or look over his shoulder. He was almost certain Khalid was merely getting his kicks tormenting him. But he was more than capable of murdering him in cold blood, Sadiq realized. Those dead yellow eyes testified to that.

Trying to appear unaffected, he reached behind him to slap the muzzle of the weapon away and quickly lengthened his stride.

Not for the first time, Sadiq found himself hoping

an enemy shell would find the bastard and blow him to hell where he belonged. Moving briskly, he passed the others in the column and joined the general and his top aides at the front.

"Sadiq." Nasrallah acknowledged him with a nod. "How are the men's spirits?"

"High, sir. How much farther until we get into position?"

"Another kilometer or so. We haven't been able to confirm everything for certain on the radio because all their frequencies are encrypted. But my men report the Marines have enough badly wounded to ensure them calling in air evacuation."

Sadiq tucked his hands beneath his armpits as he trudged along. His rifle bumped against his spine. "Do you want the rockets ready, then?"

The general glanced over at him, his eyes warm with affection. Sadiq told himself it was the fatherly sort, but Khalid's hateful words changed the look in the older man's eyes into the possibility of something ugly and disturbing. "You know me well."

Increasingly uncomfortable under the intensity of that stare, Sadiq looked away and squinted into the fog bank. "Shall I pass the word along to the others?"

"No. Only mention that they should be listening for the sounds of aircraft as we get closer. Fixed wing of course, but rotary wing as well. In this weather, we'll hear them long before we see them."

Made it hard to shoot a moving target if they couldn't get a visual. "Hopefully the fog will lift before then."

"Doesn't matter, my son. God willing, we will have the trap prepared and ready before the aircraft arrive.

Allah will guide our rockets to where they are meant to go."

"Yes sir. I'll alert the men."

"You do that." He paused. "Is everything all right with you and Khalid?"

"Of course. If you'll excuse me, sir..."

Sadiq dropped back and told the first man in line, and the soldier passed it back. The message would no doubt be garbled by the time it reached the end, but there would be time to get everyone briefed once they got closer to their target. Besides, he had no intention of going anywhere near Khalid until the fog cleared out enough to allow him better visibility. And protection. He had not suffered this much, and come all this way just to wind up the victim of an embittered mercenary disguising himself as a soldier of Islam.

# ELEVEN

DEVON AND WILL went over the pre-flight checklist and together logged the coordinates into the computer's GPS to make sure they were correct. She checked the radio frequency with the tower and ops center. Everything was a go.

"What's the viz at the LZ?" Will asked.

Devon heard the unspoken concern in his voice and understood its source. "It's expected to clear enough during our flight, so we'll be fine," she answered crisply. Until she got through the fog, however, she was going to have to rely on her instruments and FLIR to guide her over the rugged terrain.

"Okay," Will said, and she was relieved he let the matter drop. She was nervous enough for all of them and she didn't need him questioning her decision to fly the mission. She wasn't being reckless. She was being assertive. "What about our escort?"

"Apache is heading to the LZ now. But we'll probably get there before they do."

"Wouldn't expect anything different," Will sighed.

Once they were ready to go, she flipped down her night vision goggles and spoke to the crew over her headset. "Everyone strapped in back there?"

"That's affirm," McCall answered from the back.

"Sun won't be up until we're on the return flight, so

we're going in dark, low and fast. Be advised, intel reports we could encounter hostile contact in the pickup area. Be on the lookout when I give you the two minute warning."

"Roger that," the chief replied. "We're good to go."

She radioed the tower. "Angel one-niner requesting taxi."

"Roger, taxi out to helo point four, then call for takeoff."

Will upped the throttles on the overhead panel and she nudged the Black Hawk forward to the helo point. Once the wheels on the landing gear were over the proper place, she called again. "This is Angel one-niner, requesting departure clearance."

"Roger Angel one-niner, cleared for takeoff. On departure call your ops frequency."

"Angel one-niner, roger."

Working the throttles overhead, Will increased power. The aircraft vibrated as the engines opened up with a throaty roar. A wave of adrenaline rushed through her veins. Her heart pumped hard beneath her sternum when she pulled up on the collective. The bird lifted off the ground with a smooth surge. She pushed forward on the cyclic and its nose angled toward the tarmac as it flew forward, picking up speed and gaining altitude.

Clearing the airfield and the worst of the fog, she banked to the northeast and headed out toward the mountains, their distant snow-capped peaks glowing neon green in her NVGs. The increase in visibility made her breathe a sigh of relief and let her mind concentrate on flying the aircraft. Her restored confidence reminded her of why she loved this. She craved the sense of freedom and power, knowing that she was at the controls and heading out to rescue someone.

So why was her stomach getting tighter with each nautical mile closer to the destination? *Just do your job. Stay relaxed and on top of everything.*

A minute later she dialed up the new frequency and reported in to the ops center. "Angel one-niner with you now ops, and en route."

"Roger, we have no additional information for you at this time."

She took a slow breath and tried to dispel the lingering unease in her gut. *No news is good news.* Now if only the LZ would be clear by the time they arrived.

Will remained silent beside her during the flight, and the absence of their usual banter added to her tension. Was he uptight about this because of the visibility issue, or did he have a bad feeling about this mission too?

The instruments tracked their progress as they climbed, reaching their cruising altitude only twenty meters above the steadily steepening terrain. The constant pitch of the engines and rhythmic throb of the rotors helped calm her nerves. Everything was going smoothly, and the fog seemed to be thinning. Hopefully they'd be able to do a quick in and out before the sun came up.

That was the real reason she was nervous. Under cover of darkness, the bird's dark paint made the aircraft practically invisible to the human eye, and less of a target. Anyone on the ground would be able to hear them, but not see them until it was too late. If it stayed dark until the mission was completed, she could be in without posing a major risk to her aircraft and crew, and out as soon as the patients were aboard, away from hostile forces. The encroaching light made that impossible and increased the danger for all of them.

Coming up on the final turn, she glanced over at Will. He gave her a reassuring smile and she returned it, wishing it wasn't forced. She hit her last waypoint and banked to the southeast, willing her heart to slow down. "Two minutes," she informed the crew once she'd leveled out. The instant she said it, the tension in the cabin went up palpably. Will ran the engine controls up to give them optimum power if needed, and together they increased the set RPMs on the fuel control unit.

Without looking back into the cabin, she could feel rear-enders putting their game faces on, weapons at the ready and scanning the darkened terrain with watchful eyes. Devon took in a deep, slow breath and let it out. She was in one of the safest aircraft in the U.S. military arsenal with an experienced co-pilot, crew chief and a Night Stalker medic aboard. She couldn't ask for a better crew than that.

The flight clock tracked the seconds on its digital display as they approached the extraction point. "One minute," she said into her mic, her voice thankfully calm and steady as her hands.

"I'm going to have to rope in," McCall told the crew chief over the intercom radio. "Gulley's too narrow to put down in. We'll have to lift all the casualties in the Stokes litter."

"Roger that."

Devon mentally planned the insertion. Once she got them in, she'd have to hold the bird in an above-ground hover, battling gusts of wind to hold it steady with only meters of clearance between the walls of rock rising on either side. She prayed the wind didn't make the line sway back and forth or the guys would never make it down to pick up the casualties. If it swung out far enough, it could get caught in the rotors and send them all hurtling into the ground. Even without worrying about the wind gusts, she had to keep the aircraft absolutely still to avoid clipping a rotor.

*Clear your head. You've done this before.*

*Yeah, but not in hostile territory under direct threat of enemy fire,* a voice whispered in her head.

Devon forced the unsettling thought away and focused on flying the aircraft. Approaching the target area, her NVGs picked up the convoy of Humvees lined up in the distance on the narrow road, and the Marines gathered around the LZ. With Will pulling back on the power, she edged the nose up and carefully guided the aircraft into position, lowering into an above-ground hover with only a few feet of clearance between the rock walls and the tips of the rotors. "Okay, we're in position for medic dispatch." The wind gusts didn't seem too bad.

Within seconds, the crew chief had the rope out the door and McCall slid to the ground with his medical equipment. The instant he cleared the area, she pulled up and retreated a short distance to wait so they could work without being beaten with debris from the powerful rotor wash. With her hands and feet busy on the pedals and cyclic to control the bird's movement, she scanned the area for threats. *Breathe.* She pulled in a deep breath, deliberately slowing her respiration and relaxing her grip on the stick. Nothing caught her attention, so she went back to watching the computer displays.

The crew chief's voice came over the ICS, relaying the patients' conditions to the flight surgeon back at Bagram. Four wounded, three critical, just as the flight command had reported.

Then her radio crackled to life, and the ops center came on. "Angel one-niner, be advised ground forces have reported enemy movement near your location. Over."

Devon shared a look with Will. "See anything?"

"Nope," he answered, staring hard out his window. "But I'll feel a hell of a lot better once our escort gets here."

"Chief?" she asked.

"All clear back here."

She didn't see anything either, but she wondered how big a force the friendlies below had spotted. The terrain was rocky and barren. Perfect for hiding in among the boulders and crevices. Was there an A-team down there watching them? Some Delta boys maybe?

*Might be Cam.*

Her fingers tightened around the cyclic. She couldn't afford to think about him right now, and should be glad friendly forces had them in sight.

"Angel one-niner, this is Mako two. Coming up on station."

She breathed a sigh of relief. "Copy that." A minute later she spotted the Apache gunship to her seven o'clock high. It passed overhead and began a covering pattern.

On the ground, McCall used hand signals to relay a

message through the crew chief, requesting extraction. Devon maneuvered into position and held the controls steady while the sergeant in the back lowered the rescue basket. McCall and his patient spun around in the rotor wash as the basket climbed toward the open bay door.

The first patient was hauled aboard, the litter put in place by the crew chief into one of the carousel's litter pans in the back while McCall disappeared to pick up the next casualty. Once all four of the wounded were secured in the carousel, McCall was hoisted up and the crew chief gave the all clear. Relieved to be moving again, Devon pulled up on the collective, eased forward on the cyclic. The nose dropped and the tail lifted. The Black Hawk's powerful rotors pushed them forward and higher into the air. The Apache escorted them out.

Safely out of the gulley, she turned the aircraft and started northwest back to Bagram, taking a different route than the one they'd come in on. The fog was almost gone, revealing the light dusting of snow on the ground. Her heart rate settled back into its normal range, and the invisible hand clamped around her stomach finally let go. Just another minute or two and they were practically home free.

"LISTEN!"

All whispers stopped instantly. Sadiq shifted on his knees and stared out through the thinning fog. What had the man heard? Voices? Vehicles? He was just about to open his mouth and demand what they were listening for when the faint sound reached him. Like a distant roll of thunder carried on the wind.

Shelling? His hands tightened on his weapon. No, not

shells. He couldn't feel any vibrations in the ground. The sound grew louder. A rhythmic thumping that pressed against his eardrums with a hard throb. His breath caught. Rotors.

"Helicopters," someone whispered excitedly.

Sadiq looked over his shoulder at the general. He had his long-range binoculars up, scanning the sky west of their position. "Sir?"

Nasrallah lowered the binoculars. "Get ready," he told them quietly. "I want every rocket aimed and ready to fire on my command."

Sadiq pushed to his feet and took off down the line to personally deliver the message. Then he reached Khalid. "Helicopter is coming."

Khalid lifted his Chinese-made RPG onto his shoulder. "Come little birdies," he crooned with a smile.

The creepy tone in his voice made Sadiq glad that all that hatred was focused on the enemy instead of him. "The general wants everyone to wait for the order to fire."

"Does he? We'll see about that. If I get a clear shot, I won't be waiting for any order."

He hadn't expected any other response from someone like him but there was nothing he could do about it now. Sadiq rose out of his crouch and climbed over some rocks to reach the next group. The sound of the rotors was even louder now. He surveyed their position huddled among the rocks. They were spread thinly along this line, hidden from the Marines down in the valley by the sheer cliff face. If the helicopters didn't fly directly over them, they didn't have much chance of hitting them.

THE SUN'S FIRST pale gold rays were already peeking over the tops of the mountains. Devon and Will pushed their NVGs up onto their helmet mounts and pulled down their visors.

"Look at that view," Will said.

"Pretty," she agreed. And it was getting prettier with every second that took them farther away from danger. She stayed low, hugging the rugged terrain to maintain the element of surprise, and because the added weight forced her to fly at a lower altitude than she'd come in at. Thirty seconds out of the extraction zone, the radio crackled to life.

"Mako two and Angel one-niner, be advised of enemy contacts near your flight path."

Devon was shocked to recognize the familiar sound of Ryan's voice over the encrypted frequency. "Roger that," she replied, banking eastward to divert away from possible threats. He must be on the ground somewhere close by, and that meant Cam was down there too. She glanced out the right hand window at the snow-dusted terrain beneath them with a heavy heart. "It was Ryan," she said to Will.

"Yeah? Makes me feel better knowing he's got eyes on us."

Not her. She wished she could swoop down and pick them up and get them out of harm's way, but of course their mission was probably to intercept or do recon on the same force Ryan had warned her about. Had he recognized her voice too? She wished she could have said hello. She wished she could talk to Cam. She wished…

She pulled her thoughts back to the present.

"Just diverting slightly," she said to the crew, "but it

should only add a few minutes to our flight time. How's everybody doing back there?"

"Okay for now," McCall replied. "But these guys will be glad when we get to the hospital."

"Tell them we'll be there in no time."

She struggled to keep her mind on the flight instead of the danger Cam and Ryan might be facing on the ground. No sooner had she leveled out from her sharp turn than a streak of light flashed up through the air and the sensors shrieked.

"Incoming!" Will shouted. "Break right!"

Devon bit back a curse and pitched the bird hard to starboard as the rocket screamed past the nose of the aircraft. "Hold on," she warned. Will was already on the radio to the TOC, telling them they were taking fire. The Apache pilots reported the same.

Her heart pounded while she pulled up on the collective and increased altitude. The bird shot higher into the air as she continued evasive maneuvers. Her mind raced while she automatically employed her emergency training.

"Mako two and Angel one-niner, recommend you head southeast," Ryan advised from somewhere below them.

"Roger." Devon immediately turned the bird and continued to climb. "See anything?" she called out to the crew.

"Ten o'clock low," Will responded.

*Shit.* Her heart tripped. "How many?"

He craned his neck to see out the right side window. "Few dozen, and those are just the ones I can see."

"I see them," McCall said over the intercom. A second after that, the reassuring bark of his M4 came in bursts as he opened fire.

"Christ, they're everywhere down there," Will bit out.

"I know," she replied, her voice tense as she did everything possible to get them the hell out of there. The engines roared at maximum power. The Apache fired a Hellfire missile. The ground below exploded.

"RPG—break right!"

At Will's warning shout she pitched them sharply to the starboard and dove toward the ground. The round screamed past her window.

"Shit, that was close," he rasped.

"This is Mako two. We're hit."

*Oh Christ.* She craned her head around.

"See him?" Will asked.

"Yeah." She radioed the other bird. "I see smoke coming from your main rotor."

"Copy that. Losing engine function. We're returning to base."

"Just give me what protection you can until we get out of here."

"Roger that."

McCall and the crew chief continued blazing away with their rifles, but glowing tracer fire ripped through the air. Several rounds pinged off the armor plating on the Hawk's belly. Devon pressed her lips together and executed another series of evasive moves. It didn't seem to matter which way she turned, the enemy fire continued without letup. It was like flying through a nest of pissed off hornets. The Apache was way ahead of them, leaving a smoke trail behind it.

"Break left!"

She pulled the stick over, her feet instantly adjusting the pedals. A loud bang ripped through the cabin, shaking the aircraft. The sound of the engines changed, rising shrilly. "Shit," she breathed, frantically scanning the instrument panel. Couldn't have suffered a direct hit. The bird was still somewhat stable. "Shrapnel? What's hit?"

"Number two. We're losing hydraulic fluid," Will said. More bullets raked across the fuselage, piercing the metal skin, burying in the exterior wall. Bits of insulation sprayed out, falling into the cockpit like snowflakes. Freezing cold air whistled through the illuminated holes. "And fuel," he added.

Christ, had they been hit in the fuel cells? They were self-sealing, but—

"Losing power."

And altitude. No way they could make it back to base. Only a matter of time before something gave out. She had to find a safe place to put down.

Somehow she had to get them out of range of the enemy, or they'd die within moments of landing. Horrific images of the disaster in Mogadishu years ago ran through her head, of crewmen's bodies being dismembered and dragged through the streets like animal carcasses. She would not let that happen to her crew. The Black Hawk limped eastward toward the rising sun, steadily losing power and altitude. Their damaged armed escort was long gone.

A sharp whistling sound broke the tension, then an explosion rocked the whole aircraft. The concussion ripped through her body like a shockwave.

"Shit, another RPG," Will snapped.

The moment the words left his mouth the Hawk yawed wildly to the number one side, and Devon knew they'd taken a direct hit.

# TWELVE

HOLY SHIT, HE'D hit it.

Sadiq lowered the empty grenade launcher tube to the ground and stared up at the sky in disbelief. High in the air before him, a stream of black smoke trailed from the body of the helicopter as it passed by and descended into a distant canyon. No outright explosion into a satisfying fireball, but it was definitely fucked up. No way would it make it back to base. Already he could tell it was steadily losing altitude. The pilots would either have to make an emergency landing or run the risk of crashing. Either way, the bird was coming down. He and his fellow soldiers had to get to the crew before reinforcements did.

Khalid slapped him heartily on the back in congratulations. His delighted laugh rolled over him, but Sadiq barely noticed the sound over the pounding of his heart. They'd done it. They'd shot down a chopper.

Someone yanked on his upper arm. "Come on, let's go!"

Without conscious thought he shot to his feet and followed the others, rushing down into the rocky ravine. The ground was slippery with snow on the lee side of the ridge. Chunks of dirt gave way, sending a snowy waterfall of earth and rock tumbling down with their every step. He'd brought down an American helicopter.

He should have been elated, but he wasn't. A peculiar detachment gripped him. What was wrong with him? Was it exhaustion making him feel like he was moving in slow motion? His legs carried him down the ravine to another snow-covered trail at the bottom, but he felt as though he was floating.

If they'd crashed or landed in a bad spot, the pilots and crew were probably dead from the impact. If not, they would be by the time he and the others got there. Was that why he wasn't shouting and whooping like the rest of the men?

"Sadiq, come on!"

He didn't want to respond to Khalid's excited command. The bastard had enough of an attitude problem already without making him more arrogant. He quickened his pace and followed anyway, being careful to stay away from his rival while he kept his gaze on Nasrallah. At least he was confident in their leader's decisions. For an older man, the general moved fast. His stocky build didn't impede him as they raced over the boulder-strewn ground.

Sweat gathered beneath his arms and beaded on his forehead. They were jogging now, hopping and climbing over rocks like surefooted goats. The men's excitement grew with each yard they covered, as though sensing they were closing in on their target. They began chanting *God is great*. The phrase grew louder and louder, spreading with fervor throughout the ranks until the air reverberated with it. A smile spread slowly across his face, his heart thundering along with the shouts and exclamations. Finally. Finally he had done something to exact his revenge. It wasn't the precise revenge he'd wanted, but at least Americans were dead or dying by his hand.

He'd long since lost sight of the aircraft. As they cleared the next ridge, the smoke from the downed bird billowed thick and black into the morning sky, marking the position they would attack. He couldn't wait to get there. After today, his brother would be avenged. After today, they would both be free.

DEVON COULDN'T BELIEVE what was happening.

Hands locked around the controls, she threw a fearful glance at Will. His face was pinched as he stared at the instrument panel. "Losing oil pressure."

They were out of time. She couldn't see a clearing to set down in, only boulders and sheer rock faces to slam into. Her heart thudded sickeningly. Her brain refused to comprehend she was living her worst nightmare. "Angel one-niner, going down." *Oh my God, we're going to crash.* Just like her dad. "Call it in," she said tightly, fighting to stay calm. *Think, Devon. Panicking won't help. Fly the bird.*

Will immediately radioed the Mayday to the TOC. He used the code word that signified they were going down in hostile territory. "Nightmare, nightmare, nightmare. This is Angel one-niner, we are going down, do you read…"

Will's voice faded into the background beneath the scream of the engines and the pounding of her heart. Wrapped around the controls, her palms turned sweaty inside her gloves.

More loud pops broke through her concentration, then a harsh clang. The tail swung out suddenly. *Jesus.*

"Tail rotor," she blurted, fighting to regain control as they went into a torque spin. She pushed the collective straight down all the way to reduce the angle of attack on the blades and counteract the spin. No good. The tail whipped around hard in a horizontal circle. They started to drop.

With the collective buried all the way down the clutch disengaged, putting the bird into auto-rotation. Still no good. "I can't get control." The tail swung around faster, the steady increase in G-forces pushing Devon back into her seat. The world outside was a sickening blur of motion. Her stomach cramped up in a hard ball. This wasn't happening.

The muscles in her arms and shoulders strained to hold the controls steady. Sweat broke out over her face. The bird went into a tighter spin despite her attempts to wrestle control back. Gritting her teeth, she kept pulling, ignoring the burn in her back muscles. No good. The ground rushed up at them.

Next to her, Will's voice was laced with stress as he relayed their coordinates and requested rescue. She prayed they would live to make it a rescue mission instead of a recovery effort.

"Everybody brace," she bit out. The view outside the cockpit blurred into a nauseating swirl of light and shadow. She couldn't afford to look back to check on her crew and passengers. All her attention was focused on trying to auto rotate down. She couldn't even try for a run-on landing now. Best she could do was get down right-side up and hope the wheels took the brunt of the impact without killing them.

Her hands were numb, gripped so tight around the

controls they had to be bone white beneath her gloves. No chance they were coming out of this spin. "I'm gonna need your help pulling out of this fall," she yelled to Will. Their only hope now was if she could get them down without plowing into the ground. She had to maintain enough control to flare just before impact. Had to bring the nose up so they didn't hit with enough force to crush the frame and kill everyone on board.

Will nodded tightly and continued calling out the mayday, his face strained.

She spared a quick glance out her window at the ground below. Two hundred feet and falling.

Devon growled low in her throat, using all her strength to keep hold of the controls. *Come on, baby. Flatten out.* A bead of sweat trickled down her temple. She glanced outside.

One hundred fifty feet.

They were plummeting straight down into a narrow canyon. She couldn't let them hit the side of it. She had to pull them up as soon as the altitude warning system kicked in.

One hundred feet.

She had to hold the position and flare at exactly the right moment, but she couldn't steer the damn thing. "I can't hold it—"

The tail hit the wall of the canyon with a loud crunch, the violent impact making the whole aircraft shudder. The bird jerked to the side, rotors still whipping at full speed, the body turning faster in its death-spin.

"Hold on!" she yelled, bracing for the inevitable as the ground raced up at them. She clenched her fingers around the controls, determined to give them a chance, but it was going to be ugly no matter what she did.

A second later the scream of metal grinding against stone filled the cabin. They lurched violently as the tail section bounced off the canyon wall again, momentarily throwing them up and away. Pain flashed in her head. She strained to get another look out her window. Her stomach rolled.

Fifty feet.

The female voice of the altitude warning system came on. "Low altitude, low altitude, low—"

*"Now!"* Devon ordered Will, both of them hauling up on the collective to compensate for the drop in hydraulic pressure. For a breathless instant time stopped. The lever seemed to creep upward infinitesimally. Devon's teeth clenched until she thought they might shatter. Will's face was red from straining. They wrenched up on the thing together in the hopes of increasing the angle of the blades to give them a cushion. Will remained stiff and silent beside her. The blood pounded sickeningly in her ears. Were they slowing? Feet braced on the floor, she put her whole body into it. "Come *on*," she snarled between clenched teeth. Her heart slammed against her ribs.

The nose rose slightly. They lifted. *Come on. Little more*. The tail dropped a fraction, but they were still turning counter clockwise. A split second later the rear of the bird smashed into the ground. They bounced hard on the wheels.

Devon and Will both grunted as they jerked forward against their harnesses, then the nose struck with such tremendous force that for a moment she thought her spine had snapped. Her left knee struck the dashboard. A rending pain shot through it as something popped and tore inside. Her chin struck her chest so hard she knocked the breath out of herself. Coppery blood filled her mouth from where her teeth had cut her tongue. Black spots exploded before her eyes.

Will screamed, a sharp cry of agony nearly lost beneath the cacophony of rending metal. A terrible roar engulfed the cabin. The rotors tore into the rocky ground as the Hawk pitched onto its right side. Sparks flew. Pieces of broken glass, rock and debris whipped through the cockpit. Blindly, Devon raised her hands to her face to shield it from the flying shrapnel. Cuts stung her cheeks and forearms. A final, deafening bang reverberated through her body, ripping a howl of pain from her. Battling to stay conscious as the world blurred and turned gray around the edges, she flailed a hand out to cut the master electrical switch in the overhead panel. The engines' shrill cry died down. The Black Hawk slanted further onto its side, coming to a groaning, shuddering stop in its rocky grave.

# THIRTEEN

THE SEAL SQUAD leader squinted up at the sky when the first bang reverberated through the mountain air. "Ah, shit. That's not good."

Ryan couldn't answer the soft observation. He was too busy staring in horror through his binoculars at the smoke coming from Devon's damaged aircraft. He'd recognized her voice over the radio. The hidden enemy they'd been after were no doubt gleefully following the wounded bird in hopes of getting to the crash site and finishing off any survivors. Goddammit, he hadn't warned her in time.

His hands clenched around the binos. There was fuck all he could do to help her at this distance, and any air support he called in would show up too late. He flinched and held his breath when another round narrowly missed the fuselage. He could hear the stress in Dev and the co-pilot's voices over the radio, and could see the return fire coming from the open bay doors. Just when he thought she'd cleared the worst of the fire, a sharp bang made him freeze in place. Staring through the lenses, he saw a round had hit the engine housing. A tall plume of black smoke spewed from it. The Hawk began to drop. *Ah, fuck, Devon...*

The co-pilot called in a Mayday. Another round exploded. More smoke, but this time the bird clipped the cliff face and went into a deadly spin as it hurtled forward, plunging toward the ground. "Shit," he breathed, snatching up his radio with one hand, the other holding his binoculars in place. He was too far away to hear the impact, but thank God he didn't see an answering fireball. Just more coal black smoke that would draw every militant brandishing an AK and RPG for miles around. He couldn't lose visual on the crash site. Maybe they had survived.

Knowing it was Devon's bird almost paralyzed him. He'd heard every word she'd said on the radio. Ripping his radio out, he switched to the ops center frequency. "Wizard one, be advised, Angel one-niner is down. I repeat, Angel one-niner is down. Deploy search and rescue." Checking his map, he relayed the site's coordinates. The co-pilot hadn't gotten the location out before they hit.

"Roger that, Stingray. Requesting CSAR now."

He switched to another frequency, shocked by how unsteady his hands were as he turned the knob. Jesus, he couldn't get past the knowledge he'd just watched a good friend go down to enemy fire. "Angel one-niner, do you read?" He waited a beat, but only static came back. "Spike, do you read?" Nothing but dead air. Heart in his throat, he glanced over at the SEAL platoon commander who had hunkered down beside him. "No response. I can't tell if there are any survivors." From the looks of the crash, he had to accept the fact that everyone on board was most likely dead, or dying.

"Let's get in there then," the SEAL said, motioning for his men to move out. "Any survivors won't last

long without help." He radioed the ops center about
their intentions.

Ryan hurriedly packed up his gear and hoisted his
ruck into position, then fell into line with the SEALs.
Jesus, Cam was probably en route back to link up with
them right now. How the hell was he going to tell him
when he got back? He pushed it from his mind. He had
one job now—to get to the crash site and protect it from
the enemy. The terrain was the shits, lots of rock forma-
tions and loose shale. They were only two klicks from
the downed Black Hawk, but God only knew how long
it would take them to get into position. Devon might be
dead by then, if she wasn't already.

*Just move. Get in there and do your damn job.*

Even if Devon was already gone, he would get her out
of there. No matter what happened, he and Cam would
get her home again, just like they had Ty.

CAM WAS RE-PACKING his gear at Bagram when Jackson
walked in.

"You taking everything this time?"

"I lightened my load some." Jettisoning unnecessary
weight now would be a godsend once the chopper put
them in the mountains. He considered pulling out the
chicken plates in his body armor. They added another
twenty pounds. Did he really need to lug that around on
top of his weapons, ammo and med ruck? He looked up
at Jackson, thinking of Ty. They might have saved him
if he'd been wearing them. "You got your plates in?"

"Yeah, but I was gonna lose 'em."

"Leave them on." He added more packs of Ringer's

fluid just in case. It was going to be a bitch carrying that load at higher altitude, but he'd just have to suck it up.

A grim-faced lieutenant came running up to them. "Medevac was just shot down in the mountains," the man said quickly. "Your team in the field is moving there now."

Cam shot to his feet, dragging his bulging med ruck off the floor. His legs and back strained under the weight as he followed the officer at a run beside Jackson. "Chinook?"

"No. Black Hawk."

A bolt of fear hit him square in the heart. Jesus Christ, it wasn't Devon, was it? He exchanged a look with Jackson, and the other man's eyes were grave.

As his boots pounded over the asphalt, he ordered himself to calm down. There were lots of H-60 pilots that flew medevac. Didn't mean it was her.

The sick feeling in his stomach said differently.

Someone rushed up with a fistful of print-outs and shoved them at him. "No word from the crew," the man reported. "Two pilots, crew chief, two medics and four patients aboard. Enemy's moving in fast."

His mind whirled as he studied the maps and intel reports. "Who was the pilot?"

"Not sure, sir. Here's the crew authentication info."

He grabbed them and kept running because he didn't want to look until he was on the bird. No communication didn't mean they were dead, he told himself. Maybe the radios had been damaged in the crash. "How long until the team reaches them?"

"Unknown at this time. SEAL platoon is en route to

the crash site, and their CCT with them. He's already called in for air support to be on station in the area."

*Thank God.* If there were survivors, Ryan's air-to-ground fire would keep the enemy at bay until the ground forces could get there to establish a secure perimeter. "Where are we inserting?"

"You're linking back up with the team en route, then going in to secure the area."

"Roger that." On their way to the bird Jackson grabbed a cooler full of whole blood, and together they ran out to the Chinook waiting on the tarmac.

They climbed aboard and Cam recognized Liam's face staring back at him from the cockpit. His visor was up, and the somber expression on his face said it all.

It was Devon's bird.

Cam's heart dropped into his stomach then started hammering wildly. *Jesus.* He plugged his cord into the ICS to hear what was going on up front. "How far out are we?"

"Eighteen minutes, once we're airborne," Liam answered. "I've been in contact with your ground team through the ops center."

Cam bit back a sharp command to tell him to get moving and sat his ass down to go over the charts and maps with his fellow PJ. The topo map showed the crash site to be a shallow canyon, with the surrounding terrain undulating as it approached the foothills. No good place for a Chinook to put down nearby. They'd either have to fast-rope in at the site, or land several klicks away and hump it in. From the sounds of it, the crew didn't have that kind of time to wait around for them. They were going to have to go in right at the site and hope like hell the Air Force gunships Ryan called in had taken care of the enemy forces that were no doubt swarming down on the area.

"Any contact with the crew yet?" he shouted over the noise of the huge rotors. He found a pair of earphones and pulled them on.

"Negative," Liam responded over the ICS. "You boys ready back there?"

*She's not dead. She can't be dead.* "Yeah, let's go."

The radio crackled with communications between the pilots, tower and TOC, and finally the Chinook lifted its huge body off the ground. Cam planned the upcoming mission with Jackson and checked his weapons and equipment, but he couldn't bury his unrelenting fear for Devon. "Any details about the crash?" he asked Liam.

"They went down hard, but there was no explosion."

Okay. No explosion was good. But was she injured? Too far gone to make radio contact? "We picking the others up en route?"

"Negative," Liam answered. "The higher powers want you guys going in on foot to avoid another shoot down until the enemy is cleared away."

Ah, Christ. Humping the few klicks to the crash site in that terrain was going to cost Devon and the others time they didn't have. He didn't want to have to pull her dead body from the wreckage. He couldn't handle that.

Shoving aside all the negative thoughts that kept trying to burst through his concentration, he took out the crew authentication cards. Memorizing them with Jackson, he pictured her beautiful smile in his mind. *Hang on, Dev. I'm coming for you.*

The flight seemed to take forever, especially with the

sun up. Liam made several fake landings to try and fool any enemy forces watching from the ground. They'd either think they had dozens of soldiers going in, or at least be confused about the exact point where they'd inserted.

"Okay boys, this is it," Liam announced. The bird descended with a throaty roar, the rotors kicking up dust and snow in a blinding cloud. One of the crew chiefs got the rope ready and as soon as the tail ramp began to drop, he tossed it out the back. "Good to go," Liam said. "Go bring her home."

"Will do." Cam gripped the rope between his gloved hands and boots and slid to the ground. As soon as his feet touched the earth he raised his rifle and rushed to take cover beside a boulder, waiting for Jackson to join him. When the Chinook took off in a cloud of dirty snow, they radioed the rest of the team. He checked the map one last time and keyed his radio. "Moving to intercept you now."

He spotted the column of smoke rising in the distance that marked the downed Black Hawk. *Dev.* He was worried as hell, but he couldn't dwell on that now. They were in enemy infested territory and he had to stay sharp. He thanked God he had Jackson with him to watch his back. The unnatural stillness made him uneasy. They followed the bearings he'd taken with his compass, moving north-northwest. The terrain was goddamn awful. All rocks and outcroppings that took precious time climbing over and working around.

He was already sweating underneath all his layers when his headset crackled to life. "We've got a visual of you."

"Copy that." They kept walking until one of the SEALs appeared beside a group of boulders.

"Hey. Glad you guys could make it."

Yeah, he was sure they were thrilled about having to wait and link up with a couple of PJs when they had their own medic. Well too bad, because with the number of wounded they were looking at, the SEALs were going to need a hand. And he was going after Devon no matter what.

He found Ryan at the rear of the group and caught his eye. "Hear anything from her?"

"Not yet." His face was grave. "We'll get her, though."

Cam nodded, not trusting himself to speak.

"Her?" the SEAL platoon leader asked.

"Yeah," Ryan answered. "The dedicated chick that came to see us off? She's the downed command pilot."

The other man turned to Cam. "Shit man. That sucks."

*I fucking know it.*

Without slowing his stride, the SEAL looked over his shoulder at all of them. "Let's get moving. We're burning daylight."

"Don't remind me," Cam muttered under his breath, following hard on Ryan's heels. If she was still alive, he'd do whatever it took to keep her that way and get her safely to Bagram.

# FOURTEEN

SHE WAS STILL alive. The pain told her that before she
even managed to open her eyes. Fighting through it, she
tried to focus on her surroundings. Beside her Will made
deep, animalistic noises of agony. She forced her lids
apart, struggling to breathe. She was pinned forward
in her seat unable to move, and the white hot agony in
her left knee overtook everything else. Cuts and scrapes
stung across her face and arms. The adrenaline shakes
had already begun, ripping through her body in brutal
jolts that intensified her pain.

Fire, she thought dizzily. Was there a fire? She didn't
smell fuel, but automatically reached for the fire extin-
guisher. Then stopped as the cabin whirled in her vision.

No smoke. None that she could see or smell, anyway.
No fire, then? Thank God for that. Her hands went to
her harness. The thing was tight to the point of cutting
off her circulation.

"Who's hurt?" Still fighting for breath, she forced
her head to turn to look at Will.

He was still strapped into the right hand seat among
the crumpled metal surrounding him, writhing against
his restraints. Both his hands were wrapped around his
right thigh. Even in her disoriented condition she could
see the sickening amount of blood seeping out from beneath his flight gloves.

"W-Will?" she managed, lifting a shaking hand toward him.

"*Fuuuck*," he cried through bared teeth, banging the back of his helmet against the seat. His face was pasty white, eyes squeezed shut. His teeth were clenched so hard the muscles in his jaw stood out.

He would go into shock any minute from the blood loss, if he hadn't already. But at least they were still alive. She didn't know about the rest of her passengers. "Everybody ch-check in. Everyone still w-with me?" she called out.

Several groans answered her. Then McCall's voice came through with a rough, "Yeah, I think so. One of the wounded—don't know yet." She could hear the sounds of the men moving around in the back as she tried to key the radio and contact Bagram. Nothing happened.

"Radio's dead." She didn't know why she said it aloud. Will was too far gone to care, and everyone else was dealing with their own injuries or the other wounded.

Devon fumbled with the releases on her harness. It held her suspended in her seat, and when she got the last one undone she fell forward into the control panel with a cry. She clenched her teeth together, swallowing a scream as her ruined knee smashed into folded metal. She fought back the shock and the black wave at the edge of her vision that threatened to suck her under.

The crew and passengers were still her responsibility. Somehow, most if not all of them were still breathing. She had to make sure they stayed that way. She had to get them out of the wreckage and the hell away from the bird before the enemy came. And oh yeah, she knew they were coming. Dozens of them, maybe more. They'd been swarming over the rocks like black ants.

Struggling to climb over the ruined interior to get to Will, she ripped off the knee board strapped to her right thigh. The pain in her left knee made her light headed and nauseated, but she fought it back. They had to get everyone out of the bird and hidden. Before whoever shot them out of the sky got to them. She looked at his injury. The prospect of a compound fracture and the amount of blood he'd already lost alarmed her. "How b-bad, Will?" She already knew it was a potentially life-threatening injury, but she wanted to keep him alert and talking.

He didn't answer though, just kept holding his leg and breathing in rapid, shallow pants. When she got close enough, she saw the reason for his terrible suffering.

Beneath his black Nomex gloves, the white edge of his femur stuck through his torn flight suit. Her stomach rolled. "I need a medic up here," she called, "Will's got a compound fracture of his right femur."

"Hang on," McCall answered. "Be there in a minute."

She couldn't tell if the bone had pierced the femoral artery, but she wasn't going to wait to find out. She reached for his leg.

"Don't," Will growled through his teeth, shaking his head hard side to side. "Don't fucking touch it." He was breathing way too fast.

"I have to," she said matter-of-factly, hardening her resolve. "We have to get that tied off." Pushing his hands out of the way, she ripped the Velcro straps off the knee board and slipped them beneath his thigh. She placed the board beneath his knee joint, then wrapped the straps around his leg and tightened them. Will arched up with a strangled cry and lashed a hand out at her, but she ignored him and twisted harder.

"Fucking *Chriiiist*!" he howled, turning an ungodly shade of gray before leaning to the side and retching all over his seat and the pushed-in door.

Her stomach pitched at the gagging sounds and the sour stench of vomit. He cursed between retches.

"I know, I'm sorry," she said in a low voice. Her trembling hands made it hard to get a solid grip. "But I've got to stop the bleeding." Sweating now, she mercilessly twisted the straps as tight as she could get them, hoping it would make an adequate tourniquet and that the board would act as a splint until they could get him out of the bird to someplace safe.

When Will's head lolled back against the seat, she immediately checked his pulse. The fast but strong throb against her searching fingers reassured her he was merely unconscious. His face was white as flour, and his breathing was rapid and shallow. She hoped he stayed under and wasn't feeling any pain, because sure as hell moving him was going to make him come to and scream his guts out.

When Devon finished securing her makeshift tourniquet and looked back to check on the others, the crew chief was already climbing out of the twisted wreckage, dragging the first of the patients with him. His face was streaked with blood, but he seemed to be moving okay. "Where's my medic?" she called out.

"Right here." McCall crawled between the seats to get to her. Blood dripped from a gash in his chin and he was cradling his left wrist.

"How bad are you hurt?"

"I'm fine, just banged up." He glanced down at Will's leg and gave a satisfied nod as he checked his pulse. "That's good enough for now." His steely gaze rested on her face. "What about you? You hurt?"

"I'm okay. My left knee's going to be a problem though." She wasn't okay, but she wasn't as bad off as Will and the patients she'd picked up.

He moved toward her. "Let me take a look."

She shook her head, moving back to give him room. She could feel the seconds ticking past like a timer on a bomb. "No, let's just get Will out."

"Okay, but his door's crushed in. We'll have to pull him out the bay door." He pulled himself out of the wreckage while she stayed with Will.

"We'll have you out in no time," she said to soothe him, gripping his wrist tight. His lids were closed, his face lined with unspeakable agony as he began to resurface. She wished he wouldn't. "Help's probably already on the way." Base had to have received their mayday. And Ryan had to have heard them. Was he on the move right now coming to help? Air support would be a real comfort until another crew arrived to extract them.

Will nodded tightly but otherwise didn't respond. All his energy was focused on keeping pressure on his wound. Sliding and scraping noises against the skin of the bird brought her head up. The crew chief and McCall appeared above her shattered window as they moved through the cabin. She backed up to give them room, and within moments they had Will out of his harness and were lifting him through to the back. His strangled cries of pain made the hair on her nape stand up, but she understood their urgency to get him clear. They had to get out and get their bearings, then find a place to establish a defensive perimeter until help arrived.

Her handheld radio was probably dead, too, but she had to at least try. She pulled it from her vest, dialed in the emergency frequency and keyed the thing anyway. "This is Angel one-niner, requesting emergency evac, over." It didn't surprise her that nothing came back, but she hoped to God someone knew what had happened to them. Before leaving her seat, she zeroed the radio to ensure nothing important fell into enemy hands if they overtook the aircraft. Then she pulled off her helmet and grabbed an M4 rifle from the rack above the door, still partly in shock. Her 9 mm sidearm was strapped to her thigh. She couldn't believe she was going to have to use it to defend them from a hostile enemy force.

*Stop thinking and move, dammit!*

Her knee throbbed like another heart. She hadn't checked out how bad it was yet, and she wasn't going to. It hurt like a bastard, already tight and swollen beneath her flight suit. No way could she put her weight on it. She'd have to crawl or hop her way to safety.

Gearing up to withstand the torment she knew was coming, Devon gritted her teeth and began the awkward, painful climb out of her seat and through to the cabin. Sharp bolts of lightning shot through her leg as she dragged herself through the ruined cabin. She pulled in deep breaths, fighting to stay above the nauseating pain. From the amount of damage it was hard to believe anyone had survived the crash.

Inhaling deeply, she braced herself. *One. Two. Three.* She stood up with all her weight on her right leg and reached through the open bay door to pull herself up. The shocking twinge that flashed through her knee stole her breath, and she instantly wrapped her right ankle beneath her left one to anchor it.

Struggling to lift her body weight up and out the door in what amounted to a full chin-up, her arms began to tremble and then fail. Devon strained harder. *Come on. Pull! You have to get out. They're coming.*

But her muscles would not obey her no matter how afraid she was of falling into enemy hands. Her grip slipped on the door frame. Strong hands instantly closed around her wrists. She opened her eyes. McCall's face appeared above her, pale blue eyes even more startling with the darkening knot over one of them. Braced on his knees he pulled her up and free. The muscles in his arms strained beneath her gripping hands.

Cold air hit her face, stealing the breath from her lungs. She pushed as hard as she could against the frame and finally McCall pulled her free. "Thanks," she panted, scrambling down.

"Let's get a move on." He set an arm around her waist and held his rifle with his free hand as he helped her hop to where the others were gathered behind a pile of boulders. The instant they got there he set her down and looked at the crew chief. "I need you to come back with me and get all the weapons out of that bird."

"Roger that."

McCall was taking charge even though she was the ranking officer, but she wasn't about to argue with him. He had more training to cope with this sort of situation than she did. The little bit of SERE training she'd received was woefully inadequate to deal with this.

The two men ran back to the aircraft, the sounds of their boots pounding over the ground fading in the distance.

All that was left was the eerie sound of the wind and the groans from the wounded.

Gripping her weapon, Devon slid her way over to Will where he lay on his back with both hands still wrapped around his thigh. His face was gray and clammy with sweat, and his lips were pressed together in a bloodless line of agony. "How are you?" she asked.

"Hanging in there," he said weakly, and managed to meet her eyes. "Did they…get word before we…hit?"

"Yes." They had to have heard Will. Or Ryan must have at least seen them go down. Had he and Cam both watched the crash? She wanted desperately to reach them, to reassure them she was all right. She wanted to hear Cam's voice. "Anyone got an operational radio?" she called out.

McCall answered. "I already tried mine, and so did the chief. Our position must be interfering with the signal because we can't get through."

If Ryan and Cam had seen them and were close enough, they would already be on their way to help. The knowledge eased her mind. She tightened her grip on her weapon and stared out at the places the enemy might pop out from. She was a goddamn captain in the U.S. Army, and she would do her duty. All she and the others had to do was hold on until a rescue team got there.

SADIQ'S LEGS WERE heavy with fatigue when he made it up to the last rise. The rifle in his hands seemed to weigh twice what it had when he'd started out. But he was almost there. The downed chopper lay somewhere in the next canyon, just beyond the ridge he climbed. The strange numbness had disappeared somewhere along the hurried march. The excitement coming from the men was contagious. As he climbed, he forgot the weariness in his sore muscles. So close. In another few minutes they would be able to see exactly what had become of the crew.

Someone called his name. He looked up ahead and found one of the general's advisors waving him over. The man's expression was animated. Tense with anticipation. With a sudden burst of energy, Sadiq hurried up the line to meet him.

"The general wants to see you."

He must have found them, Sadiq thought, and rushed forward. He found Nasrallah perched behind cover on the top of the ridge, taking in the view before them with his high-powered binoculars. "Sadiq," he acknowledged, holding out a welcoming arm.

He hesitated the slightest instant before closing the distance between them. Nasrallah clapped him on the shoulder and brought him in tight with a one-armed hug. Sadiq fought the urge to pull away from the embrace. There was nothing illicit in the gesture. He was being paranoid, and it irritated him that he'd let Khalid poison his view of the general.

"Excellent aim." Nasrallah's light brown eyes sparkled. "I thought you might like to see your work firsthand."

Sadiq accepted the binoculars. Looking through them, he quickly zeroed in on the ruined helicopter. Its black body lay twisted and mangled, still smoking where it had smashed into the ground against the towering cliff wall. He stared into the fuselage, searching for the bodies. He frowned. "I don't see the crew."

"No. They've evacuated the area."

His head whipped up. "They're still alive?" It seemed unlikely from looking at the damaged aircraft.

"For now." The general's lips tipped up at the corners. "Only for now, my boy."

Sadiq went back to scanning the area. His eyes caught on something in the light dusting of snow covering the ground near the chopper. His heart leapt. "I see tracks."

"Heading around the side of the cliff," Nasrallah confirmed. "But they couldn't have gone far after a crash like that." He sounded certain. Sadiq didn't question his judgment. The general was an expert when it came to aircraft and their weaknesses. "Walk with me while we move out."

Sadiq wasn't about to argue, and continued the march. The ground was even rougher here than it had been when he'd fired the RPG. Gripping a slippery boulder with his gloved hands, he strained to pull his body up to the next foothold in the trail. Gaining his footing, he reached a hand down to help the next man. A strong hand gripped his forearm as he curled his fingers around the sturdy wrist. The man tipped his face upward.

The instant he met the yellow gaze looking up at him, he wanted to let go. Khalid's harsh mouth curled in amusement, as though he knew what he was thinking. Sadiq hauled him up, staying the impulse to wipe his hand against his leg. Just touching Khalid made him feel soiled. He moved away without a word.

Excited chatter broke out in the front. Several men clustered about the general. Sadiq rushed over. "What is it?"

"See for yourself." Nasrallah handed him the binoculars.

Sadiq peered in the direction the general indicated. He sucked in a sharp breath. "The crew!"

"Yes. At least four of them. Maybe more, hidden beyond that cliff."

They were too far away to get an accurate shot off. They'd have to move in closer to have any hope of hitting them. Sadiq tightened the focus of the lenses, vividly aware of Khalid sidling up next to him. He stepped closer to the edge of the trail, being careful to stay behind cover. The binoculars were incredible. Even at this distance he could see the facial features of some of the survivors. "Three of them are badly wounded." Two of them were covered in bloody bandages. They should be easy enough targets.

"Any dead?" Khalid asked with interest.

"No. At least I don't think so." He studied the rest of the group. Where were the pilots? "I see someone in a flight suit, but—" His tongue froze on the roof of his mouth. His vision tunneled around the person. Their hair was much too long to be regulation. Nearly down to their jaw. Much smaller than the others. "Merciful Allah," he breathed. His heart pounded a frantic tattoo. A woman.

"What? What is it?"

He couldn't take his eyes off her as she turned her head and he finally got a clear view of her face. He felt like someone had punched him in the stomach.

"See something?" the general asked, coming over.

Sadiq swallowed, wondering if he was hallucinating. It couldn't be her. Could it? He stared harder. His heart shuddered inside his ribcage. There was no mistaking that face. He'd memorized every line of it since the night his brother died. "It's *her*."

"Her? A woman?" Nasrallah snatched the binoculars from him and looked for himself. "The pilot?"

"Yes." He could barely get the word out of his constricted throat. His pulse pounded too fast in his neck. The rush of blood made him dizzy and nauseated.

"You know her?"

He nodded, one hand automatically coming to rest over his heart where the photo lay. Now he understood why Allah had made him take this journey into holy war. "I know her."

Nasrallah's thick brows pulled together. "What? How?"

"I *know* her," he repeated, all but shaking.

"Are you sure?"

"Positive." He needed to sit down. The ground seemed to tilt beneath his cold-numbed feet.

"This changes things."

When the words registered, Sadiq looked up at him in confusion. "How so?"

"She's a woman."

Yes, they'd already established that. "And?"

"And I won't consider executing her. We'll have to capture her."

He stared at the general. Was he serious?

"She'll be far more valuable as a prisoner than a corpse."

Sadiq leaned a hand on the boulder behind him, fighting the alarm rising inside him. He didn't want her to live. She had to die. Allah would not have brought them together otherwise.

"Send the word along the line," the general continued. "Make sure my orders are understood. I want her taken alive after we intercept them."

A loud roaring filled his ears. He stood unmoving as Nasrallah swept past him further down the trail leading down the other side of the ridge. The pilot was connected to the medic in the photo. He had to kill her to avenge Hassan.

"Don't worry."

Startled, he turned his head to look at Khalid. For once, the sly gleam in the other man's eyes didn't send a shiver of foreboding up his spine.

"He might have a problem with killing a woman, but I don't." Khalid spat in the dirt to show his disdain. "The general can't control how things go in battle. She won't make it out of that canyon alive. We'll make sure of it."

"No. I need to be the one." He had this final chance to exact revenge and he wasn't going to let it slip between his fingers, no matter what the general commanded. Or what Khalid was planning.

Something close to admiration crossed Khalid's face. "Then you will be. Allah will guide you to where you need to be."

The tightness in his chest eased. The beginnings of a smile made the corners of his mouth twitch. Khalid might be the most unlikely of allies, but for this mission to end successfully, he would take all the help he could get.

# FIFTEEN

"ANYTHING?" CAM ASKED Ryan after his fourth attempt
to establish radio contact with the crew.

"Nope. Just ops telling us they've got recent satellite images of about a hundred muj fighters on the other
side of that ridge."

Cam looked up at the forbidding outline of rock in the
distance that concealed both the enemy and the downed
crew. She wasn't dead. He wouldn't let himself think
that until he saw it firsthand. "That'll take 'em a long
time to get over."

"Let's hope."

He checked his map and compass again. They'd only
covered one kilometer in the past twenty five minutes.
The crash site was way around the other side of the cliff
base they were skirting. Craning his neck to look at the
top of it, he wondered again if it would've been faster to
climb the damn thing and rappel down the other side.

One of the SEALs out front dropped to his knee and
waved a hand to the ground. Cam instantly dropped beside Jackson and raised his weapon. Nothing disturbed
the silence. The sun's rays warmed his face. He felt completely exposed out in the middle of daylight, though
they'd been careful to stay concealed.

The SEAL point man walked out from his hiding

spot, finished with his reconnaissance. "No sign of the ragheads yet, but I saw the bird."

Cam held his breath.

"It looks pretty bad."

Ah, shit.

"Saw some tracks leading away from it, though."

His heart leaped. Somebody was still alive. He prayed to God it was Devon.

"Saddle up, boys," the commander said. They all fell back into line.

"Keep trying them," Cam said to Ryan.

"I will. She's there, man. I know she is."

The urgency screamed at him to run, to throw caution aside and sprint the rest of the way. They were taking too long to reach them.

"Almost there," Ryan said, guessing his thoughts.

Cam jogged along behind the others with Jackson, desperate to go faster, but rushing now would put them all at risk. He'd know soon enough what waited for him on the other side of the cliff.

DEVON WATCHED THE crew chief anxiously. "Keep trying. They've got to be attempting to contact us. They might have eyes on us." Maybe Ryan or another ground team, or maybe a satellite or Predator drone.

"You sure this is the right frequency?" the sergeant asked her, staring doubtfully at his handheld radio.

"I'm positive."

He opened his mouth to say something else when the radio crackled to life. Devon set her weapon down and listened intently. Her heart pounded as she stared at the medic. A voice. She was certain she'd heard the blip of a voice in there somewhere. The radio went quiet again. "Did you catch anything?"

"No." He glared at the thing in disgust and fiddled with the frequency knob. "Just more static. Damn rocks are blocking the frequency."

McCall loped over and knelt next to them. "Got something?"

"We think so." She held out her hand to the medic. "Let me try—"

The radio crackled again. The chief held it up to his ear, frowning in concentration. A soft hissing noise came through, then a garbled voice. "…copy…read?"

"We read you," he answered loudly. "But barely. You read us?"

Nothing. He met her eyes and shook his head in frustration.

"They must have heard something. They've got to be close." She'd never known hope could be so painful. It felt like a helium balloon inflating in her chest, pressing on her lungs and heart.

McCall took the radio and keyed it. "I say again, this is Angel-one niner. Anyone copy?"

More hissing. Then, "Roger that, Angel-one…"

Her heart twisted painfully at the sound of that voice. "It's Ryan!" She grabbed for the radio and pressed down on the button. "Ryan! You there?" More dead air. She looked up at the chief with a grin. "They're coming for us."

"Yeah, but when?" He nodded over his shoulder at the ridge behind them. "That's the only thing separating us from the fuckers that shot us down."

"And damn good thing too," McCall said. "Let's get

everyone ready to move outta here." He looked at her. "Can you make it without help?"

"I can hop. Don't worry about me, just carry the wounded out first and I'll do the best I can." They were going to have their hands full as it was. She'd have to find a way to manage on her own. If she had to crawl out on her hands and knees for kilometers on end, so be it.

"If help doesn't get here before we have to move, I'll come back for you ASAP."

"Okay." She smiled at him with more courage than she felt. When he and the chief left to tend to the critically wounded Marines, she dragged herself over to Will. He was resting quietly from the dose of morphine he'd been given, and the IV fluids draining into him would offset the blood loss. She laid a hand on his arm and he opened his eyes weakly. "The cavalry's on its way, Will. You'll be back at Bagram in no time to phone your wife and girls."

"Okay," he mumbled weakly and closed his eyes. She stayed perched next to him, finger on the trigger guard of her rifle and her senses tuned for any sign of a threat. She prayed help got to them soon so they could get to a better location and call in for an evac. If the militants reached them first, they'd have to fight their way out on the run.

"Shhh!"

The sharp whisper made her eyes dart over to McCall, who knelt rigidly with his weapon raised. She rolled painfully to her belly and did the same, flicking the selector to semi-auto and aiming at the gap in the rocks. She didn't think about what she was doing, or that she'd never fired a weapon in combat. Her pulse pounded in her ears. Shit, she hadn't heard a thing. Had the enemy snuck up on them? She swallowed hard, thankful Will wasn't awake. They were completely outnumbered and without reinforcements. But if anyone came at them, she wouldn't hesitate to pull the trigger.

A tense silence settled over them. Cold sweat broke out over her face and under her arms. Every muscle drew tight to the point of pain. Her finger tightened on the trigger guard. Then a clear voice startled her.

"Who's the best wide receiver of all time?"

PRESSED AGAINST THE other side of the cliff and panting from the prolonged run with all his gear weighing him down, Cam held his breath. Waiting for the answer to the authentication question based on Devon's individual crew card information almost killed him.

"Steve Largent!" came the reply. The sound of her voice filled him with relief.

*Right answer.* His heart pounded hard against his ribs and he felt dizzy. "It's her," he said to the SEAL. "It's Devon." The wave of relief was so acute his knees sagged.

Then the squad leader looked over his shoulder at him and winked. "We've got you covered. Go get your girl."

With Ryan and Jackson covering his back, he took off and cleared the edge of the cliff. The instant he saw Devon lying among the injured his already tight throat closed up, but he kept running. She pushed up awkwardly onto her side and held up a hand when she spotted him, her face lit with a joyous smile. "Cam!"

A rush of pure emotion swept through his veins. She

waved her arm, trying to sit up, but couldn't quite get there. How bad was she hurt? He tore over the ground, sprinting the entire distance to her, boots pounding over the snowy ground. Reaching her, he slung his rifle across his back before dropping to his knees and carefully hauling her into his arms. "*Dev.*" He didn't want to ever let her go again.

She let out a watery laugh and clung just as fiercely, gripping the back of his DCUs. "I'm okay. I'm okay."

He wasn't sure if she was saying it to herself or trying to reassure him. All he knew was he'd never been so relieved in his life. He allowed himself to bury his face in her hair for a moment and feel her alive and safe in his arms. Christ, he felt like crying he was so grateful that she was all right. Giving her one last hard squeeze, he set her away and pulled off his shades before cupping her face in his hands. He wiped at the tears, his thumbs leaving dirty streaks on her dusty cheeks. "Where are you hurt?"

She gripped his wrists and smiled up into his eyes. "Just my left knee and some bruises. I'm the least hurt."

"There's blood on your face and jacket."

"I bit my tongue when we hit."

He drew back when Ryan came down on one knee beside him to wrap his arms around her. "Hey, Spike. Damn it's good to see you."

"Hi," she laughed, hugging him back. She wiped at her face and shooed them away. Cam moved to the next patient, wanting to be with Dev, but her injuries weren't as critical as some of the others'. He thought his heart would explode with pride and tenderness. If he hadn't been a hundred percent certain before, now he knew for sure he was in love with her. "I'll check your knee in a little while."

She nodded and shifted onto her side, and he knew from the pained expression on her face she was hurting a hell of a lot more than she was letting on. He couldn't do anything for her right now though. He had to triage the others first. Before they could get the hell out of there he and Jackson had to patch up the wounded and stabilize the critical cases. "What's his status?" he asked her, indicating the co-pilot lying on a litter in a patch of shade close to her. Keeping her involved would help stave off any depression and shock that commonly occurred after surviving a crash.

Her answer was clear and decisive. "Compound fracture of the right femur, but he's not bleeding too badly now. They gave him some fluids and a dose of morphine, I think. He's been sleeping mostly since."

Cam nodded as he conducted his own quick assessment of the leg. Blood loss was minimal and the limb was stabilized. Good enough for now. "What about the others?" He glanced up. Jackson was already tending to one of the other wounded farther down the cliff's base.

"I think they're in pretty bad shape, but no one's told me anything specific."

He squeezed her shoulder once before climbing to his feet. "I'll be back soon." Hating to leave her, he hurried to the other wounded and took stock of the situation. One Marine was dead. They'd already covered his body and face with a blanket. The other two were definitely critical. He knelt beside Jackson, who was getting ready to administer some of the O negative blood he'd brought. "How are their vitals?"

"They're deep in shock. This one's pulse is thready and rapid. The other one's steadier, but they both need blood and an OR, stat."

Cam checked the Marine closest to him. The soldier was unconscious from blood loss due to the blast wounds he'd suffered to his lower body. He was missing a foot. Two tourniquets were wrapped around his lower thighs to stem the worst of the bleeding, but shrapnel had torn chunks of flesh from all over his legs and a few from his belly beneath the edge of his bullet proof vest. Portions of his skin were blistered.

Cam dressed the worst of the burns and added another bag of saline solution to his IV before pushing in some Hemospan to counteract hypovolemic shock until Jackson could add a unit of blood for him. The last Marine had second and third degree burns on his legs, arms and face. Poor bastard was still conscious, and in a shitload of pain. Cam checked the time mark next to the M on his forehead. If he could get another dose of morphine... From between clenched teeth a deep, constant growl came from the man's swollen throat.

"We couldn't find a vein to get an IV into him," the medic said.

Not surprising considering the extent of the burns. "I'll take care of it." Pulling out the necessary equipment, he injected some local anesthetic over an unburned portion of the man's sternum and then got busy plugging an interosseous IV into it. Once he had the line in, he taped it down so it wouldn't move when they transported him, and immediately hooked up the fluid.

The medic hovered over his shoulder, watching.

"Jesus, I didn't know you guys had that kind of training."

"Yep," he replied, starting the drip. "We know a lot of neat tricks. They come in real handy at a time like this."

Cam slipped his fingers beneath the unburned edge of his jaw to check his pulse, counting the beats along with the second hand on his watch. "Here comes some more morphine," he told him, pushing it into the line. "We're going to get you guys out of here real soon." His burns needed fresh bandaging, but for now he'd have to wait until they got to a more secure location where they could set up a casualty collection point.

Packing up his supplies, Cam cast a look at Jackson. "Need any help?"

"No, I'm good." He finished hooking up a bag of blood into the second patient, and handed it to the waiting sergeant.

"I'm going to check the walking wounded and get back to Devon."

"Okay." The young sergeant had a deep gash on his forehead, closed off with a butterfly bandage. And he was breathing through his teeth.

"Want me to put a few stitches in for you?" Cam asked.

"Nah, it'll be fine until we get the hell out of here. It's my lower back that hurts like a bitch."

"Fractured?"

"Dunno. I've still got movement and sensation in my legs—" He stopped and sucked in a sharp breath, tensing in pain. Cam checked him over.

"Would be best if we carried you out."

"No." His face was dotted with sweat when he exhaled and spoke again. "We hit pretty goddamn hard, but I can still walk out of here."

"Sure about that?"

He closed his eyes and nodded. "I can still shoot too."

"Good enough for me."

Cam glanced at the other soldier with him, a middle-aged man with piercing eyes. "What about you?" He had a good sized knot over one eye and multiple lesions on his face, but nothing that required suturing.

"I'm good to go."

Cam studied his pupils. They were evenly dilated and he seemed alert enough. "No blurred vision or nausea?"

"Not since I knew we were going to crash," he said with a grim smile.

Cam grinned. "That's good."

"I'm McCall."

"Cam Munro," he answered, shaking his hand. "You a crew chief?"

"Medic."

He looked familiar. "Have I seen you around?"

"Maybe. I'm with the 160th."

That explained it. "We're going to need your help carrying the wounded out."

"You got it."

Satisfied everyone was as stable as they were going to be for the moment, he went back to Devon. She had her M4 cradled in her lap while she kept watch over her wounded co-pilot. When she saw him coming over, she smiled.

He shrugged off his heavy med ruck and set it down at her feet. "How you doing, honey?"

"Okay." She shook her head. "I've never been so

glad to see anyone in my whole life as when you came around that corner."

"I know the feeling." He knelt at her feet and reached for her left leg. She flinched before he even touched her, and he was careful when he rolled up the leg of her flight suit. Her leg was covered in bruises. "How's your back and neck?"

"Fine. Just a bit stiff. It's my knee that hurts. I think something popped inside when we landed."

Landed. They hadn't *landed*. Jesus, he hated even imagining the crash. He'd have nightmares about it the next time he slept. "Might have done it on impact, or maybe you hit the forward instrument panel."

When he uncovered her knee, she quickly glanced away. "Can't look at it," she admitted. "Makes me feel queasy."

"No problem. I'm just going to feel around for a second, okay?" At her tacit nod he gently prodded the joint line. From the amount of swelling and obvious discoloration she'd definitely ruptured something inside, or broken a bone. "Can you bend it?"

She tried, but sucked back a sharp breath and turned pasty white. "Nope," she gasped, eyes closed. "Sorry."

"That's okay." He closed one hand around the back of her calf directly below the knee and placed the other on her thigh. "Let your leg go limp. I've got it." She did, and with gentle pressure, he applied an anterior shear force. The joint gave way without any resistance, confirming his suspicion. But near the end range she went rigid and hissed through her teeth. He looked up at her face and tested the anterior joint line with a thumb. She reflexively grabbed his wrist.

"Shit that hurts." She set her jaw. "Did I break something?"

"Might have. I think you've got a ruptured ACL, and maybe an avulsion fracture at the attachment site on the tibial plateau. Won't be able to tell for sure without x-rays, but you're not going to be able to walk on this for a long time." That made one dead and five unable to walk. Six people to carry out of here, and only thirteen of them to do it. Not good odds. That would leave only one shooter free to defend them all when they humped it out to the exfil site. Better than none, he supposed, but they had to haul ass to someplace a Chinook could get in close enough to extract them. Bracing her leg, he rummaged through his pack for a couple of tensor bandages and a chemical cold pack.

"So I'm going to need surgery?"

"I'd say that's a safe bet. But a good brace at least." He placed the cold pack against the front of her knee and wound the bandage around the joint tight enough to help keep the swelling down but careful not to cut off circulation. When he looked up at her face she was still pale, but her eyes were clear. "Want something for the pain before we go?"

She shook her head. "I can handle it, and I want to make sure I'm still sharp if anything else happens." She patted her rifle.

He didn't want her even thinking about having to fire her weapon to defend herself after what she'd already been through. "It's going to be fine. I won't let anything happen to you."

Her slender hand landed on his forearm and tightened. "I don't like that tone in your voice. Don't you be putting yourself in harm's way for me."

"You ready to head out?"

"Cam, I'm serious. Promise me you—"

"Get your gear." He climbed to his feet and hefted his ruck. "We'll be moving fast."

"Cam!" she called when he turned away, but he didn't look back at her. He couldn't promise her that. Because he'd do whatever it took to get her back to base safely.

# SIXTEEN

STARING AFTER HIM, Devon's heart dropped. She'd never seen this side of Cam. The hardened warrior part. It scared her. No, that *look* in his eyes had scared her. He was in full operational mode and she knew he would defend her and the others with his last breath.

No time to dwell on that though. It was time to move again. Grabbing her rifle, she struggled up onto her good knee. "Shit," she gasped. The shock of pain in her injured leg stole her breath and radiated through her body until she wanted to throw up.

"Let's move out, people," the SEAL leader called out. He and two of his men took up a position out front and maintained security. All the other men lifted the wounded onto stretchers or over their shoulders. Cam and the crew chief took one of the wounded Marines. Ryan and Jackson came back to lift Will. She struggled into a standing position and leaned her weight on her rifle, panting as another wave of pain washed through her. It was worse now that the initial shock and adrenaline had worn off and ten times as bad when the blood rushed into it. Jesus, how was she going to be able to walk out of here like this?

"Need some help?"

She looked up into McCall's bruised face. "I don't want to slow you down."

"You'll slow us down more without help."

He was right. She didn't protest when he encircled her waist with a sturdy arm. Slinging her weapon across her back, she stretched her arm up over his far shoulder. "I'm going to have to hop."

"That's okay. If we can't keep up this way, I'll put you over my shoulder."

He was very fit and she wasn't all that big, but moving with her extra weight across this terrain at this increased altitude would wear on him fast. "If something happens, I don't want to put you in jeopardy. Just put me down and—"

"Don't even finish that sentence," he warned, and tightened his grip. She took her first hobbling step, and her hip bumped awkwardly against his.

"I'm just saying—"

"Don't bother. None of us would ever leave you undefended, so don't waste your breath. Let's get going." They were last in line behind Ryan and Jackson carrying Will. Two SEALs brought up the rear to provide protection.

The sun was up well over the horizon now, making her squint to block the rays reflecting off the snow. She hopped alongside McCall, and they'd barely made it to the base of the far cliff before her leg was screaming with fatigue. Her heart raced like it might explode, and she was gasping for breath. Oh God, she wasn't going to be able to do this. Her body was already exhausted and they hadn't even begun the real trek. Fear tightened her muscles. She was already slowing the others down. Ryan and Jackson were already drawing away from them, and the SEALs behind were barely moving.

They had to be frustrated by how slow she was. Obviously they couldn't spare another man to help carry a litter or they would have put her on one.

Near the front of the group, Cam looked back at her. "You okay?" he called.

She couldn't spare the breath to answer, so she nodded. *You're not a quitter. You will not quit. Just keep going. Don't think about how much it hurts. You have to keep going no matter what.* She held that directive at the front of her mind and struggled on. Gritting her teeth, she pushed farther ahead, doing her best to ignore the way her leg muscles screamed and knotted with each step. The heavy E and E vest and rifle made her feel like she weighed an extra hundred pounds. Shit, she couldn't go much farther. McCall was practically carrying her anyway.

As if guessing her thoughts, he shifted his grip and came around in front of her. "Come on, I'll carry you for a bit to let your leg rest." Without so much as a grunt he bent and put her over his shoulder before straightening and falling into line. She grabbed onto the back of his fatigues to balance her weight and locked her right ankle under her left to stabilize her ruined knee. It didn't help much. He started jogging, and every bounce made her knee feel like it would explode. She swallowed a cry of agony and the edges of her vision went hazy.

*Don't say anything. Come on Dev, hang in there.* Her stomach squirmed and twisted. She pulled in a deep breath to push back the nausea and buried her face in his back when a growl came out of her throat.

"Can we get some pain meds back here?" he called.

She lifted her head and shook it. "No," she gasped out. "Don't make them stop."

But McCall was already setting her down. "We've got a lot of ground to cover." He was breathing hard as he wiped his sleeve over his sweating, blood-smeared forehead. "If it'll make it easier on you, then take it."

The whole group had stopped. Her face flushed with embarrassment. The stretcher bearers set their loads down, and then Cam jogged back to her. "Hanging in there?"

"Yes."

"She's hurting pretty bad," McCall put in.

Cam scrutinized her. "I can give you some T3s at least if you don't want morphine."

"Fine," she snapped, hating that everyone was waiting for her. The enemy was on the move. They couldn't afford to stop. She thrust out her palm. "Just hurry."

He was already fishing them out of his pack. Handing them to her, he turned around. "Take some water from my CamelBak."

She did, and forced the pills down. She hoped they'd stay down. "Thanks, I'm good now. Let's go."

Cam faced her and squeezed the back of her neck with a gloved hand. "We'll go in stages, okay? Take it one leg at a time."

Nodding, she reached for McCall but one of the SEALs in the rear came up and took his place. "I'll take her for the next bit." He hoisted her up almost effortlessly and started out. She couldn't believe how strong these men were. The muscles beneath her were like warm steel.

They walked for a long time, picking their way

through the jumbled rocks and boulders. Twice some-one switched off with the man carrying her. The drugs finally kicked in a little, making her dozy. The pain was still bad, but at least the sharp edge was gone. Over-head the sun beat down on them, making it feel warmer than it was.

They'd made it partway up the next rise when the SEAL carrying her suddenly stopped. The muscles be-neath her hands and cheek went rigid. She raised her head and tried to see over his shoulder. The point man was frozen in position with his weapon up, and the man behind him was giving rapid hand signals. The SEAL slid her off his shoulder. "Stay down," he whispered, moving away to take up a defensive position.

She scrambled onto her belly and dragged her rifle around. Any sleepiness from the codeine was long gone. Casting a sidelong glance up at Cam, her heart stuttered to see him knelt in front of his patient ready to fire. The enemy had to be damn close. Cursing under her breath, she braced her left ankle on her right and belly crawled over to Will on his stretcher. McCall came over in a crouched run and dropped in front of her.

"What's happening?"

"We've been spotted," McCall answered.

A shiver of foreboding ran down her spine. With the cliff rising at their backs, the only way out was forward or back the way they'd come. The force tracking them would have almost certainly blocked off that escape route. That left forward. She hoped there was nobody waiting to ambush them on the other side of that slope.

Movement in her peripheral vision made her whip her head to the left. One of the SEALs was moving forward, toward the brow of the hill. He was on his belly, and stopped at the exact place that marked the downward transition. He was so still it looked like he wasn't even breathing. With almost imperceptible movements he eventually cleared the top and moved out of her line of vision. Every muscle in her body coiled in anticipation. She expected to hear shots any second. Yet the silence held. And held. Until the muscles in her clenched jaw began to tremble.

Nobody moved or made a sound. She flexed her chilled fingers inside her flight gloves. Minutes later the SEAL squad leader made more hand signals, and she understood enough to know he was ordering them to keep moving. Her slamming heart slowed down fractionally as she dragged herself up onto her right knee. McCall helped her stand. Cam looked back at her once, and she nodded to let him know she was hanging in there.

The snow glistened in the sun, melting slowly now that the temperature had climbed above freezing. Inside her layered clothing, she began to sweat more. She dreaded the thought of being stuck out here when night fell if a rescue bird couldn't get to them. If she didn't dry out in time she'd be at risk for hypothermia and slow the team down even more.

*Concentrate on moving forward. That's all. Nothing else right now.*

She couldn't make the crawling sensation on the back of her neck go away. The enemy was close and had seen them. The crew chief came back to spell off McCall, and put her over his broad shoulder again. "Almost there," he said quietly.

"Where?" Was a bird coming in?

"Better defensive position."

That wasn't the answer she'd been hoping for. "Can a Chinook get in there for us?"

"Don't know."

She shut up and held on while they moved down the rocky hillside. Between the patches of snow, the dust was a monotonous light tan and fine as baby powder. Like the surface of the moon.

The whole line maneuvered down the trail to another ridge, but this time with some shelter from the sun and better visibility to scan for the enemy. The crew chief left her sitting next to Will and hurried over to help the wounded. Weapon at the ready, Devon watched the SEALs form a protective half circle around them. One of them was speaking into his radio, and she caught enough of his words to know he'd requested pick up. About damn time.

Cam checked his patients. He moved between them methodically changing bandages or adding fluid to their IVs. Her heart swelled as she watched him work, capable and sure even in this stressful environment. He looked up once and met her gaze. After handing one of the others a bag of fluid to hold, he came over. She couldn't help but notice the way his eyes never stayed still and the rock steady grip he maintained on his weapon. He hunkered down beside her. "How you feeling?"

"Looking forward to getting back to base."

"I'll bet." He unwound the tensor bandages and took out the cold pack. "This isn't doing you any good now." As he reapplied the bandage, he avoided her eyes.

"Whatever happens, you stay low and out of sight until one of us says to come out."

Her stomach plummeted like she'd just jumped off the edge of a skyscraper. "How close are they?"

His brow furrowed as he scanned the surrounding hills. "Pretty close. It'll be a race to see who gets here first, them or the chopper."

Oh my God. "But Ryan's called in air support, right?"

"Yeah, but they can't engage until we're fired upon."

Feeling sick, she couldn't think of a single thing to say. She watched as he stepped away from her to check on Will. His skilled hands moved over her co-pilot's dressings, adjusting the pressure and monitoring his pulse.

Will's eyes opened. "Thirsty." Cam gave him some water. "We going home?"

"Soon. How's your pain level?"

"Okay." He didn't look okay. His face was ashen and shiny with perspiration again. "Where—"

Devon jumped when the first round hit. It impacted with the dirt a few dozen yards to her right, and ricocheted off a boulder before burying itself in the cliff face. She instinctively rolled onto her stomach, but Cam was there. He flattened himself atop her back and shielded her head with his arms. Another round hit, answered by a burst of semi-automatic fire. The SEALs were already returning fire on the enemy position. Devon squeezed her eyes shut and fought back the scream crowding her dry throat. The firing increased until it was almost nonstop. Bullets kicked up puffs of dirt and snow, some close enough that it sprayed them.

Then suddenly, a lull descended. To her the sudden quiet was almost as terrifying as the firefight.

"Go, go, go!" someone yelled.

She raised her head when Cam got off her. What did he want her to—

"Whatever happens," he commanded the medic, "don't stop running." Before she could answer he dragged her up and handed her off to McCall. The Night Stalker threw her over his shoulder and started out at a dead run.

"Cam!" she cried, horror flooding her. He wasn't coming with them. He was still kneeling in front of Will as two men picked up the co-pilot's stretcher, guarding them with the SEALs. Fear coiled tight as McCall carried her over the ground. Then she saw them. Enemy soldiers coming over the hill at them. Swarming like locusts. Several shots pinged off rocks close to them, but McCall's stride never faltered. Grappling her rifle into position, she readied it and brought it up. She returned fire in measured bursts.

"Save your ammo!" McCall bit out. His chest heaved as he ran.

Helpless, she lowered her weapon and stared back at Cam. He got up and ran behind Will's stretcher. The SEALs moved out behind him, firing as they went to slow the advancing enemy. And still they came. Relentless and single-minded in their intent, bearing down on them like a tidal wave that threatened to drown them all.

CAM'S ONLY THOUGHT as he ran and fired was protecting his wounded. Devon and her crew were going home no matter what. Up ahead, Ryan was already on the radio requesting air support, and it couldn't come soon enough. Cam had counted over forty fighters coming over the brow of that hill before he'd started running. From the sounds of their yelling, he knew plenty more were still back there out of sight.

Up the line McCall stumbled and went to his knees. Cam saw Devon's face twist in agony. Leaving the SEALs to watch their backs, he sprinted up and hoisted her over his shoulders before dragging the medic to his feet. "Keep your head down," he yelled at Devon. The rush of adrenaline gave him added power as he tore over the ground. Cresting the next rise, Ryan ducked to the side and crouched down to consult his map. Cam saw him, but didn't slow down. He raced past Ryan and caught up to the guys carrying the badly burned Marine. "Where're we going?" one of them yelled.

"Just keep going!"

They picked up their pace and scrambled down a shallow ravine. Cam grunted, his foot slipping at the bottom, but managed to throw himself forward and keep his balance. Devon clung to him, her cheek pressed against his shoulder. He ran after the others, ran until his lungs burned and his legs felt like they were on fire. The noise of the firing slowly died down behind them. The stretcher bearers had stopped ahead, bent over and gasping for breath. Clearing a group of boulders, Cam was about to yell at them to keep running when he saw why they'd stopped. They'd run right into a fucking canyon. It was narrow, with high walls that would be impossible to scale, let alone with so many wounded on litters. About two hundred meters at the other end lay the only exit he could see. His body trembled with exhaustion.

"Put me down, Cam," Devon insisted, levering up.

He shook his head. "No. Have to…make it…to end."

"Put me down. Someone else will carry me." Her voice was thin, laced with fear. The others in the group stared up at him, waiting for direction. "Go," he ground out, jerking his chin toward the end of the canyon. They struggled to their feet, though they had to be as tired as he was, and pressed on. Normally Cam could run forever, but carrying someone over this terrain was pushing his body to its limit. He couldn't take Devon much farther without risking falling or dropping her.

"Cam!"

He slowed and turned at Ryan's voice. His buddy pounded toward them and stopped, bent over with his hands on his thighs. "Spooky's inbound," he gasped, his huge pack bristling with radio antennas.

Thank Christ. "The SEALs?"

"All okay." He sucked in a couple more breaths. "Want me to take her?"

A denial formed on his tongue, but he swallowed it. He wasn't going to endanger Devon just because he didn't want to let go of her. And he trusted Ryan to protect her with his life. With a tight nod, he shifted his grip on her. A bullet sliced over their heads.

"Shit." He dropped to his knees and let her slide off his shoulders, then went one better and climbed on top of her to return fire. She didn't move, thank God. She stayed pinned beneath him despite the rocks that had to be digging into her, made worse by his added weight. Ryan was already shooting. Cam picked off two men in front of the main body, but at this distance he doubted he'd done more than wound them. The SEALs added their firepower. The enemy advance wavered, then melted like snow. Within moments they'd retreated back over the hill.

With a break in the fighting and his breath back, Cam climbed off Devon. "You okay?"

"Yes," she said huskily. Her eyes were huge and shadowed with fear, but she was still keeping it together.

"Hang on, honey. We're going to get you out of here."

"And you too," she said with a hard frown.

Hopefully. But she was the priority. "Gotta go check on someone." While Ryan scooped her up, he shoved to his feet and ran over to the Marine with all the burns. The guy needed more fluids, and fast. Cam took another bag out of his ruck and hooked it into the line. The interosseous IV was doing beautifully despite how much the patient had been bounced around. It enabled him to get more fluid into the patient in a short amount of time. "Let's go," he told the stretcher bearers. They started for the end of the canyon while he checked the tourniquets on the next wounded Marine's legs.

Jackson was back with the third Marine and Will, and Cam waved the others on. Ryan came up with Devon, and he could tell with one look at her pained grimace that her knee was killing her. "Let me give you some morphine."

She shook her head emphatically. "They're my crew and we're probably going to be in another firefight. I'm responsible for them and—"

"And we'll take care of everything."

"I don't want anything."

He didn't have time to argue about it. Biting back a retort, he set out behind Ryan, guarding their backs. The ground was flatter here, and easier to navigate. They made good time until a bloodcurdling yell rose up behind them. High-pitched and eerie. More like a wailing than a war cry. His nape prickled. *Fuck, here they come again*. Ryan set Dev on the ground and immediately came around to defend her. Turbaned men appeared on the far slope, charging headlong down the hill.

From his knees Cam kept firing aimed shots until he was out of ammo and had to reload with a fresh magazine. He shoved the thing into place and got back into the action. He hit three men with four shots. They all went down, but more kept on coming. The force grew and swelled like a giant wave gathering. "Devon, move," he bit out. "I'll be right beside you, but we have to move. Understand?"

"Yes." She got up on her hands and knees and started crawling. Her guttural cries of pain tore into him, but he couldn't help her until he stopped the action. Dammit, there were too many of them coming out of the mountains. "Where the hell is that Spooky?" he shouted to Ryan.

"Inbound," he yelled between shots. "Should be on station any minute."

Yeah, well, if the pilot didn't get there in time, there wasn't going to be anyone on the ground team left to defend.

# SEVENTEEN

RYAN'S VOICE WAS calm when he answered Cam, but his mind whirled. Where the hell was his fucking air support? It should have been here by now.

Cursing under his breath, he held his rifle with one hand and ripped out his radio with the other. "Blade three, this is Stingray, do you read?" He couldn't hear shit over the popping of the gunfire, but hopefully they could hear him on the other end. "Blade three, do you copy?" Ducking behind a group of boulders for cover, he plugged his free ear to hear the pilot over the noise of the firefight if they responded. He glanced up into the low cloud cover. He couldn't see it yet, but the Spooky had to be close. Was it already in range?

Somebody replied, but with all the noise he couldn't make out what they'd said. "Say again?" No answer. He made his voice deliberately calm and clear. "Do you have a visual on the target yet?"

A second's delay, then someone answered. "Negative. Will be on station in three minutes."

He went dead still at the sound of the husky female voice coming through his radio. Even with the noise of battle around him, he recognized it instantly. He knew exactly who the pilot was. But three minutes? God damn. "Copy that, Blade three. Proceed to these coordinates." After consulting with his map and laser range finder, he rattled the coordinates off. Then he lobbed a smoke grenade to mark their location. "Ground team is east of orange smoke. Targets are approaching from our west, closing in on four hundred yards. You are cleared to engage. Be advised, you will encounter small arms fire."

"Roger that, Stingray. Blade three out."

He set his radio on his knee and looked up at the sky. Fuck, now Candace was in the fight, and she was going to have to come in low to get a good visual on the enemy position. That would expose her aircraft to shoulder-fired missiles and the RPGs the enemy were only too happy to use. He hoped to God her flares and chaff would be enough to protect the aircraft from ground-to-air missile fire.

Picking up his rifle, he glanced over at Cam. He was lying over one of the wounded Marines, using him as a shooting platform to lay down suppressing fire. A total pro, cool as ever under pressure. Ryan goddamn loved him for it. The sharp, rhythmic crack of his precise double taps carried over the din, but Ryan had no idea how effective the rounds were. Devon was on her belly behind them, aiming her own weapon.

His training kicked into high gear. He couldn't focus on the firefight right now. All he cared about was directing that Spooky to the right place and making sure he kept giving Candace accurate up-to-the-minute intel on the enemy's position. Every one of the service members on the ground depended on him getting it exactly right the first time. In his job, he rarely got second chances.

He had a B-52 circling somewhere high above in a holding pattern at 40,000 feet, but the enemy was too close. It made using the two thousand pound JDAMS on board impossible. Damn shame. Even one of those babies would have taken care of business nicely. But the Spooky's howitzers and guns were going to have to clear most of the enemy off that hill if they were going to have a chance in hell of escaping. There was no way they could outrun a bunch of zealots on their home turf. Not while carrying the wounded. And neither he, Cam, Jackson nor the SEALs would quit the rescue operation until they'd either won the day or been wiped out.

The SEALs fell back. As Ryan watched, a round hit one of them, knocking him over. The SEAL got up but he was moving slow. His buddies immediately moved into a protective formation around him. "Munro!" Ryan yelled.

"I see him!" During the next lull, Cam got up and ran over, staying low to the ground. Ryan aimed his weapon at the slope and prepared for the next wave of the attack. He glanced at Cam to see fresh blood staining his hands and uniform. Shit. The SEAL was hurt bad. Now they had one more person to carry.

The pot shots started again. Sporadic at first, but growing in intensity. This time the shooters stayed hidden among the rocks to give them better protection. Wouldn't be long before they mounted another full-out assault. Crazy bastards never knew when to call it a day.

But then, neither did he. Or his teammates.

More shots whizzed past him, and his radio chirped. "Blade three on station. Target acquired."

*Fucking A.* "Roger that." Tilting his head back, he made out the silhouette of the Spooky as it broke through the cloud deck. He couldn't hear the drone of the props over the shooting, but he was ecstatic to see it. "Incoming!" he yelled.

Everyone hunkered down, and moments later the big aircraft came roaring in. The men on the hill fired a few RPGs at it, but the gunship launched its countermeasures. They lit up the midday sky with brilliant white fireworks and trails of smoke. Descending even lower, it banked once in a final turn and opened up with its Gatling guns. The big rounds plowed into the ground with a throaty roar among the enemy. Bodies fell everywhere. "Yeah!" He grinned up at the airplane as it swept past overhead. "That's a direct hit," he confirmed on the radio.

"Roger that. Banking to make another pass."

Hell yeah. Another pass or two like that and they'd be able to crawl out of the canyon if they wanted to.

DEVON RISKED RAISING her head as the gunship approached for the second time. The first enemy wave on that hill was decimated. Dead or probably wishing they were, writhing on the snow-patched ground. A sense of unreality hit her. She shook herself. *Oh no you don't. You're not going to get all shocked-out in the middle of this firefight.* She bit the inside of her cheek to counteract the numbness, and forced herself to focus on the remaining targets left scrambling up the hill.

Will stirred beside her. Was he awake? With the SEALs all busy, he lay undefended and helpless. She had to protect him. Using her elbows, she clawed her way over the short distance to him and laid across his belly like Cam was doing with one of the other wounded. Her co-pilot jerked awake, staring at her with startled brown eyes. When he saw the plane coming in above them, his mouth fell open.

"Stay still," she told him, staring down the barrel of her rifle. The men on the hill had scattered like dry leaves in a gust of wind. Were they all gone? Must be a cave or something she couldn't see in the hills, because there were fewer bodies than she'd expected. Her heart thudded hard. Something caught her eye. There. Someone was coming out of the rocks. The muzzle of his rifle swung out. Letting out the breath she'd been holding, she fired.

"Hit him?" Will managed.

She licked her lips, squinting at the militant's unmoving body. She ignored the guilt trying to worm its way into her conscience. Was he dead? "He's down." *Now stay down, damn you. Leave us the hell alone.* She looked around to find out where the others were. Ryan was still over next to Cam, talking on the radio. She hoped he was calling for another strike. She'd love to have the main body of the enemy force cleared off before they had to move again. The Spooky's infrared sensors would pick up on any remaining enemy heat signatures.

Sure enough, the aircraft did a big circle and came back.

"Incoming!" Ryan yelled again.

She immediately flopped over Will's torso and covered his head. He gripped her upper arms tight. "You hold on, Will. Think of your girls."

The Spooky didn't open up with its guns this time. It fired a missile. She braced and shut her eyes as the warhead streaked through the air with a shrill scream and impacted with the side of the hill. The explosion ripped apart the quiet. She raised her head. Rock and debris shot up into the air like an earthen geyser. The shockwave rippled through the ground and rattled her teeth. Blood rushed in her throbbing ears. She lifted her upper body away from Will. Nothing moved up on the leveled hill. Only a plume of smoke trailed up into the clear air. In the sudden stillness the noise of battle faded abruptly, and when she moved her head back to look into the sky the Spooky was winging away overhead. Was it leaving, or turning around? She prayed it had finished off most of the enemy.

Approaching footsteps made her look over her shoulder. Cam crossed the ground between them, an amused grin on his face. "What's so funny?" she demanded. Unless he was happy because the enemy had just been blown to hell, she couldn't think of any reason why he should be smiling. Her heart was still galloping in overtime, but he looked like he was on the verge of laughing.

"Nothing," he answered. "Just you."

"What?" She winced as she rolled off Will and onto her side to face Cam. He knelt and helped prop her injured leg on top of her good one.

His eyes glowed with affection and maybe even pride as he gazed at her. He shook his head. "You're something else."

Compared to everyone else, she wasn't doing a hell of a lot. Still, his compliment boosted her spirits. "Where's the Spooky going?"

"To refuel. Ryan's got another one coming on station for standby."

A moment later Ryan dropped down beside them. He

grinned at her, his teeth a startling white in his camouflaged face. "Remind me to thank your pal when we
get back."

What? She jerked her head around to stare after the
retreating plane. "Ace?"

"You betcha."

The drone of the Spooky's four prop engines died
away in the distance. *Thanks Ace. See you soon.* She
looked at Cam. "So…are we clear?" Because she would
really love to feel his arms around her right now.

He nodded. "For now. But we're not going to wait
around long enough to find out if anybody's still out
there. Let's get moving."

Hell yes. She grabbed the strong hand he offered
and let him pull her up. Holding his hand was better
than nothing.

# EIGHTEEN

SOMEONE MOVED BESIDE him in the darkness. He could hear men moaning and screaming. Shaking, Sadiq scrambled to his feet and picked his way through the smoking rubble. That explosion had damn near killed him. Everything hurt, even his insides. It felt like someone had beaten him with a sledgehammer. It was dark in the cave, but enough light came through tiny holes in the pile of collapsed rock to allow him to see where he was going. He almost wished he couldn't see. Wounded and dead lay everywhere. Body parts too. What remained of the cave stunk of blood and burning flesh.

He slipped on something. Looking down at his feet, his gaze landed on the bloody remains of someone's guts beneath his boots. Gagging, he stumbled over more bodies to where the other survivors were trying to dig their way out of the rock. He could see the light streaming in through a narrow gap. Some men were crying, others whispering among themselves. He pushed his way through the knot of men and took hold of one of the rocks. It encased them like a tomb.

Using the heavy stone as a lever, he shoved it beneath a tall boulder and pried it loose enough that others could grab it. They toppled it over. He jumped back as part of the roof came down, raining rock and pebbles on their heads. One hit him in the cheek, nicking his skin, and fine dust filled his eyes. Coughing and scrubbing at them, he managed to move two smaller pieces of rock away from the exit. Someone took his place. Excited voices came from outside the hole. A second later a face appeared in the gap, followed by a hand. The man in front of him grasped it, and in the light Sadiq could see the raw, bloody wounds on the man's arm and hand.

More men outside rushed over to help. The gap widened with each rock pulled away. "Get back!" he barked, pulling the two closest to him back out of the way to avoid another small cave-in. The moment the hole was big enough, men started pouring through it.

When it was his turn he placed one boot on a boulder beneath the opening and reached up. Someone grabbed his wrist and helped pull him out. Emerging into the light, he sucked in a full breath of cold, clean air and crawled over the jagged rocks. His head swam as he looked around. Across the small ravine where the other cave had been, a pile of smoldering rock lay. It was completely destroyed. If the mess in his own relatively untouched cave was any indication, no one could have survived in there.

He glanced around in shock. Men were bleeding everywhere he turned. His own hands and shirt were spattered with blood. He touched a finger to his torn lip, and it came away covered with glistening scarlet.

How many of them were left? He didn't know. Hushed voices carried on the wind. He turned his throbbing head, squinting as his eyes focused on a plateau above him. Nasrallah stood there. He was all right. Sadiq put a hand to his chest, relieved, and made his way over to a spot where he could climb up, wincing at the pain.

He found Khalid standing a few yards behind the general and his advisors. His predatory eyes lit as he watched Sadiq struggle up the side of the hill. Mocking and rueful. And not a damn mark on him. How the hell had the bastard managed to be clear of the airstrike? Sadiq looked away and focused on putting one foot in front of the other. The muscles in his legs were knotted. So tight he half expected them to rip off the bone.

Nasrallah's face went slack when he finally saw him. "Help him, hurry," he urged, sliding his way over. One of his lieutenants clambered down and helped tow him up. Nasrallah took Sadiq's face between his hands and gave a gentle shake. "I knew you did not die. I knew it in my soul."

Sadiq nodded, fighting the urge to pull away. He was already queasy, and being held in what felt like an intimate embrace made the crawling sensation in his belly worse.

The general released him. "Not to worry, Sadiq. We have many men left yet who will continue the fight." He gazed up at the sky a moment, his expression growing almost dreamy. "There are always more men willing to fight." He handed him the binoculars. "Look at our enemy. They think they have defeated us. That they have nothing more to worry about than waiting for the next bird to pick them up. But they are wrong."

Khalid approached, eyes gleaming with anticipation. "The woman is there," he said, nodding to the east. Wordlessly Sadiq took the binoculars from the general. The Americans were on the move again in the canyon, heading for the exit. Sadiq's jaw clenched. They'd been close to trapping them there. If they'd had more time they could have divided again and circled around to entrap them. Now he didn't know how they'd ever catch them in the open. Once they cleared the end and moved to more open, flatter ground, someone would come in to evacuate them.

"I am quite familiar with these hills," Nasrallah murmured. "There is another way to get to far end of that canyon. A short cut. We need to keep moving and link up with the others. The battle is not lost."

Sadiq nodded, not really paying attention to the general's words, but glad they could still possibly mount another attack. The magnification of the lenses made his field of vision crystal clear despite the buzzing in his head. He could see the woman. She was still conscious, laid over a soldier's shoulder as he carried her. He tightened the focus to better see the face that had haunted him for so long. His eyes caught on the ID patch affixed to the man's shoulder. *No.* He sucked in a breath so sharply that Nasrallah put a steadying hand on his shoulder.

"What is it?"

He couldn't answer. His vision tunneled, narrowing until all he saw was the strip of material on the man's shoulder and the two letters stenciled there. They made Sadiq's soul shudder.

*PJ.*

The letters ricocheted in his skull like shrapnel.

"What is it?" The grip tightened on his arm.

He couldn't breathe. The light wind blew over his face and ruffled his hair, but all he was aware of was the terrible pressure in the center of his chest, as if his lungs were filled with concrete, and the frantic slam of his heart. Rage and pain swirled up from deep inside, threatening to choke him. "He has to die." He barely recognized his own voice, so low and rough. It was as though someone else had spoken. His skin tingled and burned as he stared, unblinking, his eyes growing so hot they teared up. "He. Must. *Die*."

"And he will, my son." Nasrallah patted his shoulder. "Once we get the woman, they all will."

Yes, they would. Including the woman and the PJ, *all* the other Americans in that canyon would die. But Nasrallah didn't understand. This new development changed everything. The woman was no longer Sadiq's primary target. Even if he had to sacrifice himself to make sure it happened, that PJ would die by his hand.

THE QUIET WAS starting to grate on her nerves. No contact from the enemy should have been reassuring, but it wasn't. She couldn't shake the sensation that someone was watching them, following them just out of view behind the unforgiving shield of rock. Ryan carried the front of a stretcher behind her. She couldn't hear any engines overhead, but someone had to have eyes on them, at least part of the time. A patrolling AWACS. Maybe a satellite.

Her stomach and ribs were bruised from being bounced against hard shoulders, and every jolt shot needles of fire through her left knee. Cam held her securely with one arm clamped across the backs of her thighs. It comforted her to be able to curl around him and hang on. But when the hell were they going to get to the extraction point? The sun was already starting to descend in the west. In another hour or two it would sink below the tops of the hills, and drop the temperature with it. She'd left her helmet with the NVGs back on the Hawk. If a rescue didn't come in soon, she wouldn't be able to see if she had to shoot again.

At the next clearing the SEAL squad leader called another halt. Cam set her down with a weary sigh. He had to be exhausted from carrying her for such a long time. "Can I do anything? Rub your shoulders?" she asked.

He took a few sips of water from his CamelBak and offered some to her. "Just get some rest while you can."

Near them, Ryan set his wounded man down and immediately got on his radio. McCall was working on one of the Marines.

"There must be something I can help with." She felt so useless. The able bodied men were worn out, and all the other wounded were worse off than she was.

"Gimme a minute." He left to make another round with Jackson. After working on the wounded SEAL for a few minutes, he looked up at her and waved her over. She climbed painfully to her right foot and bit back a growl when the blood rushed to her knee. She managed a hop, but in a moment Cam was there to clamp a strong arm around her waist. His stamina amazed her.

"He won't take any pain meds," he said nodding towards the SEAL, "but he's hurting pretty bad." Cam set her down beside the wounded man and helped her into a sitting position, tucking his ruck beneath her knee to support it. "He needs some fluids. Can you hold the bag?"

"Yes." She took it and held it up so the tube wouldn't

get kinked. Cam moved on to the next patient. The SEAL stared up at her through pain-glazed eyes, his lips compressed in a bloodless line. The thick wad of bandages covering his left hand were soaked with blood, as were the ones on his shoulder and side. One of the rounds must have hit him beneath the bottom of his Kevlar chest plate. He might be down, but she knew if another firefight broke out he'd be up and into the action before she could blink. "Do you need some water?"

He closed his eyes and nodded. Devon rummaged through his ruck and dug out some water. She cradled the back of his neck and made sure he sipped it slowly, doing her best to ignore the waves of pain radiating through her leg. Out front, the remaining SEALs and her crew chief were out in a defensive perimeter. She saw Cam stop to talk to Ryan for a moment before he made his way back to her.

"Any word on the air support?" she asked.

"Yeah. Gunship coming on station had to return to base because of mechanical problems."

Damn. "Any word on whether we're being followed?"

"They're still out there. But Went's call for an extraction is working through the channels right now."

The squad leader turned back to them and motioned with his arm. "Let's move."

Stifling a groan, Devon smoothed a hand over the wounded SEAL's damp hair before handing off the bag of fluid and taking Ryan's hand when he came over for her. "You and me this time, Dev."

She patted his sturdy shoulder. "Just try and give me a smooth ride, will you?"

"Do my best."

They forged ahead, stopping only to take short breaks to let the stretcher bearers rest. When Cam took Ryan's place and settled her over his shoulders, she sighed in relief at being able to touch him. "Only a little further to the LZ," he told her.

She brightened. "They're really coming?"

Over his shoulder he gave her one of the lopsided smiles she loved so much. "Yeah. Just a little longer and I'll get you on that bird for a nice shot of morphine."

Sounded damn good to her. She gritted her teeth and focused on breathing to distract her from the hard throbs of pain every time Cam's steps jarred her leg. The sun had already disappeared over the tops of the hills. The dying rays coated the edge of the ridges with a blood red line.

Cam stopped moving. She tensed and braced herself up on her forearms. Out front the squad leader was on full alert. He and the others were on one knee with their weapons raised. Cam knelt and slid her off him, lifting his own rifle as he set her down. Rolling to her belly, she did the same.

Her heart beat crazily against her ribs. *Please no more. I can't take any more.*

Popping noises came in the distance. Shots, but too far away to pose any real threat.

Except it meant the enemy was still there and coming after them.

Her stomach knotted.

"What's the story, Went?" Cam said in a loud whisper.

Ryan's low voice carried over to her, but she couldn't make out what he was saying. Her eyes swept ahead to the distance. The LZ was so close. She could see the relatively flat area a few hundred yards beyond the SEALs. That had to be it. If they could just get there before the remaining enemy force caught up with them, the Chinook might be able to pick them up without incident.

More shots echoed in the still night air. She could hear men shouting at each other in the distance. The hair on her nape stood up. Ryan stopped talking, and his tight expression filled her with dread. He ran over to the SEALs and talked for a minute, then came back to her and Cam.

"Well?" Cam asked. "What's the status?"

Ryan's jaw tensed before he answered. "Command won't risk another bird. LZ's too hot for rotary wing aircraft."

"Hot?" Dev was incredulous. "It'll be a hell of a lot hotter if they wait."

"Yeah, well, bottom line is no one's coming for us until dark."

Because the enemy wouldn't be able to see them in the dark. "When will it get dark enough out here?"

"Eighteen hundred hours. Maybe."

Shit. That meant they had at least another few hours to kill before a bird would attempt to come in for them. She looked up at Cam in disbelief.

Without a trace of frustration or concern, he waved an arm at Jackson. "Thatcher. Set up a CCP over behind those rocks. We'll treat there and provide suppressive fire."

"They have to send in a gunship at least," she argued. "They can't just leave us here without air support."

He slung his weapon and picked her up in his arms

to carry her to the casualty collection point. The other stretcher bearers moved their patients. When everything was in place inside the protective perimeter, Cam knelt in front of her and took her face between his hands. "We're still okay, honey." His eyes burned with intensity. He stroked her cheekbones. "No matter what happens, I won't leave you. I'm going to make sure you get out of here."

Why did he keep phrasing it like he wasn't getting out with her? She opened her mouth to set him straight. Before she could get a single word out he got up and ran ahead to stop the enemy bearing down on them.

# NINETEEN

CAM WAS ALREADY in firing position when one of the
SEALs spoke over the inter-squad radio. "Enemy sniper,
two o'clock, hundred and fifty meters."

To Cam's right, someone fired a single shot. A muf-
fled cry rang out.

"Sniper down."

The darkness opened up. A hail of bullets ripped
overhead. The arcing tracers glowed neon green in the
lenses of his NVGs.

"Eleven o'clock."

Cam took aim and fired. The man running toward
them threw up his arms. He arched backward with the
impact of the bullet and fell. He didn't get up. "Target
down."

The minutes stretched out endlessly. They fired
on the enemy with carefully aimed shots to conserve
ammo. The only talk on the radio was reporting targets
and hits. In his peripheral vision he saw Ryan lying
flat next to one of the SEALs, his radio held to his ear.
Christ, they had no eyes other than the circling AWACS
high overhead. The crew had radioed to provide an es-
timate of remaining enemy forces. Fewer than eighty,
as far as they could tell. With only ten shooters on the
forward line, that made a hell of a lot of kills for each
of them. If the numbers were right.

"Thatcher, how's it going back there?" He squeezed off another shot. The target dropped but flipped over and started crawling away. *Shit. Only wounded him.*

"Everybody's still stable."

"You covering Crawford?"

"You know it."

"Command finally cleared our birds." Ryan's voice came over the radio. "ETA eleven minutes."

About fucking time. "Roger that." He kept his eyes pinned on the enemy moving among the rocks in the distance. Bastards weren't stopping even though they probably couldn't see shit. He fired off two more rounds, taking down two men. "Thatcher, get the patients ready for evac. I'll be there shortly."

"Roger that."

He would get Devon and the others on that bird at the first possible moment. And he wouldn't get on it with them until every last one of the wounded was safely aboard.

OVER THE DIN of battle, Sadiq was sure he heard the sound of helicopters coming in. A growl of denial lodged in his throat. His targets could *not* get away. Not yet.

Holding tight to the general's binoculars, he crawled on his hands and knees over to the closest wounded man. Sadiq sucked in a harsh breath. Poor bastard had been shot through the throat. His fingers clawed at his throat as the blood poured out in a sickening stream. His mouth was open, gasping for air but not getting any, and his body thrashed around in terror. The bulging eyes stared up at him, full of panic. Begging for mercy.

Sadiq picked up the man's rifle. Without pausing, he put a round through the man's forehead. The body went instantly limp, his earthly suffering ended.

Bullets zinged past his head. He hit the ground. Two more men rushed down the hill as more rounds sliced through the air. Both men threw up their arms and cried out as they fell, rolling in the dirt. Sadiq flattened himself on the ground, and scrambled over to grab their weapons and ammo. He was out—he needed more to stand any chance at living through this fight. And those damned helicopters were bearing down on them. With more men and more guns. Electronic sensors and gadgets that made it impossible to hide.

He shoved a full magazine into his rifle and dragged himself behind cover. Men shouted and screamed around him in the chaos. Any sense of order was long gone with the chain of command broken and darkness closing in. The muzzle flashes were the only way he could tell where his fellow soldiers were. They still outnumbered the enemy by a large margin, but the Americans held their ground.

Sadiq could smell the panic swirling through the air around him as he swiveled on one knee and fired at the distant enemy. Men in the ranks were fleeing, he could see them charging back up the hill and over the rise. Their desperate flight was futile and sickening. Moving now made them easy targets to an enemy using night vision technology. They fell by the dozen trying to claw their way to safety.

"Fucking bastards!"

The English words surprised him so much he spared a quick glance behind him. His shocked eyes found

Khalid sprawled on his belly nearby. He'd been wounded in the arm. Sadiq could see the slickness of the blood soaking his sleeve. "Khalid—get to the general," he cried, rolling to fire more rounds.

He eyed a large boulder a few yards away. If he could get to it, he might be able to hide enough of his body that the helicopters wouldn't see him. And even if they did see a heat signature, they might not fire if he stayed still long enough. He could play dead.

The aircraft appeared, three shadows in a dark sky. One large one and two smaller ones. Frustration beat at Sadiq. The woman and the PJ would get away if the aircraft landed. He couldn't allow that. He had to get them before they loaded onto the helicopters.

In answer to his prayers, some of the men began firing RPGs into the air. They shrieked toward their slow moving targets. He didn't hear any impacts.

His gaze strayed to the jagged boulder. It wasn't that far away. He could make it.

His hands tightened around the rifle and binoculars. Drawing on all the power in his legs and arms, he threw himself out from behind cover and dove toward the bigger rock. His arms stretched out. Forearms splayed to cushion his fall. Reaching for safety.

A bullet struck him high in the shoulder. He screamed as it tore through muscle and bone. The force of the impact drove him back. He hit the ground with a thud. Struggling up on one elbow, another round plowed into his belly. It burned like hellfire. The pain stole his breath and brought the darkness crashing down upon him. His hands clutched his belly. Warm, sticky blood flowed out under his fingers. Fighting to stay afloat, he forced his legs to propel him toward shelter. Inch by excruciating inch he moved, while bullets pinged off rocks around him. His legs trembled and weakened. He couldn't make it. The pain was too much.

He cast a helpless glance over at Khalid. "Khalid—help me," he cried out. His voice was already raspy and weak.

In the glimmer of moonlight filtering through the clouds, those terrible yellow eyes fastened on him for a moment. A grim smile curved that evil mouth. And then Khalid turned and ran up the hill, leaving him there to die.

He had never felt this alone and afraid. The fear thickened. Tightening like a choke hold around his throat.

*This is not my destiny. I am not meant to die this way.*

Rage and fear began to replace the awful despair smothering him. Using his remaining strength, he dragged his bleeding body into the shelter of the boulder and dropped in exhaustion. Shivers coursed through him in uncontrollable waves. The helicopters buzzed above him. Their powerful engines made the ground shake.

He watched their black shapes as they passed overhead. The big one came in to land and evacuate the enemy. The other two circled above, their guns raking over the hill to finish off anyone still moving. Bullets hit the ground to his left in hard thuds.

*I will not die like this*, he promised himself. *Not like this. I will avenge my brother.*

He would not go without taking the woman and the PJ with him.

# TWENTY

THE RHYTHMIC WHAP of the incoming Chinook's blades was the sweetest sound she'd ever heard. The roar increased until it almost drowned out the noise of the gunfire. Then out of the darkness appeared two Pave Hawks leading the rescue bird. The Chinook landed, and a group of soldiers charged out to form a protective perimeter. Rangers maybe? Thank God. She tightened her hold on Will's cold hand. "Hear that, Will? They're here. We're getting out of here!"

He offered a weak smile and squeezed her hand feebly. "Thank God."

She couldn't stop smiling, and a surge of satisfaction swept through her when the Hawks opened up with their fifty-cals from the open bay doors. The glowing red tracer rounds sliced through the night air along with the measured fire from the Rangers, SEALs and PJs. She scrambled up onto her good knee and waited. Cam leaped over the boulders with Jackson. "Stay down," he yelled at her as they hoisted Will's stretcher into the air and got into position to make the charge to the waiting bird. The volume of fire increased exponentially out front. Covering fire.

"Go, go!" Cam yelled.

Devon watched with her heart in her throat as they

took off amidst the sporadic enemy fire and raced for the Chinook.

*Do something.*

She still had ammo left, and she damn well would do something helpful instead of waiting around to be carried to the bird. She slid on her belly to a spot beside the protection of the boulders and aimed her weapon. She couldn't see much without NVGs, but she could see the muzzle flashes coming from across the ravine.

When another volley fired, she pulled the trigger. The flashing on the other side stopped. Had she hit the target? Her breaths were shaky and rapid. Was Cam okay? More muzzle flashes. She fired again. Men ran into the casualty collection point to grab more stretchers. McCall and the crew chief raced past. Two of the SEALs came back with Jackson and Ryan, and evacuated two more stretchers.

She ignored them and laid down whatever fire she could to help protect them. Overhead the Pave Hawks continued their air-to-ground assault, the distinctive bark of the fifties adding to the chaotic noise. When she was out of ammo, she stopped to reload and realized she was alone. All the other wounded had been taken out. The Rangers had boarded the Chinook. Her heart slammed so hard it made her hands shake.

"Cam would never leave you," she told herself fiercely. She hated herself for ever doubting his promise.

She kept firing, heartened that some SEALs remained out front. It wasn't like they'd deserted her. Her gun clicked when she squeezed the trigger. Empty. Shit, out of ammo again. She reloaded. Her gaze swept past the SEALs toward the Chinook. She cried out in relief when she saw Cam running flat out toward her. He moved like a blur, weapon firing. He came barreling into the rock shelter and skidded to his knees beside her.

"Come on," he yelled over the noise.

Still holding her weapon, she grabbed a fistful of his uniform as he levered her onto his shoulders. Amidst the whine and ping of the rounds landing around them, he ran for the Chinook. She kept firing in bursts toward the enemy, and stopped only when she felt the heavy rotor wash beating at her back. A howl of agony ripped from her throat as Cam flipped her off his shoulder and all but tossed her into the cabin. Someone grabbed her under the armpits and hauled her backward away from the ramp as Cam jumped inside. Black spots swam before her eyes.

"Talk to me, Spike."

She turned her head at Ryan's voice. "I'm okay!"

He moved away toward the cockpit. The inside of the bird was so crowded with bodies she couldn't tell who was who. The pitch of the big engines changed, rising to a shrill scream as the bird struggled to take off. Fighting back the pain, she found Cam at last near the ramp and met his stare. The gunners were still firing from their positions. The bird shuddered and strained under the burden of all its passengers.

Oh God. They were overweight. The engines were already maxed out.

Cam exchanged a long look with Jackson, then pushed his way over to her. She grabbed his upper arms and leaned forward to shout. "They need to throw some ammo and equipment out, or—"

"Listen to me." His eyes were the most intense she'd

ever seen them. She stilled. He surrounded her with his arms for a second before kissing her hard and pulling back. He shook her once, staring down intently at her. "I love you."

Her heart stopped beating. *He wouldn't.* She read the intent in his eyes. "No, don't—"

"Hang on to this for me," he shouted. He yanked out the chain she'd given him and put it in her stiff hand. Then he turned and disappeared down the tail ramp.

She threw out a hand to grab him. Stop him. But her fingers only grabbed air. "*Cam!*"

He didn't stop. Didn't so much as hesitate as he jumped off the tail ramp and joined the SEALs still on the ground around the Chinook. "Cam, *no!*" Heedless of the pain in her leg, she pulled herself toward the closing ramp. Desperate to get to him before it was too late.

She tripped on someone's leg and went down, crying out in agony as her wounded knee smashed into the steel floor. Hard hands gripped her waist. Yanked her up and back. She fought them.

"Dev, don't."

*Ryan.* Mindless, she ripped at his restraining hands. "Let me go! He's going to get killed!"

Ryan hauled her up and into his arms, holding her tight as the Chinook lifted off the ground. She fought him with all her strength. "Is he on the Hawk?"

"Dev—"

"Is he on one of the fucking Hawks!"

"I...I don't know." He held her tighter. Cutting off her breath. She weakened and stopped fighting.

Her body was stiff with denial. She was sobbing now, hysterical. "W-we have to g-get him."

"He'll get out, Dev. I promise you."

The pain was suffocating. She couldn't breathe. Couldn't ease the splitting sensation in her chest. The tears flowed fast and hot down her cheeks. They soaked the front of Ryan's fatigues as the bird rose into the dark sky and left the man she loved behind.

SADIQ FOUGHT THROUGH the thick layers of blackness toward consciousness. The beat of his heart echoed in his ears as his body began to register the pain. Through the wildfire burning in his chest, he heard the sound of the big helicopter taking off. He forced his heavy eyes open and turned his head to the side. A sharp rock dug into the side of his cheek, but he couldn't summon the strength to brush it away. How much blood had he lost? His limbs felt heavy as lead. He didn't know if his wounds were mortal or not, but he knew they were bad. It hurt to breathe. Like someone was driving a spike into the front of his ribs.

He blinked to focus his hazy vision. Two of his dead comrades lay next to him. He was alone. Khalid and the general had left him to die.

A shocking anger began to take hold. Wiping away the fear like it had never existed.

Forcing slow, shallow breaths, he focused on the enemy leaving the field. Was he going to slowly die out here all alone? Watch his enemies escape while he lay helpless and in agony?

*Never.*

He summoned all his strength and rolled to his side. Pain exploded in his chest. He fought to stay above it. Stay conscious. The faint light from the half moon revealed the behemoth silhouette of the helicopter perched on the ground. The sound from its engines grew louder, but it didn't take off. Sadiq blinked, then squinted as men jumped out of the aircraft and rushed back toward his position. What were they doing? Coming back to kill all the wounded or take him prisoner? He groped for his rifle. His cold hands met nothing but dust and rocks. Had he lost it? He couldn't remember.

The aircraft's engines roared and lifted the beast into the air. The throb of its rotors pressed in on his eardrums and reverberated in his torn chest. His ribs felt like they would split open.

The noise gradually faded. The helicopter rose further into the air as it flew away, accompanied by its two escorts. In the vacuum of silence left in their wake, he made out the sounds of the remaining ground force talking to each other. Their voices were indistinct, too far away to identify, but the words carried clearly on the night air. He needed a weapon. He would not die without a fight.

His knife. His trembling fingers closed about the scabbard at his hip. The handle was like ice against his palm. But he didn't have the strength to move. Dragging himself away would deplete the little energy he had left.

"Roger that, will hold position for extract."

He tensed and held his breath. His right arm came up to sweep the area around him. He'd been holding the general's binoculars when they'd shot him. They had to be close. Unless Nasrallah had come back and taken them with him before he retreated.

The tips of his fingers brushed cold metal. A gun barrel. From the man next to him. He closed his fingers around it. His hand bumped something else, and he recognized the contours of the binoculars. Dragging them over, he raised them with shaky hands. There was just enough light to see. He had to squint to make out the black outline of the men moving toward him. The binoculars wobbled in his grip but he steadied them, determined to learn exactly what he faced. He counted the men approaching him. Nine men. Nine Special Operations soldiers. Who were they?

The moon broke through the mottled clouds. Its silver light gilded their bodies and weapons. Glinted off the night vision goggles mounted on their helmets.

In the soft glare, one of the soldier's shoulder patches reflected back at him. He stiffened, a surge of blood rushing to his head. What did it say?

*PJ.*

It was him. He was still here. For some reason he had jumped off the helicopter before it took off.

Prickles raced over his skin. The woman was gone, but the PJ remained.

Sadiq dropped back in exhaustion and released the binoculars. He stared up at the night sky, studying the pattern of light and shadow created by the clouds shifting over the face of the moon. Was this Hassan's doing? Or Allah's? He had no other explanation. The odds were too incredible.

The soldiers came closer. Edging their way toward him.

Sadiq lay still waiting for the moment to strike. He would lie in wait like a coiled snake. The hatred warmed his cold body, thawing him from the center outward. He could feel the blood rushing through his veins. Feel the air pumping in and out of his aching lungs. The pain faded away.

One more chance. A higher power had granted it to him, and he would use the last seconds of his life to take the PJ with him into death's dark embrace.

# TWENTY-ONE

ALONE IN HER hospital room, Devon was ready to scream. No one would tell her anything. Once they'd loaded her off the Chinook, a couple of nurses had stuck her in this room and left her there before rushing out to help with the other more seriously wounded. Ryan had rushed past her with one of the wounded Marines, and she hadn't seen him since. He might have already left the hospital to go to the ops center for a debriefing. Or he might have even loaded up and headed back to get Cam and the others.

*Please God let Cam be flying back to base right now.*

The raw emotion on his face when he'd told her he loved her was burning a hole in her gut. She clenched handfuls of the blanket the nurses had tucked around her and craned her neck to look out her door whenever she heard footsteps running down the hallway. But she didn't see anyone she recognized, and no one came into her room.

She debated whether to climb out of the bed and hop down to the nurses' station to get some answers when Erin walked in. "Hey."

Devon grabbed her roommate's hands. "Where's Cam? Have you heard anything? He didn't get on the bird with us—he jumped out because we were overweight. Do you know if he's all right?"

Erin shook her head. "I'm sorry, hon, but I don't know anything. I just thought I'd come and check on you while I had a free minute. They're probably going to need me in the OR soon." Her green eyes were full of concern. "Are you all right?"

What was a ruined knee compared to the pain she was in now? The ache in her throat was so bad she couldn't speak for a moment. When she did, her voice was hoarse. "He went back out there to make sure I got to base. He promised he'd get me back, no matter what—" She buried her face in her hands and sobbed.

Erin leaned over the bed and wrapped her arms around her. "He's going to be okay, Dev. They're going to send someone in for the rest of them. Don't forget he's trained for this. Well trained. The best in the Air Force prepared him for this. You have to believe everything's going to be okay."

Dev shook her head. Erin didn't get it. "You don't know what it was like out there," she cried. The fear kept welling up, making her heart race even faster. Increasing the pressure beneath her ribs until it felt like an elephant was sitting on her sternum. "Oh God, I can't lose him! I *love* him."

Erin stroked her hair. "I know you do. But he'll be back. Don't give up. He needs you to hang on and be strong for him."

Erin's words slowly penetrated her frightened brain. She was right. Cam would want that from her. Expect that from her. Sitting up, she hitched in a breath and wiped at her wet face. "I'm fine. Promise me you'll tell me if you hear anything."

"I promise." Erin edged off the bed. "Is there anything I can get you? The doctor will come as soon as he can to take a look at that leg."

"No, there's nothing." Nothing would help unless she got word Cam was all right. She'd already refused pain meds. She wanted to keep a clear head in case—

Just in case.

Left alone in the silent, sterile room Devon covered her eyes with her hands. She prayed as hard as she could while the tears tracked down beneath her shaking fingers.

IN AN OFFICE off the debriefing room, Candace rolled her head around to ease the tension in her neck and shoulders. It didn't help. Today had been the longest day of her military career, and it wasn't even over yet.

She'd given her verbal report along with her pilot commander. But when it was over she'd still had no idea if the ground team had made it out once they left to refuel. No one had called them back in, but she didn't know if that was a good thing or a very bad sign.

She couldn't stop thinking about what she'd seen. Those enemy fighters had literally covered those two hills when they'd opened fire. The Hellfire missile had dispatched most of them to hell, but her aircraft's heat seeking radar had still picked up on numerous targets. Whether they were alive or dead remained a giant question mark in her mind.

Sighing, she took the pen on the desk to fill out her After Action Report. The office door opened. That annoying combat controller walked in. Ryan whatever his last name was. Yet her heart leaped with joy before she could control it. If he was there, then the ground team must have made it back safely. But when his warm brown eyes locked on hers like a laser guided missile, she froze.

His hard expression made her uneasy. He was tall, over six feet, and broad through the chest and shoulders. In full combat gear with his face streaked with grime and camouflage paint above where the thick stubble ended, he looked dangerous. And somehow too gorgeous for words.

"Hi," she managed when he kept staring. Her voice sounded very small, so she lifted her chin. The last thing she wanted was to appear nervous in front of him.

"Hey." He crossed the room toward her, and she had to resist the urge to retreat a step or two. Something besides his appearance unnerved her. He made her feel threatened on several levels. Not that she was afraid he'd hurt her or anything. It was the power and sexual intensity coming off him that made her balk. He had danger signs all over him, despite how worn he looked.

Swallowing, she found her voice. "You all right?" He looked okay.

"Yeah, thanks to you."

He knew she'd been up there. A flush spread across her face and neck. A compliment from a man like him was the last thing she'd expected. She reached up to rub the back of her neck to cover her awkwardness, but it was damn hard meeting the full power of his stare. If there was such a thing as an A type personality, he was an A plus, topped off with more alpha than she knew how to handle. "How's Dev? All I heard was that she was injured in the crash."

"Dunno. Haven't seen her since we got back, but she's probably having tests done right now."

"Why, what happened to her?"

"Screwed up her left knee during impact. Might have broken her leg too."

God, poor Devon. She couldn't imagine going through a crash, let alone trying to outrun and then hold off the enemy with a broken leg. She needed to see her, ASAP, and throw her arms around her best friend. "I'm heading to the hospital as soon as I'm done."

He studied her carefully. "What you did out there took guts."

She looked away. "I just did my job."

"While under small arms and RPG fire."

"It was the pilot commander's decision to stay."

He shocked her by putting a hard finger beneath her chin and tipping her head up until she met his eyes. "If it'd been you in the left hand seat, you would have stayed too."

How did he know that about her?

"You saved our asses today. All of us."

She didn't know what to say. She was just glad she'd been able to help protect them and clear off some of the enemy so the Chinooks could come in. "Wish we'd gotten there sooner."

"Your timing was perfect, believe me." A slight grin softened his features. The shadows lifted from his eyes. "Thank you."

"You're welcome," she mumbled automatically and firmly pulled her head away from his hand. Retreating a step brought her up against the metal desk, but she didn't care as long as it meant having some space between them. Her fingers closed convulsively around the edges of it.

"I don't bite you know." His eyes gleamed with amusement. And—was that respect?

She scowled despite the inner glow of pride that look in his eyes created. "I know." *Back off, buddy.*

"I might nip a little if you let me, though." His voice dropped to a sensual murmur. "But real softly so I wouldn't mark your tender skin."

For a moment she couldn't get her breath. He didn't take a step toward her, but she felt caged nonetheless by his masculine presence. It alarmed her. He held her motionless with nothing but his stare.

She straightened her spine and shot him a warning glare. "You know what? You just reminded me why I don't like you."

He grinned like he got a giant kick out of needling her. Or maybe it was her response that he found funny. "Well I like you."

"That's because I'm not rude and obnoxious."

"Well there is that. But I think it's mostly to do with the fact that I'm standing here breathing because of you."

"Ah. So gratitude makes you rude? I'll have to remember that if I'm in the area next time you get in a tight spot."

His expression instantly became contrite. Then remote. Like he'd flipped a switch. "I was just teasing you. I didn't mean any offense."

Part of her softened at the sincerity in his expression and tone, but she hardened her heart. He might come in a pretty package, but underneath that dreamy wrapping laid the heart of a warrior and a sexual appetite to match. She knew his type. No doubt he went through women faster than she went through her fashion magazines. Well she wasn't interested in being one of his play things. She straightened and started to walk past him. "I'm going to see Devon. Is Cam with her?"

He paused before answering. "No."

She stopped and looked at him over her shoulder. "Is he in a briefing?"

"No."

Her heart stuttered when his somber expression registered. The shadows were back. Swirling in his eyes. "Then where is he?"

Ryan hesitated, wiping a hand over his face. He didn't look at her. "He's still out there."

She put a hand to her stomach. "What?" That couldn't be right. It would kill Devon if he didn't come back alive. "As in MIA?"

"Not quite. He and Jackson jumped out because we were too overweight to take off."

She couldn't believe what he was telling her. "But they won't just leave him—"

"More crews are headed out there right now." The unguarded flash of pain in his eyes ate at her. "We wanted to go back for him, but the fire was too heavy. The escorts were ordered out with us to provide protection." He dragged a hand through his mussed hair and shifted his weight. He seemed to struggle with himself for a minute. She didn't dare say anything, waiting for him to speak.

He let out a rough sigh. "I should have been the one to jump off, but I was crammed too far forward. He was out the door before I knew what was going on. He should be standing here right now. And I should still be out there to call in air support."

"PJs and SEALs can do that on their own."

"Yeah, but we could've used Cam's medical skill on the return flight." He shook his head. "It should be me out there, not him."

She studied his drawn expression. God, he'd already lost one of his best friends over here. Having to leave another one behind must be killing him. Before she could talk herself out of it, she crossed the room and stood directly in front of him. "He'll be all right." Her voice rang with a conviction she didn't feel. "They'll find him." She prayed he'd still be alive when they did. He had to be, for Devon's sake. And for Ryan's as well.

His smile was weary and sad. Full of guilt and regret. "Yeah."

Not knowing what else to say, she turned around to go. She was almost to the door when he spoke again.

"Will you do me a favor?"

She stopped. "Depends what it is, but go ahead."

"When you see Dev, don't tell her yet. I want to find out the latest intel before I go back to the hospital. I'll tell her myself about Cam if he's not back by then."

He had a better chance of finding out what was going on than she did. "Okay." She didn't envy him that task, but she respected him for wanting to deliver the news in person. He seemed exhausted standing there. He had to be worried sick, though he'd still found the energy to mask it long enough to flirt with her. She'd probably regret being nice to him later on, but…

"Do you need anything?"

His head came up. Those penetrating mahogany eyes touched hers. "Sorry?"

She folded her arms and shrugged. "You must be tired. I could get you something to eat, or at least a cup of coffee. If you want."

He seemed surprised by the offer. "I'd love some hot coffee."

"How do you take it?"

"Just black."

She went to fetch it, berating herself with every step down the linoleum hallway. What the hell was she *doing*?

When she got back to the glass door Ryan was slumped in a chair with one elbow propped on the table, his head in his hand. Her heart turned over. He looked up as she entered, and the grateful smile he offered set off a tingling of warmth in her belly.

*Oh no you don't*, she scolded her body. *He's trouble and we're staying the hell away from him.*

"Thanks." He took the cup from her.

She was careful not to touch his fingers during the transfer. "You're welcome."

"And thanks for being so nice to me."

She shrugged. "Sure. Just try to remember my good deed the next time you're tempted to be rude to me, Sergeant."

His grin flashed before he swallowed a sip of the coffee. "Yes ma'am."

# TWENTY-TWO

THE NURSE TOOK the thermometer out from beneath Devon's tongue and stepped away from the bed. "Slightly elevated."

Yeah, because she was freaking out and her body was going haywire. She *should* have a damn temperature.

"We'll get you down to x-ray when we can."

Devon nodded impatiently at the nurse, not bothering to open her eyes. It was all she could do to stay above the pain, and not just in her knee. A steel vise was locked around her chest, slowly crushing her. She couldn't find anyone who knew anything about Cam, but someone had confirmed another bird had been dispatched to extract them. Had he gotten on the last chopper? She felt like screaming. Instead she pressed her lips together and focused on breathing in and out. *He's fine. He's on his way back*, she kept repeating. She had to believe it. Wouldn't accept the possibility of anything else.

The edges of Ty's lucky quarter dug into her damp palm. Whatever happened, she wouldn't lose hope. That's all she had left.

"Captain Crawford?"

She opened her swollen eyes at the quiet greeting. The translator, Saiid, stood in the doorway looking at her with a sympathetic expression. "Yes?" She really didn't feel like talking right now.

"I understand if this isn't a good time, but the elder you spoke to the other day insisted I come to you. He says he has something important to tell you."

She closed her eyes for a moment. Did she really have the strength to talk to him right now? All she wanted was to know Cam was all right and then to be left alone for a while. An unfamiliar voice spoke from beyond the doorway, but she couldn't make out what the speaker said.

Saiid cleared his throat and she faced him with a sigh.

"How important is it?" If it was gratitude for her flying him and his grandson to the base, she didn't need a thank you.

"He's quite insistent."

Devon scrubbed a hand over her face. "Fine, tell him it's okay." One quick conversation wouldn't kill her. And there was always a chance it would provide a distraction for a few minutes. Please God, let it distract her from the terrible fear gnawing at her.

Saiid beckoned with his hand and a moment later the old man tottered in, pausing in the doorway to say something to Saiid. "He wishes to know if you will be all right," the interpreter said.

"Yes, it's just my knee." She resisted the urge to wave them both away. "What can I do for you, sir?"

The man straightened after Saiid translated, and began to speak. Saiid glanced at him sharply, his brows lifting, and he listened for a few more moments, spellbound.

Devon frowned at him. "What? What's the matter?"

"I… He says he has a confession to make."

A confession? Devon pushed up on her elbows to sit

more upright as she met the old man's black stare. His voice was low and calm. Almost soothing. And he never once looked away from her eyes.

"He says he recognized you when you came to see him in the hospital."

*I knew it.* Her hands gripped the edge of her blanket. "How is that possible?"

The old man continued for some time, and Saiid's expression made her belly draw tighter with every breath. Finally, he translated. "He has seen you before. In a photograph."

"What?" she whispered. "No way." That was impossible.

The old man nodded vigorously, and Saiid continued. "The photo was of you and your husband, standing in front of a helicopter like the one you flew."

The air locked in her lungs. "My husband?" Did he mean Ty?

The old man glanced at Saiid for clarification, but then scowled and gestured impatiently with his hand.

"Your husband," Saiid repeated, watching him. "He was standing with his arm around you."

Devon lifted a shaky hand to her mouth. Dear God, she knew the picture he meant. Cam had snapped it a few days before he and Ty deployed to Afghanistan. Ty had carried it with him in his uniform. "But how…?" The only way the old man could have seen it was if he'd known Ty. She swallowed the painful lump in her throat. "Did you know him? The man in the photograph?"

The weathered face was solemn, the eyes sincere and direct.

"No. But he was there the night he died," Saiid responded.

Hot tears blinded her. She blinked hard, focusing intently on the old man. "You saw him? Did you see how it happened?"

Saiid's voice was lost beneath the pounding of her heart as he translated. Then that white turbaned head bobbed emphatically.

"Yes."

Tears slipped down her cheeks too fast for her to wipe them away, but she didn't care. "Tell me what happened," she begged. "We were told he bled out, all alone."

The man watched Saiid as he relayed the message, but then turned his keen gaze on her and emphatically shook his head.

"He says no."

"No what?" she demanded. No he wasn't going to explain? No, Ty hadn't bled out?

"No, he was not alone," Saiid clarified.

"You mean the Taliban had him?" She almost couldn't get the words out.

Another shake of his head. "No Taliban," he said firmly in a heavy accent, pointing to himself.

"Who had him, then?"

The man kept pointing at himself, watching her. She bit back a sob. Oh God, she wanted to think Ty had been with someone. She wanted to believe someone had been there to offer what little kindness they could when he drew his last breath.

The old man repeatedly stabbed a gnarled finger into his chest and said something else. Saiid swallowed and met her eyes. "He...he says *he* was with him when he died."

She sat up higher, grabbing the bedrail for support. Her other hand dashed at the tears on her face. "*You* stayed with him?"

He nodded. She clapped one hand over her mouth to stifle a whimper, then covered her eyes instead. Every hair on her nape stood on end. The chances of meeting were so small. How could this be? She was losing it, and she wanted to be left alone to cry in private.

Before she could summon the control to ask him anything else, the old man broke from his position in the doorway and crossed to her bedside. The soles of his sandals scuffed the floor. He sought her free hand and pried her curled fingers off the cold metal rail. He pressed her hand tightly between his. The skin of his palms was rough and leathery, and felt warm. He spoke, his voice soft and soothing. Though Saiid had to translate them, the words were directed at her.

"He was a very brave man, and he was not alone when he died. If you like, I will tell you what happened."

Blinking at him through her tears, she managed a nod.

THE SOLDIERS WERE close now. Close enough for him to see their shadowed faces. They were fanned out, stopping to look at the dead. He fought back the anxiety eating at him as they drew nearer. They rolled the bodies over with their feet. Checking for Nasrallah? Sadiq's lips curved in a satisfied smile. They would never find him. The general was long gone by now, sheltered in some secret location in one of the nearby villages. The people would never give him up.

In the faint moonlight, he stared at the spot where the block letters were stenciled on the soldier's sleeve. Coiled and ready, his mind swept back to that terrible night when he had lost everything that mattered to him. He called up his brother's face, remembering every beloved line of it as they ate dinner in their uncle's house.

"I HEAR SOMETHING," his brother, Hassan said.

Sadiq turned his head toward the door of their uncle's mud brick house. He heard it too. Distant voices floating on the night air.

"Taliban."

They both shoved to their feet and grabbed their old Russian-made weapons from near the door. Their uncle emerged from the back room, his face a mask of concern. "We have to keep them away. The Americans are still in the area."

Sadiq glanced to the doorway beyond his uncle's shoulder. "Are the children—"

"My wife and children will stay hidden until they leave. Hurry." He waved a hand at them and together they stepped outside. To the east, the twilit sky was an ocean of indigo and purple, with the first few stars winking to life. To the west and south, a great bank of fog was closing in, slowly swallowing everything in its path. Already it curled around their feet with ghostly tendrils.

"We don't want any trouble here," his uncle said firmly. "Don't antagonize them. We have nothing to offer them here, and soon they'll be on their way to another village."

The distant voices lost in the fog grew louder. Within minutes, the first man wearing a black turban materialized through the smoky veil. He was tall, with a thick black beard and eyes that glittered in the light from the oil lamps some of the men held. Sadiq stayed next to Hassan while his uncle went out to speak to him. More Taliban appeared, coming out of the mist like ghosts. He suppressed a shiver of unease, his fingers tightening around the old rifle.

Apparently satisfied, the Taliban leader stepped away and motioned with his hand for his followers to join him. Sadiq's stomach tightened. They were going to check the houses, to make sure no Americans were hidden there. He thought of the many books in his uncle's house, and the ones he'd brought with him for his little cousins. The Taliban forbade girls to attend school or receive formal educations. He took an involuntary step back toward the house when one of the men started toward it. Hassan laid a hand on his shoulder and shook his head.

"But the children…"

"I know," his brother whispered. "We'll stay close by until he leaves."

The man re-emerged a few minutes later, and Sadiq let out the breath he'd been holding. He'd been so afraid of—

Shouts came from down the hillside. The Taliban instantly gripped their weapons and gathered at the edge of the dirt road. More shouts. Then sharp popping noises. The reports echoed up the valley.

He went cold. "Who are they shooting at?" he said to Hassan.

All hell broke loose.

"Get down!"

He dove to the ground as a spray of bullets hit the house in front of him. Men were running, yelling. Women and children were screaming in fright inside the houses.

"Sadiq!"

He opened his eyes. Hassan rushed toward him, his expression full of fear. "Get up! We have to draw them down the hill away from the village."

He started to shake his head no, but Hassan grabbed him by the front of his shirt and hauled him to his feet. His brother dragged him out behind cover and they ran for the line of small trees bordering the village. Tracers arced overhead, glowing bright red in the darkness. His feet slipped and skidded over the loose shale. He followed his brother to shelter behind the ruins of some older houses that had been wiped out by heavy rains in the spring. Gulping in air, he made out the shadowy forms of the Taliban moving farther down the hill into the valley. Hassan pushed to his feet and then dropped into a crouch as if he was going to follow. Sadiq threw an arm across his brother's chest. "Don't."

"We have to protect the village."

"Then we should go back up the hill, not into the valley. It's the Taliban's fight, not ours. Let their fighters worry about the Americans."

Hassan hesitated. "All right. Go."

Halfway to the relative safety of the houses, he

spared a glance over his shoulder to check for Hassan. He barely heard it coming.

The only warning he had was the shrill whistle a second or two before the explosion. A missile exploded somewhere down the hill. The blast of hot air lifted him into the air and slammed him onto the ground. Sadiq lifted his head, searching for some sign of his brother.

"H-Hassan..." he called, but his voice was weak. He struggled to his feet and looked around. "Hassan!" His heart pounded sickeningly.

Villagers milled about like a herd of lost goats. Women wrung their hands and wailed as small children clung to their skirts. Men stood about in groups staring at the destroyed houses. Sadiq wanted to yell at them to move, to do something other than stand around and make more targets for the Americans that had unleashed their deadly missile.

He spotted his uncle in one of the groups and staggered over. "My brother," he gasped when he caught his eyes. "I can't find him." He stumbled over toward the edge of the slope and peered over. The old man came over with the lamp and Sadiq's heart plummeted. The lower half of the hillside was gone. Its smoking remains lay beneath him like a gaping maw. "Hassan!" he cried. There was no answer but the distant gunfire down in the valley where the Americans battled the surviving Taliban element.

Over and over he called his brother's name. But when the answer came, it wasn't his brother's voice.

"Over here!"

Heart in his throat, he scrambled through the fog down further to where the old man knelt with his lamp

next to something. Unable to believe what he was seeing, Sadiq dropped to his knees beside his brother. "Hassan..."

"I'm all...right..." he wheezed.

Sadiq ripped off his shirt and pressed it hard against
the multiple wounds in Hassan's chest.

"The children..."

"Are safe." He kept the pressure up, agonized that
there was nothing more he could do. Out here in the
middle of nowhere, Hassan didn't have a chance. His
eyes stung with tears of fury and regret. "Don't talk.
Help is coming." The old man brought a blanket and
Sadiq wrapped it around his brother's chest as tight as
he could, then added his hands atop the bloody wounds
and used his body weight to slow the bleeding. He didn't
know how long he stayed that way but the distant sound
of rotors brought his head up. Two helicopters. The villagers all retreated up the hill except his uncle and the
old man. Sadiq stared up at the hidden night sky. His
muscles tensed. Was it more Americans coming back
for another air strike?

The helicopters' noise increased but he couldn't see
anything through the thick blanket of fog. Then the wind
from its rotors swept over him. Cool, moist air blew over
his face. He stayed crouched over Hassan as a hulking
black shape landed a few hundred yards away, nearly
invisible behind its gray shroud. A minute after that five
soldiers appeared through the curtain of fog. Big men,
all carrying automatic rifles. The helicopter's engines
powered up and lifted it into the air

He didn't move. The men came closer, spreading
out as they approached, scanning the area. The gog-

gles mounted on their helmets made them look like alien beings.

Three of the men continued past to check the area, but the other two came up to where Hassan lay. Sadiq kept his hands where they were as his uncle and the old man raised theirs to show they were unarmed. The soldiers checked them all for weapons, then pushed the goggles back onto their helmets and crouched down.

"We have one civilian down and in need of transport," one of them said into his microphone.

"My brother," Sadiq said. The man's eyes snapped to his. Startled and so pale a green they almost glowed in the lamplight.

"You speak English."

He nodded. "He's wounded in the chest."

"Let me take a look. I'm a medic."

Sadiq looked at the patch on the man's uniform sleeve, the letters PJ reflecting in the lamplight.

"I'm good here," the man said to his partner. "Go ahead and see if there's anybody else."

"You sure."

"Yeah," he said, already tearing apart his medical bag. When the other soldier left, the man met Sadiq's gaze again. "What happened?"

"A missile I think. It hit the hillside and he was too close." His throat closed up, suddenly choked with tears.

The man didn't answer. He pulled on some thin, clear medical gloves and took Hassan's pulse. "Move your hands." Sadiq lifted his hands from his brother's chest. Hassan raised up with a terrible gurgling sound, and Sadiq grabbed his hand.

The medic lifted the crude bandages and checked

the wounds, his lips pursing. Without a word he took some dressings from his kit and applied them to Hassan's weakly rising and falling chest. "Ask him if he wants something for the pain."

"We have opium if he wants it. He needs to be taken to a hospital."

The medic's pale green eyes were full of quiet empathy. "I'm sorry, but he wouldn't survive the flight." He began packing up his gear.

Sadiq grabbed his sleeve. "You're not leaving?"

"There's nothing I can do for him except give him some morphine."

"He doesn't need morphine—he needs a hospital!"

The medic closed his hand around Sadiq's forearm. "I'm sorry. I'll come back and check on him after I see the others."

The others? Sadiq's head swam. What the fuck did the others matter when there was a patient in dire need right in front of him? "You call yourself a medic? Do something!"

He shouldered his rucksack. "Keep pressure on it and give him some opium if you want. I'll come back later and give him something if he still needs it."

If he's still alive by then.

The medic didn't say it, but his meaning was more than clear. Before Sadiq could utter anything further, the man left.

Shaking, Sadiq stayed over his brother though the hand in his grew lax and ice cold. The wheezing slowed and then quieted. The almost imperceptible movement of his chest stopped. His brother was gone. He knew it but he couldn't force himself to let go. If he let go, he would be accepting it, and he couldn't. Hassan had given up everything for him.

A horrible, rending pain tore through his chest. The cry ripped free, the howl of a wounded animal. That bastard medic had left Hassan to die when he could have saved him.

More gunfire broke the stillness. Gritting his teeth, Sadiq hauled Hassan into the shelter of one of the undamaged houses. The gunshots faded into stillness. Moans rose up on the air, ripe with suffering. He peered through the fog and spotted the glow of the lantern. It wasn't moving. Had the old man been hit?

Sliding down once again, he carefully traversed the hillside, closing in on the light. He could make out the shape of the old man, bent over two writhing bodies. The scent of blood hit him. When they finally came into view, he stopped and stared.

The old man was bent over the medic who had abandoned Hassan, pressing something against his lower abdomen and speaking in a low voice. The medic was breathing heavily and clutching his belly, eyes clamped shut and teeth bared in a grimace of pain. Beside him lay another village man with his legs bandaged, moaning piteously.

"What are you doing?" Sadiq demanded.

The old man pushed something between the American's parted lips.

"You're giving him opium?" he asked incredulously. How dare he ease the American's pain after what he'd done!

The medic shook his head weakly and mumbled something unintelligible, but the elder insisted and forced it into his mouth. He looked up at Sadiq. "He crawled here to help Jamil, though he is badly wounded. He was talking on his radio. They will be sending in help. We must get them up to the village and wait until the helicopter arrives."

Sadiq stared down at the suffering medic with pure malice. "He can lay here until he bleeds out like my brother did."

"You know Hassan was too badly wounded," the old man admonished. "This man risked his life to help Jamil. I saw him get hit a third time while he was putting on the bandages. He bandaged himself then got back up and tended to him."

"I don't care." The hatred was all consuming, so strong it made him dizzy.

"Ask him what we can do for him."

"No." He would not translate for the man responsible for Hassan's death.

The old man's eyes hardened. "Then go and get others to help move them."

"I won't help him," he growled.

"It is your duty as a Muslim to help those in need."

He ignored the lecture, but ran back to the village and found an old Russian handgun. Sadiq's fingers curled around the cold grip. It felt good in his hand. Hassan's death required retribution. The Quran said so. He was more than willing to deliver Allah's judgment to the American who had barely lifted a finger to help Hassan. He didn't remember making the journey down the hill. The gun was almost hot in his hand, warmed by his body heat. His gaze never wavered from the wounded medic, lying still now on the ground. The pistol's cylinder made a metallic click when he cocked the hammer back.

The old man's head snapped up. "What are you doing?"

"What needs to be done." He raised the pistol, the muscles in his arm taut with strain.

The old man raised a hand to ward him off. "He is already dead."

The gun trembled in his grip. "What?" he whispered.

"He is dead. The wounds were too much."

No. The trembling spread throughout his arms and into his torso, down to his legs. It could not be. Hassan's death had to be avenged. Without that justice being served, his spirit would never get to heaven.

Helpless fury swept through his body, with no hope of being diffused. "Put the gun away. What you would do is against Allah's will."

He drew a deep, unsteady breath. With a snarl of anguish, he threw the weapon down and advanced on the dead medic. Straddling his body, he repeatedly punched his face, chest and belly, ignoring the old man's hands trying to hold him back. He kept hammering until he was gasping for breath and dripping with sweat. And still it wasn't enough. He ripped the American's fatigues open and rifled through his clothes, taking his weapons and valuables. He stripped his watch off him and shoved it into his pocket.

Doing one last sweep over the body, his fingers touched something smooth and cool beneath the bullet proof vest that hadn't saved the victim. Frowning, he pulled out the photograph.

"What you are doing is wrong," the old man said

harshly, shaking his head in disgust. "Defiling him will only make the Americans harsher with our people."

Sadiq barely heard him, staring transfixed at the photo. Looking at it was like being kicked in the stomach. The dead medic stood with his arm around a woman, who wore a flight suit. A helicopter sat parked behind them, the same as the one that had inserted him earlier. An icy hatred settled in his gut. Both of them were smiling, their toothpaste commercial teeth white and perfect. As though excited to go out on their next mission and kill more civilians in Pakistan's tribal region. His fingers tightened, crinkling the edge of the picture. I will never forget, he vowed. To his brother and to God.

SADIQ SHOOK AWAY the dark memory. That was all in the past. The moment of atonement was at hand. The soldier drew nearer. Coming toward him in the night as though guided by Allah's hand. Through the numbness, a sense of elation swept through him. *I will free you, Hassan. Even with my last breath.* Goose bumps rose all over his chilled skin. The fire inside him raged hotter.

The PJ was marked for death.

## TWENTY-THREE

CAM CAREFULLY ROLLED another body over with the toe of his boot to ID him. The heavily bearded man was young. Through his NVGs, Cam studied the face. Whoever he was, the dead man was not Nasrallah or one of his deputies.

He shifted his grip on his weapon and moved on, grateful to be able to keep moving to stay warm. It was cold enough to make him uncomfortable. They'd been out here for over two hours since the rescue birds left, and still no sign of the warlord the SEALs wanted. He knew in his gut they wouldn't find him out here on the battlefield. The SEALs must know it too.

The squad leader came on the radio, his voice low so it wouldn't carry. There might still be survivors tucked away where they couldn't see them. "Extraction in twelve minutes. Meet back at the LZ."

"Roger that." He'd be glad to get back to base. They were all low on ammo and he was dying to see Devon.

His glance stopped on another group of bodies lying in a shallow dip. The two men on the ends were obviously dead. Their limbs were frozen in place and bent at awkward angles. The one in the middle drew his attention. He swore he saw vapor rise up from the man's nose. Was he still breathing?

Cam went on full alert and motioned for one of the

SEALs to head over. His steps were silent as he approached, his finger resting on the trigger. The young man's bearded face was turned toward him. Eyes closed. He looked peaceful enough that he could have been sleeping. Cam caught the scent of blood before he reached the group. His eyes fastened on the man's hands. They were wrapped around a rifle.

He could see the SEAL in his peripheral vision. His weapon was also aimed at the group of bodies.

Inching closer, Cam never took his eyes off the hands.

When one of the dead men suddenly twitched and sucked in a gurgling breath, Cam jumped. He jerked the barrel of his rifle toward him, heart pounding. For that split second, all his attention was riveted on the dying man.

Before he could blink, the man in the center lunged upward with a guttural snarl. Everything went into slow motion. Cam swung around. The man had his rifle up. He squeezed off a burst of rounds. Cam ducked as he brought his own weapon up. Rounds whizzed past his head. The SEAL grunted and fell. Cam's finger squeezed his trigger as a booted foot came up and knocked the muzzle away. The momentum threw Cam sideways. He splayed out a hand to catch himself and hit the ground hard on one knee. The man was yelling. In English.

*"Die, PJ!"*

Cam didn't have time to think or wonder how the guy knew what he was. He twisted around to fire and caught the glint of a knife in the man's other fist. It swung downward at his throat in a vicious arc. He threw up an arm to block it. The outer edge of his forearm smashed against the man's wrist. The blade narrowly missed his neck. Cam threw his upper body back and out of range.

Two rounds slammed into the ground beside them. From the other SEALs somewhere in the distance. A third hit the man in the chest. He screamed and hit the ground. Somehow he managed to bring up the muzzle of the rifle.

Cam couldn't get his weapon up fast enough to shoot the bastard. He lashed out a hand to slap the barrel away. The man's strength was shocking as he centered the muzzle on Cam's chest. Cam started to roll, dragging his gun up to fire. A shot rang out. The bullet hit the man between the eyes, but his finger locked around the trigger as he fell. Two rounds spat out. They punched into Cam's belly like a sledgehammer. Pain exploded in his gut as he dropped to the ground in a wash of blackness.

DEVON GLANCED AT the clock on the wall for what seemed like the thousandth time since arriving back in her room. The tests were all done, and the doctor had confirmed she had ruptured ligaments and an avulsion fracture of the tibia. She didn't care about her knee. She wanted answers about the ground team. She wanted to know Cam was okay.

A team had come in to debrief her, but hadn't told her anything about him. When they'd left she'd broken down and cried some more. She was sick of crying, but all she could think about was Cam lying out there bleeding to death, waiting for the sounds of the rescue bird's rotors. Like Ty.

But no, Ty had at least had the elder with him, hadn't he? The knowledge was cold comfort to her right now.

Candace rubbed her back soothingly. At least she had her friend to talk with about what had happened out there. At least Ace understood. The minute hand had to be stuck on that clock. God, it had been hours since they'd pulled her from the field. There had to be some news about the ground team.

Footsteps sounded in the hall, and a moment later Ryan appeared in the doorway. Alone. "Ryan!" She held out a hand.

He stopped short when he saw her. Her stomach plummeted at the look on his face.

She bolted upright away from Candace, wincing when a burst of pain shot through her knee. "Where's Cam?" She fought the hysteria that threatened to overtake her. He didn't answer right away. "Where is he?" Her voice was shrill but she couldn't control the sudden spike of fear.

Ryan stared at her helplessly, his eyes tormented. He took a step toward her.

Scalding tears blurred her vision, so hot they burned like acid. She held out a hand to ward him off. "God damn you, Ryan. *Don't* you stand there and tell me he's dead. Don't you dare tell me he's—"

He grabbed her up in a tight hug, and pressed her face into his shoulder with one strong hand. "Command received a transmission that they took more enemy fire. There's some wounded. Maybe some KIA."

Fuck that. "No!" she yelled, shoving at him. "He's not dead! I'd know if he was dead." She slammed her fists down on his shoulders, but Ryan wouldn't let her go. He just curled around her, as if he was trying to absorb her pain.

"I wish I had an answer," he said thickly, "but I don't." His fingers clenched in her hair. "We just have to hang in there, Dev."

She clutched the back of his T-shirt in her fists. "I c-can't lose him." She was shaking so hard her teeth chattered. Cold all over. Going into shock. "I c-can't."

"Shhh," he whispered. "Don't give up on him. Hold on with me."

She buried her face in the hollow of his shoulder and held on, fighting to breathe. Candace perched on the edge of the bed and laid a hand against her shuddering back. Her friend's voice washed over her. "We'll stay with you. We're not going to think he's gone unless we hear it from the top."

Too far gone to speak, Devon reached for her hand and nodded.

# TWENTY-FOUR

CAM WATCHED HER from the hospital doorway for a moment, his heart constricting when he saw her tear-ravaged face. *Ah, sweetheart.* "Hey, baby."

Her head jerked off her pillow. Her eyes went wide and for a split second she stared at him like she was seeing a ghost. "Cam!" She bolted upright like she would have leapt off the bed, and held her arms out. He caught her before her foot hit the floor and wrapped her up tight in his arms, ignoring the ache in his bruised belly. With her held close to his chest, all the pain disappeared. They were both alive and she was warm and safe up against him.

"I've got you," he whispered, holding her tight and squeezing his eyes shut. Shit, he'd never been so thankful for anything in his entire life. He barely noticed when Candace and Ryan walked out and closed the door behind them.

"Are you hurt?" She pulled back and ran her hands over him, searching for injuries. "Are you okay?"

"I'm okay."

She was crying. Jerking with it. Her arms wrapped around his neck so hard she almost cut off his circulation. He didn't complain. She let out a hiccup. "I thought you died. They told us you were MIA, that there'd been casualties…"

Her pained whisper cut through him like a knife. When he'd hit the ground, for a moment he'd thought he was dead. If those rounds had hit a few inches lower, his body armor wouldn't have done shit to save him. "No, baby, not me. I told you I wouldn't leave you."

"What happened?"

"I took a couple rounds in the stomach."

Her face blanched. "What?" She looked down at his front and laid a hand over his belly.

"I wasn't paying attention like I should've been." His abs hurt like hell and had to be black and blue beneath his body armor. Hell, his insides were probably bruised too. Taking two point blank rounds to the gut wasn't a lot of fun, even with Kevlar. But at least he was alive.

"You're sure you're okay?"

"Yeah. The plates took the brunt of the impact. Just banged up underneath is all."

She didn't seem convinced. "You should have them look at you. Maybe you've got internal damage and they should do an ultrasound or—"

"Baby, I'm fine. I swear." He hugged her and nuzzled her temple.

Still holding him, she let out a soggy chuckle. "I love you. I don't know what I'd do if anything happened to you."

"I love you too." He stroked her hair with one hand, thinking of the tattered photograph in his chest pocket. He really shouldn't say anything to her about it until after the debriefing, but she had a right to know what he'd found. "Dev…"

"What?" she whispered.

"The guy who shot me knew what I was. He spoke

English, knew I was a PJ. It was like he'd been waiting for me."

She stared up at him, listening to every word.

"When I searched him after, I found this in his pocket." He pulled out the photo and showed it to her.

Devon gasped and grabbed it. Her face was white and her eyes were huge. "It was him! Jesus, it was that Sadiq guy."

"What?" She knew him?

"The elder said—"

"What elder?"

She shook her head impatiently. "The elder said Sadiq took this picture off Ty's body."

He listened incredulously as she relayed the events of that horrific night. When she was done, she looked up at him with haunted eyes. "He couldn't kill Ty, so maybe…" She swallowed. "Maybe he recognized your ID patch and wanted to kill you instead."

Her words echoed in his skull. It wasn't impossible. If the story was true, then his part in it made a weird kind of sense. Had that asshole been out there hunting him the whole time? A shiver snaked down his spine. "Jesus." He held her tighter, trying to take it all in.

"But you're safe."

He kissed the top of her head. "I'm safe." *And damn glad the bastard's dead.*

Devon pulled back and smiled into his eyes. Then she held his head between her hands and kissed him. Hard. Quick, ecstatic kisses that spoke of her love and the fear she'd felt. Cam settled her back on the bed without breaking contact and kissed her just as desperately. Love wasn't near strong enough a word for what he felt for her. The emotion swelling in his chest was a thousand times more powerful. And painful. She was part of him.

He lifted his head and brushed at the tear marks on her cheeks. "What a bitch of a day, huh?"

"My worst and best all in one."

He looked down at her knee that the medical staff had wrapped into a brace. "What's the verdict?"

"Exactly what you said it was. Maybe you should be a doctor."

He grinned. Putting a hand on the back of her neck, he shook his head. "I was so damn proud of you out there today. Using your co-pilot as a shooting platform to lay down suppressive fire. You'd make one hell of a PJ, honey."

She flushed and opened her mouth to respond when someone knocked on the door. Cam looked over his shoulder. Jackson stood on the other side of the door. He cracked it a few inches. "Hi, ma'am," he said to her.

Devon laughed at his politeness. "Oh my God, don't call me that—especially after what we all went through today. Come on in."

"Thanks, but…" He looked at Cam. "They want us now. Sorry, man."

Damn. He didn't want to leave. He faced Devon. "Do you have a surgery scheduled yet?"

"Not that I know of. They're pretty busy around here."

He stroked her soft cheeks, drinking in the sight of her. Even with her eyes swollen from crying and her nose red she was still the most beautiful woman in the world to him. "I'll be back as soon as I can, okay?"

"I'm counting on it." She put a hand against the side of his face and leaned up to kiss him one last time.

DEVON GLANCED UP at the clock again, fighting off the dread. Something was up. He hadn't come back yet. She glanced over at Candace, asleep in the pullout chair beside her bed. They'd waited for over two hours, but Cam hadn't returned. She doubted the debriefing would take that long. Trepidation fluttered in her belly. Was something wrong?

Erin poked her head in. "How you feeling?" she whispered.

Devon forced a smile. "Just sore. But relieved to the tips of my toes. I guess you heard Cam made it back okay?"

She crossed to the bed. "Yep, and I'm damn glad for both of you." But her happy expression faded.

Devon tensed. "What?"

"A team's coming in to move you shortly."

Something stilled inside her. "Move me? To where?"

"To Landstuhl, for surgery."

She sat up, wincing when her knee throbbed. "What, now? Can't it wait until morning?"

"They're flying some of the less serious cases out to free up some OR space. You're scheduled to be on the flight."

*No*, she wanted to cry. That would put her a continent away from Cam, and then after surgery they'd probably send her stateside to recuperate. She'd be on the other side of the world from him. It might be months before she saw him again. She glanced over at Candace, who was wide awake and taking in every word. She put a hand on Erin's arm. "But Cam's still being debriefed, and—"

"No, he's not." Her expression was almost guilty.

Devon's heart started a slow, sickening thud. "What do you mean? Where is he?"

"He got called out again."

"What?" She refused to believe it.

"I don't know the details, but I saw him and your other friend heading out with all their gear."

"Who?"

"The combat controller."

Oh shit, had they gone back out to hunt down the last militants? Or to follow up a lead on Nasrallah?

"Dev."

She looked over at Candace, fighting down the panic. "What?"

"I'll get the message to Cam when he comes in. He'll be able to get in touch with you once you're in the hospital in Germany."

She would have thought she was out of tears, but they boiled up anyhow. "Oh my God...I can't *believe* this."

Erin squeezed her hand. "I'm so sorry, hon. We'll get word to him as soon as we can, okay?"

A sinking feeling took hold. She wasn't going to get to say goodbye.

When the team came to transport her, she closed her eyes and turned inward. They loaded her onto the C-130 with the other wounded and soon she was flying westward away from Bagram, back to civilization. With her arm laid across her eyes to hide her tears, she wondered if Cam could hear the plane from wherever he was on the ground.

# TWENTY-FIVE

*Washington D.C.*

LIFTING THE BAG of frozen peas she was using as an ice pack, Devon winced at the mess revealed beneath the bandages she'd unwound from her left knee. It was swollen to twice its size, mottled with purple and yellow bruises, and bearing five inch-long surgical incisions closed by Steri-strips.

The wounds might be small, but that was because the real damage was on the inside where the surgeon had drilled holes in her bones. He'd threaded through a tendon he'd harvested from her own hamstring, then anchored them in place with two inch-long titanium staples. Right now, that was all that held her knee joint together. Not to mention the screws that now held the piece of her tibial plateau in the spot it had been before the accident.

Damn, it *hurt*.

She tossed the cold, soggy bag of veggies onto the dish towel she'd left on the coffee table and let out a weary sigh. At this point in her recovery the pain wasn't bad enough to keep her awake unless she moved wrong. She was going out of her ever-loving mind being stuck all by herself until the Army docs cleared her to go home. Her big accomplishment for the day had been crawling into the shower to wash her hair and shave her legs for the first time since the surgery. And she'd sat on the shower floor the entire time. She had to admit she felt the best she had since the accident, but the depression was wearing on her.

The doctors had told her she had at least six to nine months before she'd be able to even think about getting behind the controls of a bird. Even longer before she could return to active duty. Which meant she had a hell of a long wait before she could get back to Bagram and be near Cam.

He'd called her twice since her arrival stateside, once the day after her flight, and the other two days afterward. *I'm sorry, baby*, he'd told her. *I wish like hell I could be there for you.*

It wasn't his fault. God, she wouldn't even be alive if it wasn't for what he and the others had done out in the field. Thinking back to that awful day made tears clog her throat.

*For godsake, stop crying like a little girl.*

She blamed it on her fatigue level. She was tired and uncomfortable and depressed, not to mention lonely as hell. Every minute spent apart from Cam made her miss him all the more. The ache in her heart was worse than the pain in her knee, and was made almost unbearable by the knowledge it might be months before she saw him again. No way could she go back to Bagram right now, not that the military would give her clearance anyhow. If they'd been married, maybe, but not just because they were in love and she missed him so much she ached.

The phone rang in the kitchenette. Startled, she grabbed her crutches and struggled onto her right foot, moving as fast as she could. Very few people had her number. Her heart started to race. Maybe it was Cam.

If it wasn't, it was either her mom or her eldest brother. They were due in within the next few days, and she couldn't wait for the company.

Reaching the breakfast bar, she balanced on one crutch and snatched the cordless phone up. Her knee pounded like a drum from the rush of blood. She winced. "Hello?"

A second's pause filled the line. "Hey, beautiful."

She closed her eyes as her heart rolled over in her chest. "Hey."

"How you feeling?"

"Okay." God it hurt to hear his voice. "How are you?"

"Doing the best I can, but I miss you like hell."

She bit her lip. "I miss you too." Damn, hearing his voice put her a second away from bawling.

"I wasn't sure if I'd catch you at home."

Home? She smothered a bitter laugh and glanced around her hotel room. "I'm here all day today. No appointments." No appointments, no friends except for her current neighbor, seventy-three year old Mrs. Roberts who came by twice a day to check on her. No cable TV, and only two news station. Most of the time she couldn't stomach watching it because they were always broadcasting stories of death and destruction from Afghanistan. The only thing that had saved her sanity was the Internet connection and the laptop another patient had lent her. She checked her watch. Would be almost seven in the morning his time. "You just getting in?" She couldn't disguise the note of concern in her voice.

"No, I didn't go out last night."

"Oh, that's g—"

A sharp knock interrupted her. She glanced toward the front door in annoyance. Much as she appreciated Mrs. Roberts' kindness, she couldn't answer the door without putting the phone down because she needed both hands to use her crutches. She hated the thought of losing even one second of her airtime with Cam.

"Dev?"

"Sorry." She jammed the phone between her ear and shoulder, determined not to miss a moment of hearing his voice. It was all that got her through the endless days. "Someone's at the door. If I accidentally hang up on you, call me back."

"It's okay, I'll wait. Or I can just call back."

"*No*." The word came out much sharper than she'd intended. "Just bear with me. I'm multitasking."

Mrs. Roberts knocked again. "Coming," Devon called, shoving down her annoyance as she hobbled to the door. "You still there?" she asked Cam.

"Yep. Not going anywhere."

She managed not to fall and do any more damage to herself on the tricky transition from carpet to slippery white eighties-style tile in the foyer. Propping herself up on her crutches, she unlocked the latch and deadbolt. She swung the door open, expecting to find her blue-haired neighbor on her doorstep. Instead she met a pair of sparkling eyes the color of the ocean.

She dropped the phone with a gasp. "Oh my God, *Cam*—" She launched herself at him. Her eyes filled with tears when his arms closed around her. A deep chuckle rumbled from his chest.

"Hey, Spike." He held her tight, her toes dangling

a few inches off the floor. His body was warm and solid and he smelled like sin. The muscles in his arms bunched as he squeezed her. His grip was hard enough that it almost bruised, but it was exactly what she needed.

"Oh God," she repeated roughly, burying her face in his neck, clinging tight.

"Surprise," he whispered against her hair.

"What are you doing here?"

"I managed to get a few days' leave. You've got me until seventeen hundred hours Thursday night when my flight leaves."

A choked laugh escaped her. Then she raised her head to look at him, and his expression stole the air from her lungs. Yearning and hunger, so strong it echoed inside her. He let her slide down the length of his body, until her right foot touched the cold tile, but he didn't let her go. She couldn't wait another second. Tilting her head, she leaned up on tiptoe to kiss him. Cam groaned and cupped her face. He held her steady around the waist with one arm as he raised her up again and got them across the threshold into the apartment.

When he went to set her down, Dev wrapped her good leg around his hips and the kiss turned desperate. The glide of his tongue against hers sent shivers racing across her skin. He kept walking, his free hand moving to her hips and he broke the kiss just long enough to locate her bedroom down the short hall from the kitchen.

It was awkward holding onto him without banging her knee, but he solved that by bending down to scoop one arm beneath the knees and the other around her back. She smiled up at him, her belly doing a little flip

at the effortless show of strength. His lips brushed over
hers gently and the next thing she knew, he pulled back
the covers and laid her down against the soft flannel
sheet. Before she could protest the loss of his embrace,
he piled up two pillows beneath her injured knee. Lying
down beside her, he propped himself up on one arm to
look at her and smooth her hair back.

"God I've missed you," he whispered.

Devon took his face in her hands and drew him down
to kiss him, curving her back and tugging to bring him
closer. She missed his warmth and strength. Wanted to
feel his weight pressing her down into the softness of the
mattress. Instead he pulled her hands away and sat up.

"Wha—"

"Shh." Cam's eyes trailed over her body, pausing
at her knee. His long fingers were gentle against her
bruised skin. "Sore?"

"It's better than it was."

"Poor baby," he said softly, caressing her swollen
skin. The brush of his palm against her bare thigh made
her suck in a sharp breath.

Cam lifted his stare, his eyes burning with love and
leashed heat. She reached for him again, pulling him
down into her arms. The instant he stretched out and
came down on top of her a loud moan boiled out of her
throat. She'd waited a long time for this… He growled
against her ear, his big body vibrating with tension.

His lips feathered a path across her jaw and down
her throat, his tongue flicking out to tease her skin. She
squirmed closer, arching into him. He felt like heaven,
warm and solid and strong. Even better than she remembered. Her hands ran over his wide shoulders and

down his back, tracing the thick ridges of muscle on either side of his spine. Without warning he sat up on his knees and gripped the bottom hem of his T-shirt, tearing it over his head before dropping it to the carpeted floor. Devon pulled in a deep breath and stared at his naked torso. Her fingers went to the contoured muscles of his chest and glided down over his ribbed abdomen. A delighted shiver went through her at the knowledge she was going to have all that raw power up against her naked skin in a matter of moments.

Cam leaned down and took her face between his hands as he brought his mouth down on hers. He kissed her hard, the pulsing hunger between them growing wilder until the heat of it licked over her skin. The silken stroke of his tongue against hers made the muscles in her core contract sharply, sending a flood of warmth between her legs.

Empty and aching, she raised her good knee and pushed up off the bed to press against his thick thigh. She moaned again, growing desperate, and he swallowed the sound, one hand fisting in her hair to hold her still for his kiss. When his other hand slid between her breasts and down her belly to the hem of her shirt, she lifted her back to help him, wishing he'd hurry. He pulled it over her head and threw it aside, his eyes fixed on her black lace bra. The muscles in his jaw flexed as he stared at her, making the ache inside her even worse.

She started to reach behind herself to undo the clasp, but he stopped her, grabbing her hands in one of his. When she looked up into his face, her breath caught. He was panting, his chest rising and falling with his uneven inhalations, his eyes glittering with raw lust. A primitive thrill raced through her that she could elicit that reaction from a man like him.

Before she could say anything, he squeezed his eyes shut and leaned down to press his face into the side of her neck. The grip on her hair tightened to the point of pain. She licked her lips. "Cam?"

He shook his head, a tight movement of denial.

"Cam, what's wrong?"

He cursed and held her tighter. "*Help* me," he rasped.

Her senses dizzy from the scent and feel of him, it took a few moments for the words to register. She stroked her fingers through his thick, soft hair. "Help you?"

His head moved against her hand, as much a show of helpless pleasure as it was a nod. "Help me slow down."

She shook her head. "I don't want you to slow down—"

"I want to be gentle," he said roughly, his warm breath tickling her neck. "But I'm so fucking turned on right now all I can think about is pounding into you."

His words sent another wave of heat pooling between her thighs, bringing a strangled whimper to her throat. "Cam, it's okay." God, she was *so* okay with that. Her voice was breathy, full of need. That's what she wanted, to feel him filling her, stretching her. She wanted to feel his muscles bunch and shift as he moved in and out of her, wanted to hear the sounds he made while he found pleasure in her body.

"No." He raised his head, and the sincerity in his expression made her heart turn over. He looked almost tortured. "You're not ready."

"Yes I am." She'd never been readier in her life.

His eyes burned bright enough to sear her skin. "I want to take care of you first. I'm not going to last five seconds when I get inside you, so *help* me, dammit. Tell me what you need."

Loving him more than ever, she reached up and touched his flushed cheekbone. "Just you. That's it." She didn't care if he only lasted five seconds as long as she got to feel him inside of her. They could work on the finesse part later.

The muscle in his jaw twitched before he finally sat up. He hooked his fingers in the waistband of her shorts and drew them down her legs, pausing to carefully pull them over her sore knee. He tossed them over his shoulder without looking up from her black lace panties. His throat moved visibly when he slid his hands beneath her to undo her bra and gently pull it off.

Already hard with arousal, her nipples stiffened even more under the intensity of his stare. The ache grew painful. "Cam, just—"

He covered her mouth again, this time for a kiss so slow and seductive she melted for him. That's what it felt like, as though everything inside her was turning liquid. When he finally drew his tongue over her lips one last time and lifted his head, she couldn't move. Spellbound, she watched his lashes lower as he turned his attention to her neck and shoulders. He touched her collarbone with reverent fingertips, and she held her breath. The anticipation was driving her insane, but it was the most delicious thing she'd ever experienced.

His fingers trailed lower, barely skimming over the surface of her skin, raising goose bumps in their wake. His expression was totally absorbed, one hundred percent of his attention focused on what he was doing. Beneath his worshipful gaze and careful touch, she felt like the most beautiful, desirable woman on earth. With a sigh, she allowed her lids to flutter closed as the pads of his fingers grazed the lower swell of her right breast. He touched her delicately, the tenderness of it at odds with the hunger on his face and the rigid lines of his body.

But she couldn't wait anymore. Her back curved to push her breast into his hand, and she groaned in relief the instant her distended nipple came into contact with his hard palm. He cupped her gently, flicking his thumb across her nipple, looking up into her eyes to gauge her reaction.

Devon sank her teeth into her lower lip and stared back at him, the molten heat turning her limbs heavy. "More," she whispered, tugging the back of his neck to bring his head down. She wanted to be in his mouth, to feel the drag of his tongue against her aching flesh. But he refused to be rushed. He stayed where he was, his mouth inches from her tingling, desperate nipple, and turned his attention to the other one. She tightened her grip on his nape and pulled. "Cam, don't tease me."

Bracing his weight on one arm, he finally allowed her to tug his head down and gently took her into his mouth. The scorching heat and satin smooth caress of his tongue made her cry out. Her fingers clenched in his hair, her spine arcing to increase the pressure against her nipple. He sucked slow and firm, each pull of his mouth sending bolts of sensation between her legs. She moved restlessly, and the hamstrings in her left leg grabbed in a vicious spasm. Devon gasped and went rigid, fighting the pain as it warred with the pleasure. Instantly Cam lifted his head and one hand moved to grip the back of her thigh, squeezing the muscles with just enough pressure to ease the contraction.

The pain faded, and she let out a sigh of relief, relaxing back into the mattress. His fingers continued to rhythmically massage the tight muscles. "Baby, I don't want to hurt you." His voice was deep. Full of repressed hunger.

She looked him straight in the eye with a disbelieving stare. "Don't you *dare* stop." She'd die if he did. "Do that again," she urged, curling her spine and bringing his head down, moaning softly at the feel of his mouth enveloping her once more. Oh, that was *good*.

"So beautiful, Dev," he whispered against her skin. He caressed and laved the curves of her breasts, sucking her nipples until she cried out and moved her good leg restlessly. She needed him to touch between her legs. "Stay still."

The hand on the back of her injured leg stroked upward, leaving a trail of fire in its wake. *God.* All she wanted was to get him naked and pull him inside of her, but he was taking his own sweet time getting to that. His clever fingers skimmed up her inner thigh to her hipbone, pausing to caress the edge of her panties, following the line of lace down, down to where she wept and ached for his touch. Then back up, torturously slow. "Cam—you're killing me," she quavered, pressing her head back into the pillow and praying for patience. Her heart was pounding.

"I'm loving you," he corrected in a hot whisper, then took her nipple deep into his mouth as his palm brushed over the damp lace covering her core.

Devon cried out and dug her fingers into his shoulders, silently begging him to take her. "Just pull them off—"

He smothered her desperate plea with another scorching kiss, sliding his fingers beneath the edge of the lace to graze her slick flesh. She forgot how to breathe. Every cell in her body cried out for mercy, but he kept stroking, making her hotter and wetter, sliding up to circle her swollen clitoris before trailing down to tease her entrance. A strangled whimper came out.

"Shh. I want you ready."

"God, I *am*," she moaned, mindless with need.

"Sure?" he whispered against her lips, pulling back just far enough to avoid her famished kiss and tease her with another luscious stroke of his tongue.

"Yes!" God, she was going to attack him if he didn't get a move on, her stupid knee be damned—

The slow, firm stroke of his finger inside her made every muscle in her body go rigid. She panted, clenching her eyes shut against the exquisite frustration of having not quite enough pressure, not quite enough friction. Dammit, she needed *more*. She was so close…

Reaching out blindly, she grabbed hold of his waistband and yanked at the button and zipper hiding what she needed more than she needed her next breath. Her hand closed around the rigid length of him through his boxer briefs, and her whole body tightened in agony. He was long and hard, and hot enough to scald her palm through the fabric. She couldn't wait to feel him moving inside her. Pushing aside the soft cotton underwear, she wrapped her fist around him, savoring the feel of the slippery drops weeping from the tip.

Cam's lids dropped down, his expression a study in pained ecstasy as she squeezed and stroked. His finger continued its wicked torment in and out of her body, but at least now they were both suffering. The muscles in his chest and shoulders stood out sharply, and his breathing was heavier. She wanted to touch and kiss and lick every inch of him, but all that would have to wait. Right now she needed him inside her before she died from the emptiness. When his finger slid up around her throbbing clit this time, her patience snapped.

"Don't make me wait any more," she demanded hoarsely.

Cam lifted his lids and stared down at her. His magnificent body was rock hard with unrelieved tension, his eyes blazing with it. Then, thank God, he pulled his hand free of her panties and dragged the rest of his clothes off. She barely had enough time to see him in his full naked glory before he hooked his fingers into the waistband of her panties and ever so slowly dragged them down her legs. His eyes stayed on the flesh he'd revealed between her thighs, and something very close to a growl tore from his chest.

Empty, aching, she reared up to grab him around the shoulders and dragged him down to her. The instant their naked skin touched she moaned and wrapped her right leg up and around his hips, opening for him. Waiting. Needing.

Reaching back, he fished a condom out of his pants and tore it open. His gaze moved slowly up her trembling body until he met her eyes. The fierce emotion she saw there made her eyes sting. Taking her hand, Cam gently brought it to his thick erection, handing her the condom. Stealing a glance down at the pulsing length of him, she smoothed the condom over the swollen head and rolled it down the length of the shaft. Cam shuddered once, bending to kiss her. Releasing him, she lightly caressed the tight sac beneath and swallowed his rough groan. Her tongue rubbed over his while she gripped his ass and pulled him to her.

"Please," she breathed, lifting her hips, rubbing the head of his erection over her wet folds. "I need you."

He brushed his fingertips over her hot cheek, his eyes smoldering. "I'm going to take care of you."

She shivered at the ironclad vow. "I know."

Stretching out full length on top of her, Cam lowered his weight onto his elbows and settled between her thighs. She felt the heat of him against her, the pressure as he moved into place. Then heavy, blissful stretching as he filled her inch by slow inch. Gasping, she curled her lower back to bring him deeper. The shift in angle made the glow inside burn hotter. Her muscles grabbed hold of the thick intrusion greedily, bearing down on him, increasing the heat and the ache. She moaned and tightened around him, holding on for dear life. Nothing had ever felt this good.

The muscles in his arms and back trembled as he pushed in as deep as he could go, until all of him was buried inside her. His head sagged and a deep, primitive snarl ripped free. Sparks of light exploded behind her tightly closed lids. His hands burrowed into her hair, holding her head still while he kissed her hard and deep and wild. Then he began to move. Hard, steady strokes that ignited every nerve ending in her body.

Devon clutched him throughout the rhythmic pumping, sobbing out his name while the incredible pressure built within her. He was right there with her, moaning and shaking in her arms, pushing her higher up the cliff with each sinuous movement of his body. She felt the wetness of her tears on her cheeks, but was too lost in the pleasure to care. He slid a hand between their bodies and without stopping the delicious glide in and out of her, stroked gently over her quivering bud, caressing her core with each heavy thrust.

The pleasure built, taking over her body in a black velvet wave, then broke, sending her flying. The sharp contractions radiated throughout her body, blotting out the sounds of her shattered cries. When the pleasure finally subsided she was so limp she could hardly hold him. Devon lifted heavy lids to watch Cam as he thrust deep one last time and threw his head back. He let out a strangled roar and stiffened, his body shuddering hard in the grip of his own release. Finally he sagged down on top of her and buried his face in her neck. His heavy breaths sent shivers scattering across her sensitized skin.

Too blissed out to move, she contented herself with kissing his damp temple and enjoying the feel of his smooth skin beneath her exploring hands. She could do this for hours and never get bored.

Drawing in a deep breath, Cam raised his head and looked into her eyes. "God, I love you."

She grinned at the adoration on his face and in his tone. "I love you too." Question was, what the hell were they going to do about it?

Cam gently disengaged and dropped a tender kiss on the tip of her nose. "Be right back."

Sighing in contentment, she couldn't wipe the smile

off her face as she watched him cross the floor to the connecting bath. When he came back out, he prowled over to the bed, completely unashamed of his nakedness. She let her gaze travel over the muscular length of him, a little thrill racing through her, and held her arms out wide. With that lopsided smile she loved so much, he crawled in and rolled her gently into his arms. She snuggled up with her cheek resting on the hard curve of his shoulder and breathed in his scent.

His hand stroked up the length of her spine, warm and protective. "I knew you'd feel this good."

"Did you?"

"Yep." Her eyes fluttered closed. "Know what else?"

"Hmm." She was half asleep, drowsy and satisfied.

"I love that you're not shy with me anymore."

She giggled, a high-pitched burst that came out before she could stop it. He laughed, too, a deep purring sound in his chest and gathered her closer, tucking another pillow beneath her sore knee. She fell asleep to the feel of his reverent hands stroking over her hip and thigh.

CAM SIGHED AND stared up at the ceiling in the darkness, enjoying the feel of Devon's naked skin against his. Being apart from her while she'd gone through surgery and the first part of her rehab had weighed heavy on him. Holding her went a long way toward assuaging the guilt he carried around from not being there for her, but he kept thinking about how she'd come apart beneath him earlier. The look on her face as she'd come was the most beautiful thing he'd ever seen. He shifted as his erection came to life. She stirred, nuzzling her cheek against his chest. His pec flexed in reaction and he felt the smile spreading over her face. "Thought you were sleeping," he whispered. "Didn't I tire you out enough?"

"No."

He laughed. "Guess I'll have to try harder next time."

"Please do." She pushed up on one arm to grin at him.

When she kept staring, he brushed her hair away from her cheek. "What?"

"Guess we don't have to worry about the fraternization problem now, huh. At least not until I can get back to Bagram."

"Guess not." Her hair was silky and cool beneath his searching fingertips. "But there is a way to solve that issue for good."

She looked up at him with a shocked expression, and he held his breath. It wasn't an outright proposal, but he wanted her to know he was ready to make that commitment to her. A loving smile spread across her lips and his heart turned over in his chest. "There is, isn't there?"

"Yes." He curved a hand around her nape and tugged her down for a kiss.

She met his lips for a moment, but pulled back. Her eyes held a devilish gleam as she changed the subject. "By the way, I never got to see your tattoo."

He stilled in surprise. "My tattoo?"

"Yeah, don't all you PJs have green feet back there somewhere?" She patted his butt.

Of course she'd know about them. She'd have seen Ty's. He pushed the thought from his mind. "Maybe. What's it worth to you?"

"I'll show you after you show me."

Chuckling, he rolled onto his stomach and let her

look at the four-toed green feet permanently inked on his right ass cheek. His whole graduating class had gone together to get them and carry on the PJ tradition started during Vietnam.

"Very cute," she remarked. Her slender fingers trailed over the design and slid lower, brushing between his thighs.

"Glad you like it," he managed. The light touch made his swelling dick push into the mattress.

A sharp knock at the door ruined any chance of getting to use it. Cam lifted his head and half-turned over to check the clock. Devon pushed up onto one elbow. "You expecting someone?" he asked.

"No. What time is it?"

He sat up, grabbed his discarded clothes and tugged them on. "Almost nine. Want me to answer it?" He pulled his shirt over his head, covering himself.

"Sure, but I have no idea who it was. Could just be my neighbor." Pushing up higher on her elbow, she ran a hand through her disheveled hair.

Another knock. Less patient. "Devon?"

She froze at the male voice. "Oh God." She scrambled into a sitting position, wincing as she moved her injured leg.

"What? Who is it?"

"It's my brother." She grabbed for her shirt.

"Is that a bad thing?" She'd said they were close.

"It is if I don't get to the door in the next five seconds."

More pounding on the door. "Devon? I know you're in there. Christ, have you fallen or something? Answer me or I'll— *One*."

"Oh shit, he's counting." She threw the covers back.

Cam smothered a grin. "I'll get it. Take your time."

"No, I should—"

"*Two.*"

"Hang on!" she called, scrambling from the bed and grabbing her robe from the bench at the end of the bed as he left the room.

"*Thr—*"

Jogging to the door, Cam unlocked it and pulled it open. A clean cut black-haired man a few inches shorter than him stood in the hallway. The family resemblance was strong. His eyes were an identical smoke gray to Devon's. His worried expression transformed into shock, and then hardened in anger as he stared at Cam. "Where's my sister?" he growled.

"She's—"

Dev's brother wasn't listening. His stare moved right past Cam as Devon hobbled out of the bedroom on her crutches. Her face was flushed, but she put on a bright smile. "Hi, Kev."

"Hi." His eyes moved back and forth between her and Cam. They narrowed on him in distrust, and Cam didn't blame him. "Who the hell are you?"

"I'm Cam." He offered a hand, but the other man ignored it. Devon gasped and took a halting step forward, but Cam stopped her with an upraised hand. "It's okay, honey."

"No it's not," she said, aiming a glare at her brother. "Kevin—"

"Stay out of this." Kevin folded his arms across his chest, never looking away from him. "Cam who?"

"Technical Sergeant Cam Munro, U.S. Air Force."

When that didn't earn him any leeway, he stole a quick glance at Devon before facing her scowling brother. Maybe she hadn't told her family about him. Well, he was going to set the record straight right now. He faced the brother and met the hostile stare squarely. "I'm the guy who's going to marry your sister."

Devon gasped but he didn't look at her to see her reaction. In the sudden silence, Kevin's eyebrows shot up. "Is that right."

Cam met Devon's startled expression for a moment and smiled. Raised an eyebrow.

"Yeah," she said, "that's right." His heart swelled when she smiled back at him.

"Well." Kevin grinned and held out his hand. Cam gripped it hard, and her brother laughed. "In that case, it's damn nice to meet you, Cam."

"Damn nice to meet you too."

Devon went over to hug her brother. "Hey, you."

"Hi, munchkin. Congrats, kid."

"Thanks." She looked over her shoulder at Cam. Her eyes glowed with love. "I'm a very lucky girl."

# EPILOGUE

*Arlington National Cemetery*

THE LIGHT DECEMBER wind blew fat snowflakes into her face as she walked once again between the rows of white headstones toward Ty's grave. She held the grips of her crutches tightly. Someone had visited it recently, because a bouquet of frostbitten red roses lay against the stone. Bending as best she could, she wiped the snow from the curved top and brushed it off the flowers. Her fingers shook.

*Stop stalling. Say what you came here to say.*

"Hey, Ty," she said softly. "I brought you something."

She placed the completed framed cross-stitch at the base of his headstone. As though the wind had breathed life through the glass, the angel seemed to glow behind it. The golden thread in her wings sparkled in the wintry light, almost like she was alive.

"I finished it in Germany, but I wanted to bring it here myself. And this as well."

Reaching behind her neck, she undid the repaired clasp of her necklace and removed it. The silver quarter gleamed in her palm, the metal warmed by her body heat. She slid it off the chain and set it carefully on top of his headstone. "It came in real handy over there." Leaving it with him felt right this time.

Raising her head, she looked out at the unending sea of white headstones. There were more in this section than there had been the day of his funeral. She traced her gloved fingers over Ty's name. "Had a close call over there, but Cam came and got me out. He saved me. Just like you saved *your* wounded." Her throat tightened at the thought of how he'd died. "I'm sorry I didn't come for you when I got the call. Cam says you'd tell me I did the right thing, and I hope that's true."

The chill from the marble seeped through the lining of her glove, but she didn't withdraw her fingers. She needed the tactile connection, as though it could link her to him. "I wanted you to hear it from me before someone else said anything, but…" She swallowed. "We're getting married. Sometime next year. I love him and he's really good to me, Ty. I guess we have you to thank for introducing us in the first place."

Footsteps crunched in the snow behind her. She swiveled around. Cam walked over, his eyes solemn as he approached his best friend's grave. The sight of their footprints in the snow made her smile. Two sets plus the circular marks of her crutches, his feet so big compared to hers. They mirrored her path through the snow. Someone to watch over her and walk beside her through the rest of her life.

"You tell him yet?" he asked.

"Yes." She rose, and Cam instantly put an arm around her waist to steady her. Having said what she'd come to tell Ty, she stepped back to let Cam have his turn.

"Well now you know our news," he said quietly, the snow catching in his short hair. "I'm gonna take good care of her, buddy, just like I said I would. I promise."

Devon smiled and squeezed his shoulder in a silent thank you. She only had one more day left with him before he went back to Afghanistan. Loving a hero like him wouldn't always be easy, especially when he deployed, but he would always take care of her. Whatever hardships lay in store, he was more than worth it. She intended to love him to pieces and support him as best she could.

"We'll come and see you when we can. You might be gone, but you're not forgotten," Cam said, rising. He turned to her with an outstretched arm and a gentle smile. She slid her arm around his waist and laid her head against his chest as they stared down at Ty's grave.

"You were a wonderful man, Tyler Bradshaw."

"Yeah you were," Cam agreed. "Miss you, buddy."

She was silent a moment. "I think he'd be happy for us."

Cam kissed the top of her head. "I know he is."

Staring at his headstone, she could almost hear Ty's voice speaking to her. *My death wasn't your fault, Dev. And it's way past time you let me go. Be happy, and take care of him for me.* The words were so clear they made her eyes sting.

Devon hugged Cam close and let the remaining tightness in her chest go. She sighed when his arms came around her, surrounding her with his strength, his warmth.

*I will take care of him*, she silently vowed to Ty. *I'll love him with everything in me.*

Cam was her future. She'd come here to make peace with her past. To let go of it so she could move forward and get on with living her life. Tilting her head back, she smiled up at Cam.

    *Mission accomplished.*

\* \* \* \* \*

# ABOUT THE AUTHOR

Kaylea Cross is an award-winning author of military romantic suspense. Her books have won the Heart of Excellence Award, Laurel Wreath Award, and have twice been shortlisted in the EPIC Awards. A Registered Massage Therapist, Kaylea is an avid gardener, artist, Civil War buff, special ops aficionado, belly dancer and former nationally carded softball pitcher. She lives in Vancouver, British Columbia, with her husband and two little men.

Her books always feature alpha military heroes, and showcase the incredible capabilities of our men and women in uniform. She loves researching so much that despite her fear of flying, she even braved a few helicopter rides so she could interview the pilots and experience flying in a helo firsthand. To get through it, the whole time she secretly imagined she was a spec ops soldier heading into enemy territory.